FOR STANLEY, DEATH IS AN INSPIRATION

Stanley looked dispassionately at the body of Ethel Carpenter, speculatively, calculatingly, without pity. There was no doubt she had died of a stroke. It was cruelly unfair. No one profited by her death, no one would be a scrap the happier, while Maud who had so much—twenty thousand pounds—to leave behind her . . .

A thought struck him. Who but he knew that Ethel Carpenter had ever arrived? And immediately this idea was followed by another, terrible, daring, wonderful and audacious.

Why couldn't it have been Maud lying there? Stanley clenched his hands. *Why not do it? Why not. . . ?*

ONE
ACROSS,
TWO
DOWN
Ruth Rendell

BANTAM BOOKS

TORONTO • NEW YORK • LONDON • SYDNEY • AUCKLAND

*This low-priced Bantam Book
has been completely reset in a type face
designed for easy reading, and was printed
from new plates. It contains the complete
text of the original hard-cover edition.*
NOT ONE WORD HAS BEEN OMITTED.

ONE ACROSS, TWO DOWN

*A Bantam Book / published by arrangement with
Doubleday & Company, Inc.*

PRINTING HISTORY

Doubleday edition published August 1971

Bantam edition / September 1974
2nd printing .... May 1975
3rd printing .... June 1981
4th printing .... May 1987

ISBN 0-553-25975-X

Published simultaneously in the United States and Canada

PRINTED IN THE UNITED STATES OF AMERICA

O   13 12 11 10 9 8 7 6 5 4

For my son

Come into the garden, Maud,
    For the black bat, sight, has flown,
Come into the garden, Maud,
    I am here at the gate alone.

ALFRED, LORD TENNYSON

1. Blank Puzzle

1

Vera Manning was very tired. She was too tired even to answer her mother back when Maud told her to hurry up with getting the tea.

"There's no need to sulk," said Maud.

"I'm not sulking, Mother. I'm tired."

"Of course you are. That goes without saying. Anyone can see you're worn out with that job of yours. Now if Stanley had the gumption to get himself a good position and brought a decent wage home you wouldn't have to work. I never heard of such a thing, a woman of your age, coming up to the change, on her feet all day in a dry-cleaner's. I've said it before and I'll say it again, if Stanley was a man at all . . ."

"All right, Mother," said Vera. "Let's give it a rest, shall we?"

But Maud, who scarcely ever stopped talking when there was anyone to listen to her and who talked to herself when she was alone, got out of her chair and, taking her stick, limped after Vera into the kitchen. Perching herself with some difficulty—she was a large heavily-built woman—on a stool, she surveyed the room with a distaste which was partly sincere and partly assumed for her daughter's benefit. It was clean but shabby, unchanged since the days when people expected to see a ganglion of water pipes protruding all over the walls and a dresser and built-in plaster copper requisite fitments. Presently, when the scornful glance had set the scene for fresh propaganda, Maud drew a deep breath and began again.

"I've scraped and saved all my life just so that there'd be something for you when I'm gone. D'you know what Ethel Carpenter said to me? Maud, she said, why don't you give it to Vee while she's young enough to enjoy it?"

Her back to Maud, Vera was cutting meat pie in slices and shelling hard-boiled eggs. "It's a funny thing, Mother," she said, "the way I'm an old woman one minute and a young one the next, whichever happens to suit your book."

Maud ignored this. "Why don't you give it to Vee now, she said. Oh no, I said. Oh no, it wouldn't be giving it to her, I said, it'd be giving it to that no-good husband of hers. If he got his hands on my money, I said, he'd never do another hand's turn as long as he lived."

"Move over a bit, would you, Mother? I can't get at the kettle."

Shifting an inch or two, Maud patted her thick grey curls with a lady's idle white hand. "No," she said, "while I've got breath in my body my savings are staying where they are, invested in good stock. That way maybe Stanley'll come to his senses. When you have a nervous breakdown, and that's the way you're heading, my girl, maybe he'll pull his socks up and get a job fit for a man, not a teenager. That's the way I see it and that's what I said to Ethel in my last letter."

"Would you like to sit up now, Mother? It's ready."

Vera helped her mother into a chair at the dining room table and hooked her stick over the back of it. Maud tucked a napkin into the neckline of her blue silk dress and helped herself to a plateful of pork pie, eggs, green salad and mashed potato. Before starting on it, she swallowed two white tablets and washed them down with strong sweet tea. Then she lifted her knife and fork with a sigh of sensual pleasure. Maud enjoyed her food. The only time she was silent was when she was eating or asleep. As she was starting on her second piece of pie, the back door slammed and her son-in-law came in.

Stanley Manning nodded to his wife and gave a

sort of grunt. His mother-in-law, who had temporarily stopped eating to fix him with a cold condemning eye, he ignored. The first thing he did after throwing his coat over the back of a chair was to turn on the television.

"Had a good day?" said Vera.

"Been up to my eyes in it since nine this morning." Stanley sat down, facing the television, and waited for Vera to pour him a cup of tea. "I'm whacked out, I can tell you. It's no joke being out in the open all day long in weather like this. To tell you the truth, I don't know how long I can keep on with it."

Maud sniffed. "Ethel Carpenter didn't believe me when I told her what you did for a living, if you can call it a living. A petrol pump attendant! She said that's what her landlady's son does in his holidays from college. Eighteen he is, just a student doing it for pin money."

"Ethel Carpenter can keep her nose out of my business, the old bag."

"Don't you use language like that about my friend!"

"Oh, pack it up, do," said Vera. "I thought you were going to watch the film."

If Stanley and Maud were in accord over one thing it was their fondness for old films and now, having exchanged venomous glances, they settled down among the tea things to watch Jeanette MacDonald in *The Girl of the Golden West*. Vera, a little revived with two hot cups of tea, sighed thankfully and began clearing the table. Altercation would break out again, she knew, at eight o'clock when Stanley's favourite quiz programme conflicted with Maud's favourite serial. She dreaded Tuesday and Thursday evenings. Of course it was only natural that Stanley, with his passion for puzzles, should want to watch the quizzes that took place on those nights, and natural too that Maud, in common with five million other middle-aged and elderly women, should long for the next development in the complicated lives of the residents of "Augusta Alley." But why couldn't they come to an amicable arrangement like reasonable people? Because they weren't reasonable people, she thought, as she began the washing up. For her part, she couldn't care less about the television and sometimes she hoped the cathode ray tube would break or a valve go or something. Certainly the way things were, they wouldn't be able to afford to get it seen to.

Jeanette MacDonald was singing "Ave Maria" when she got back into the living room and Maud was accompanying her in a sentimental cracked soprano. Vera prayed for the song to end before Stanley did something violent like bringing Maud's stick down on the table with a thunderous crash, as he had done only the week before. But this time he contented himself with low mutterings and Vera leant her head against a cushion and closed her eyes.

Four years Mother's been here, she thought, four long years of unbroken hell. Why had she been so stupid and so impulsive as to agree to it in the first place? It wasn't as if Maud was ill or even really disabled. She'd made a marvellous recovery from that stroke. There was nothing wrong with her but for a weakness in the left leg and a little quirk to her mouth. She was as capable of looking after herself as any woman of seventy-four. But it was no good harking back now. The thing was done, Maud's house sold and all her furniture, and she and Stanley had got her till the day she died.

Maud's petulant angry wail started her out of her half-doze and made her sit up with a jerk.

"What are you turning over to I.T.V. for? I've been looking forward to my 'Augusta Alley' all day. We don't want that kid's stuff, a lot of schoolkids answering silly questions."

"Who pays the license, I'd like to know?" said Stanley.

"I pay my share. Every week I turn my pension over to Vee. Ten shillings is the most I ever keep for my bits and pieces."

Stanley made no reply. He moved his chair closer to the set and got out pencil and paper.

"All day long I was looking forward to my serial," said Maud.

"Never mind, Mother," said Vera, trying to infuse a little cheerfulness into her tired voice. "Why don't you watch 'Oak Valley Farm' in the afternoons when we're at work? That's a nice serial, all about country people."

"I have my sleep in the afternoons, that's why not. I'm not upsetting my routine."

Maud lapsed into a moody silence, but if she wasn't to be allowed to watch her programme she had no intention of allowing Stanley uninterrupted enjoyment of his. After about five minutes, during which Stanley scribbled excitedly on his pad, she began tapping her stick rhythmically against the fender. It sounded as if she was trying to work out the timing of a hymn tune. "Dear Lord and Father of Mankind," Vera thought it was, and presently Maud confirmed this by humming the melody very softly.

Stanley stood it for about thirty seconds and then he said, "Shut up, will you?"

Maud gave a lugubrious sigh. "They played that hymn at your grandfather's funeral, Vera."

"I don't care if they played it at Queen Victoria's bloody wedding," said Stanley. "We don't want to hear it now, so do as I say and shut up. There, now you've made me miss the score."

"I'm sure I'm very sorry," said Maud with heavy sarcasm. "I know you don't want me here, Stanley, you've made that very plain. You'd do anything to get rid of me, wouldn't you? Grease the stairs or give me an overdose?"

"Maybe I would at that. There's many a true word spoken in jest."

"You hear what he says, Vera? You heard him say it."

"He doesn't mean it, Mother."

"Just because I'm old and helpless and sometimes I hark back to the old days when I was happy."

Stanley leapt to his feet and the pencil bounced on to the floor.

"Will you shut up or do I have to make you?"

"Don't you raise your voice to me, Stanley Manning!" Maud, satisfied that she had ruined Stanley's quiz, rose and, turning to Vera with great dignity, said in the voice of one mortally wounded, "I shall go to bed now, Vera, and leave you and your husband in peace. Perhaps it wouldn't be expecting too much if I was to ask you to make me my Horlick's and bring it up when I'm in bed?"

"Of course I will, Mother. I always do."

"There's no need to say 'always' like that. I'd rather go without than have it done in a grudging spirit."

Maud wandered round the room, picking up her knitting from one chair, her glasses from another, her book from the sideboard. She could have got all these things by walking behind Stanley, but she didn't. She walked between him and the television set.

"Mustn't forget my glass of water," she said, and added as if she was boasting of some highly laudable principle, as salutary to the body as it was demanding of strength of character. "I've slept with a glass of water beside my bed ever since I was a little mite. Never missed once. I couldn't sleep without my glass of water."

She fetched it herself, leaving a little trail of drips from the overfull glass behind her. They heard her stick tapping against the treads as she mounted the stairs.

Stanley switched off the television and, without a word to his wife, opened the *Second Bumper Book of Advanced Crosswords*. Like an overworked animal, worn out with repetitive tedious labour, her mind empty of everything but the desire for sleep, Vera stared at him in silence. Then she went into the kitchen, made the Horlick's and carried it upstairs.

Sixty-one, Lanchester Road, Croughton, in the northern suburbs of London, was a two-storied red brick house, at the end of a terrace, and built in 1906. There was a large back garden, and between the living room bay and the front fence a strip of grass five feet by fifteen.

The hall was a passage with a mosaic floor of red and white tiles, and downstairs there were two living rooms and a tiny kitchen, as well as an outside lavatory and a cupboard for coal. The stairs ran straight up without a bend to a landing from which opened four doors, one to the bathroom and three to the bedrooms. The smallest of these was big enough to accommodate only a single bed, dressing table and curtained-off area for clothes. Vera called it the spare room.

She and Stanley shared the large double bedroom at the front of the house and Maud slept in the back. She was sitting up in bed, the picture of health in her hand-knitted angora bedjacket. But for the thirty or so metal curlers clipped into her hair, she might well have entered for and won a glamorous grandmother contest.

Perhaps the bottles and jars of patent and prescribed medicaments on the bedside table had something to do with the preservation, indeed the rejuvenation, of her mother, Vera thought, as she handed Maud the mug of Horlick's. There were enough of them. Anti-coagulants, diuretics, tranquillizers, sleep inducers and vitamin concentrates.

"Thank you, dear. My electric blanket won't come on. It needs servicing."

Turning away from her draggled and exhausted reflection in Maud's dressing table mirror, Vera said she would see to it tomorrow.

"That's right, and while you do you can ask them to look at my radio. And get me another ounce of this pink wool, will you?" Maud sipped her Horlick's. "Sit down, Vee. I want to talk to you where *he* can't hear."

"Can't it wait till tomorrow, Mother?"

"No, it can't. Tomorrow might be too late. Did you hear what he said to me about doing me in if he had the chance?"

"Oh Mother, you don't really think he meant it?"

Maud said calmly, "Stanley hates me. Not that it isn't mutual. Now you listen to what I've got to say."

Vera knew what was coming. She heard it with slight variations once or twice a week. "I'm not leaving

Stan, and that's that. I've told you over and over again.
I'm not leaving him."

Maud finished her Horlick's and said in a cajoling
tone, "Just think what a life we could have together,
Vee, you and me. I've got money enough for both of us.
I'm telling you in confidence, I'm a wealthy woman by
anyone's standards. You wouldn't have to go to work,
you wouldn't have to lift a finger. We'd have a nice new
house. I saw in the paper they're building some lovely
bungalows out Chigwell way. I could buy one of them
bungalows outright."

"If you want to give me some of your money,
Mother, you can give it to me. I shan't argue. God
knows, there's plenty we need in this house."

"Stanley Manning isn't getting a penny of my money," said Maud. She took her teeth out and placed them
in a glass; then she gave Vera a gummy wheedling smile.
"You're all I've got, Vee. What's mine is yours, you
know that. You don't want to share it with him. What's
he ever done for you? He's a crook and a jailbird."

Vera controlled herself with difficulty.

"Stanley has been to prison once and once only,
Mother, as you very well know. And that was when he
was eighteen. It's downright cruel calling him a jailbird."

"He may have been to prison just the once, but
how many times would he have been back there if all
those people he works for hadn't been soft as butter?
You know as well as I do he's been sacked twice for
helping himself out of the till."

Getting to her feet, Vera said, "I'm tired, Mother, I
want to go to bed and I'm not staying here if all you can
do is abuse my husband."

"Ah, Vee . . ." Maud put out a hand and managed to make her wrist quiver as she did so. "Vee, don't
be cross with me. I had such high hopes for you and
look at you now, a poor old drudge tied to a man who
doesn't care whether you live or die. It's true, Vee, you
know it is." Vera let her hand rest limply in her mother's and Maud squeezed it tenderly. "We could have a
lovely house, dear. We'd have fitted carpets and central

heating and a woman in to clean every day. You're still young. You could learn to drive and I'd buy you a car. We could go for holidays. We could go abroad if you like."

"I married Stanley," said Vera, "and you always taught me marriage is for keeps."

"Vee, I've never told you how much I've got. If I tell you, you won't tell Stanley, will you?" Vera didn't say anything, and Maud, though seventy-four and for many years married herself, hadn't yet learnt that it is no good telling secrets to a married person if you want them to remain secrets. For, no matter how shaky the marriage and how incompatible the partners, a wife will always confide other people's confessions in her husband and a husband in his wife. "My money's mounted up through the years. I've got twenty thousand pounds in the bank, Vera. What d'you think of that?"

Vera felt the colour drain out of her face. It was a shock. Never in her wildest dreams had she supposed her mother to have half that amount, and she was sure it had never occurred to Stanley either.

"It's a lot of money," she said quietly.

"Now don't you tell him. If he knew what I was worth he'd start thinking up ways to get rid of me."

"Please, Mother, don't start that all over again. If anyone heard you they'd think you were going daft in the head. They would."

"Well, they can't hear me. I'll say good night now, dear. We'll talk about it again tomorrow."

"Good night, Mother," said Vera.

She didn't think any more about what her mother had said on the lines of taking her away from Stanley. She had heard it all before. Nor was she very much concerned that Maud suspected Stanley of murderous inclinations. Her mother was old and the old get strange ideas into their heads. It was silly and fantastic but it wasn't worth worrying about.

But she did wonder what Stanley would say when —and that would have to be when she was less tired— she told him how much money Maud had in the bank.

Twenty thousand! It was a fortune. Still thinking about
it, and thinking how even one-twentieth part of it would
improve the house and make her lot so much lighter,
Vera stripped off her clothes and rolled exhausted into
bed.

2

Maud was an old woman with dangerously high blood
pressure and one cerebral thrombosis behind her, but
she wasn't affected in her mind. The ideas she had that
her son-in-law might kill her if he got the chance weren't
the fruit of senile maunderings but notions of human behaviour formed by Maud in her impressionable teens.

She had gone into service at the age of fourteen
and much of the talk in the kitchen and the servants'
hall had dealt with unscrupulous persons whom her fel-
low servants suspected of murder or the intention of
murder for gain. Cook often insisted that the valet in the
big house across the square would poison his master as
soon as the time was ripe merely for the sake of the
hundred pounds promised to him in the old man's will,
while the butler countered this with horrible tales of
greedy heirs in the great families that had employed
him. Maud listened to all this with the same receptive
ear and the same gullibility as she listened to the vicar's
sermons on Sundays.

It seemed that from the butler down to the tweeny,
no servant was without a relative who at some time or
another had not considered popping arsenic in a rich

aunt's tea. A favourite phrase in the servants' hall, on the lines of Eliza Doolittle's statement, was:

"It's my belief the old man done her in."

And it was Maud's sincere belief that Stanley Manning would do her in if he got the chance. Enlightening Vera as to the extent of her fortune had been a temptation she hadn't been able to resist, but when she awoke on the following morning she wondered if she had been unwise. Vera would very likely tell Stanley and there was nothing she, Maud, could do about it.

Nothing, that is, to silence Vera. Much could perhaps be done to show Stanley that, though he might kill her, he wouldn't profit from his iniquities. With these things uppermost in her mind, Maud ate the breakfast Vera brought to her in bed and when her daughter and son-in-law had left for work, got up, dressed and left the house. With the aid of her stick she walked the half-mile to the bus stop and went down into town to consult a solicitor whose name she had found in Stanley's trade directory. She could easily have brought her own wool and seen to the servicing of her electric blanket at the same time and saved Vera's feet, but she didn't see why she should put herself out for Vera when the silly girl was being so obstinate.

Back in the house by twelve Maud ate heartily of the cold ham, salad, bread and butter and apple crumble pie Vera had left her for her lunch and then she settled down to write her weekly letter to her best friend. Ethel Carpenter. Like most of the letters she had written to Ethel since she came to live in Lanchester Road, it dealt largely with the idleness, ill manners, bad temper and general uselessness of Stanley Manning.

There was no one, Maud thought, whom she could trust like she could trust Ethel. Even Vera, blindly devoted to that good-for-nothing, couldn't be relied on like Ethel who had no husband, no children and no axe to grind. Poor Ethel had only her landlady, owner of the house in Brixton where she occupied one room, and Maud herself.

Ah, you valued a friend when you'd been through

what she and Ethel had been through together, thought Maud as she laid down her pen. How long ago was it they'd first met? Fifty-four years? Fifty-five? No, it was just fifty-four. She was twenty and the under housemaid and Ethel, little, innocent seventeen-year-old Ethel, the kitchen maid at that sharp-tongued cook's beck and call.

Maud was walking out with George Kinaway, the chauffeur, and they were going to get married as soon as their ship came in. She had always been a saver, had Maud, and whether the ship came in or not they'd have enough to get married on by the time she was thirty. Meanwhile there were those delicious quiet walks with George on Clapham Common on Sundays and the little garnet engagement ring she wore round her neck on a bit of ribbon, for it wouldn't have done at all to have it on her finger when she did out the grates.

She had George and something to look forward to but Ethel had nothing. No one knew Ethel even had a follower of her own or had ever spoken to a man, bar George and the butler, until her trouble came on her and Madam turned her out of the house in disgrace. Ethel's aunt took her in and everyone treated her like dirt except Maud and George. They weren't above going to see her at the aunt's house on their evenings off, and when the child came it was George who persuaded the aunt to bring it up and George who contributed a few shillings every week to its maintenance.

"Though we can ill afford it," said Maud. "Now if she'd only stop being a little fool and tell me who the father is . . ."

"She'll never do that," said George. "She's too proud."

"Well, they do say that pride goeth before a fall and Ethel's taken her fall all right. It's our duty to stick by her. We must never lose touch with Ethel, dear."

"If you say so, dear," said George, and he got Madam to take Ethel back just as if she were a good girl without a stain on her character.

Those were hard days, Maud thought, leaning back her head and closing her eyes. Twelve pounds a year she

got until the Great War came and made people buck up
their ideas. Even when the master raised her wages it
was hard going to get a home together and in the end it
was George's good looks and nice manners that gave
them their start. Not that there had ever been anything
wrong between him and Madam—the very idea!—but
when she died George was in her will, and with the two
hundred and fifty he got and what Maud had saved
they'd bought a nice little business down by the Oval.

Ethel always came to them for her holidays and
when Vera was born Ethel was her godmother. It was
the least she could do for Ethel, Maud confided in
George, seeing that she'd been deprived of her own
daughter and wasn't likely ever to get a husband of her
own, second-hand goods as she was.

What with George's charm and Maud's hard work
the shop prospered and soon they could think themselves comfortably off. Vera was sent to a very select
private school and when she left at the late (almost un-
heard-of) age of sixteen, Maud wouldn't let her get a
job or serve in the shop. Her daughter was going to be a
lady and in time she'd marry a nice gentlemanly man, a
bank clerk or someone in business—Maud never told
people her husband kept a shop. She always said he was
"in business"—and have a house of her own. Meanwhile she gave Vera all the money she wanted within
reason for clothes and once a year they all went down to
Brayminster-on-Sea—dear old Bray, as they called it—
and stayed at a very genteel boarding-house with a view
of the sea. Sometimes Ethel went with them and she was
just as pleased as they when her goddaughter found fa-
vor in the sight of the boarding-house keeper's nephew,
James Horton.

James had the very job Maud envisaged as most
desirable in a son-in-law. He worked in the Brayminster
branch of Barclay's Bank, and when during the winter
months he occasionally came up to London and took
Vera on the river or to the theatre matinée, Maud
smiled on him and began discussing with George what
they could do for the young couple when they fixed the

day. A deposit on a house and two hundred for furniture was Ethel Carpenter's recommendation and Maud thought this not unreasonable.

Four years older than Vera, James had been a petty officer in the Royal Navy during the war. He had a nice little sum on deposit at the bank, was a dutiful son and churchgoer. Nothing could be more suitable.

Maud had old-fashioned ideas and thought young people should only be allowed to know each other if they had been properly introduced or if their parents were old friends. It was with horror, therefore, that she learned from Mrs. Campbell, the wife of the fishmonger down the road, that Vera had been seen about in the company of the young barman at the Coach and Horses whom, Mrs. Campbell alleged, she had met at a dance.

It was all George's fault, Maud told Ethel. If she had had her way, Vera would never have been allowed to go to that dance. She had tried to put her foot down but for once George had asserted himself and said there was no harm in Vera going with a girl friend and what could be more respectable than the Young Conservatives' annual ball?

"I'm sure I don't know what James will say when he hears about it," Maud said to Vera.

"I don't care what he says. I'm sick of James, he's so boring. Always on about going to bed early and getting up early and saving money and keeping oneself to oneself. Stanley says you're only young once and you might as well enjoy yourself. He says money's there to spend."

"I daresay he does when it's someone else's. A barman! My daughter sneaking out with a barman!" Although she sometimes permitted George to enjoy a quiet pint in the Bunch of Grapes with Mr. Campbell on Friday nights, Maud had never in her life set foot in a public house. "Anyway, it's got to stop, Vee. You can tell him your mother and father won't allow it."

"I'm twenty-two," said Vera, who, though her father's daughter in looks and generally in temperament, had inherited a spark of her mother's spirit. "You can't stop me. You're always on about me getting married but how can I get married when I never meet any men? Girls can't meet men when they don't go out to work."

"You met James," said Maud.

Afterwards she wasn't sure which was the worst moment of her life, the time when Mrs. Campbell told her Stanley Manning had served two years for robbery with violence or the time when Vera said she was in love with Stanley and wanted to marry him.

"Don't you dare talk of marrying that criminal!" Maud screamed. "You'll marry him over my dead body. I'll kill myself first. I'll put my head in the gas oven. And I'll see to it you won't get a penny of my money."

The trouble was she couldn't stop Vera meeting him. For a time nothing more was said about marriage or even an engagement but Vera and Stanley went on seeing each other and Maud nearly worried herself into a nervous breakdown. For the life of her, she couldn't see what Vera saw in him.

In all her life she had only known one man she could fancy sharing her bed with and by this yardstick she measured all men. George Kinaway was six feet tall with classic Anglo-Saxon good looks apart from his weak chin, while Stanley was a little man, no taller than Vera. His hair was already thinning and always looked greasy. He had a nut-brown face that Maud prophesied would wrinkle early and shifty black eyes that never looked straight at you. Well aware of who wore the trousers in the Kinaway household, he smiled ingratiatingly at Maud if ever he met her in the street, greeting her with an oily, "Good morning, Mrs. Kinaway, lovely morning," and shaking his head sadly when she marched past him in cold silence.

She wouldn't have him in the shop or the flat above it and she consoled herself in the knowledge that Stanley worked in his bar every evening. The main disadvantage of Vera not having a job was that she was at liberty to meet Stanley during the day, and barmen work peculiar hours, being free for most of the morning and half the afternoon. But Maud thought that "anything wrong," by which she meant sexual intercourse, only ever took place between ten and midnight—this belief was based on her own experience, although in her case she regarded it as right and proper—and it was during those two hours that Stanley was most busily occupied. It was with horror and near-incredulity, therefore, that she learnt from a weeping Vera that she was over two months pregnant.

"Poor Ethel all over again," sobbed Maud. "That such a disgraceful thing should happen to my own child!"

But foolish and wicked as Vera had been, she mustn't be allowed to suffer as Ethel had suffered. Vera should have her husband and her house and a decent home for her baby. Vera should be married.

Instead of the big wedding Maud had dreamed of, Vera and Stanley were married quietly with only a dozen close relatives and friends as guests and they went straight off home to the little terraced house in Lanchester Road, Croughton. There was little Maud could do to humiliate Stanley but she had seen to it that when she and George put up the money for the house, the deeds were in Vera's name and Stanley was made to understand that every penny must be paid back.

They had been married three weeks when Vera had a miscarriage.

"Oh my God," said Maud at the hospital bedside, "why ever were we so hasty? Your father said we should wait a bit and he was right."

"What do you mean?"

"Three weeks we should have waited . . ."

"I've lost my baby," said Vera, sitting up in bed, "and now you'd like to take my husband away from me."

When she was well again, Vera took a job for the first time in her life to pay back the money she owed her parents. For Maud was adamant. She didn't mind giving Vera a cheque now and then to buy herself a dress or taking her out and giving her a slap-up lunch, but Stanley Manning wasn't getting his hooks on her money. He must pull up his socks, make a decent living and then Maud would think again. . . .

As soon as she realised this would never happen, she set out to get Vera away from him, a plan which was far more tenable now she actually lived in the same house with her daughter. She pursued it in two ways: by showing her how difficult her present life was, making it even more difficult and maintaining an atmosphere of strife: and by holding out the inducements of an alternative existence, a life of ease and peace and plenty.

So far she had met with little success. Vera had always been stubborn. Her mother's daughter, Maud thought lovingly. The little bribes and the enticing pictures she had painted of life without Stanley hadn't made a chink in Vera's armour. Never mind. The time had come to put the squeeze on. It hadn't escaped Maud's notice that Vera had turned quite pale at the mention of that twenty thousand pounds. She'd be thinking about that now while she stood in that dreadful place, shoving re-texed, moth-proofed coats into polythene bags. And tonight Maud would play her trump card.

Thinking about it and the effect it would have made her sigh contentedly as she laid her head back against the pillows and switched on the second bar on the electric fire with her good foot. Vera would realise that she meant business and Stanley . . . Well, Stanley would see it was useless getting any ideas about helping his mother-in-law out of this world.

Funny, really. Stanley wanted to get rid of her and she meant to get rid of Stanley. But she was going to get in first. She had him by the short hairs. Maud smiled, closed her eyes and fell at once into deep sleep.

3

Of the fifty motorists who pulled in for petrol at the Superjuce garage that day only five got service from Stanley. He didn't even hear the hooters and the shouts of the half-dozen out of the other forty-five who bothered to wait. He sat with his back to them in his little glass booth, dreaming of the twenty thousand pounds Maud had in the bank and which Vera had told him about at breakfast.

When George Kinaway had died, Stanley had waited excitedly for the contents of the will to be made known to him. He could hardly believe his ears when Vera told him there was no will, for everything had been in her mother's name. Impatient like most people of his kind, he prepared for another long bitter wait and his temper grew sourer.

The tobacconist's had been given up and Maud had retired to luxury in a small but sumptuous detached house at Eltham. Stanley never went there—he wasn't invited—and he showed small sympathy when Vera, lunched and cosseted by her mother, returned home from a day at Eltham full of anecdotes about Maud's high blood pressure. Through the years this was Stanley's only consolation and, being a man of more than average intelligence who could have excelled at any of several well-paid careers if he had only put his mind to it (if he had had a chance, was the way he put it), he set out to study the whole subject of blood pressure and

hardening of the arteries. At that time he was working
as a factory night watchman. No one ever tried to break
into the factory which was on its last legs and contained
nothing worth stealing, so Stanley whiled away the long
hours very pleasantly in reading medical books he got
out of the public library.

It was therefore no surprise to him when he arrived
home one morning to be greeted by Vera with the news
that her mother had had a cerebral thrombosis.

While pulling long faces and being unusually kind
to his wife, Stanley began calculating his inheritance.
There ought to be at least eight thousand from the sale
of Maud's house as well as a tidy sum in the bank. The
first thing he'd buy would be a large car just to put the
neighbours' noses out of joint.

Then Maud got better.

Stanley, hope springing eternal, agreed that she
should come and live with them in Lanchester Road.
The extra work, after all, would fall on Vera and if the
eight thousand didn't immediately fall into his lap, there
was bound to be a share-out. No one, in Stanley's view,
parked themselves on a relative without paying their
way, and if Maud was sticky, he would drop her a gentle
but unmistakable hint.

Two days after she arrived, Maud explained her
intentions. With the exception of ten shillings a week,
her whole pension would be handed over to Vera but
her capital remained where it was, comfortably invested.

"I never heard such a diabolical bloody liberty,"
said Stanley.

"Her pension pays for her food, Stan."

"And what about her lodgings? What about the
work she makes?"

"She's my mother," said Vera.

The time had come to put that phrase into the past
tense. Not murder, of course, not actual murder. Since
he had knocked that old woman on the head and taken
her handbag when he was eighteen, Stanley had never
laid violent hands on anyone and when he read of murder in the newspapers he was as shocked as Vera and as

vociferous as Maud in demanding the return of the
death penalty. As in the case of that shot police constable, for instance, P. C. Chappell, who had died trying
to stop thugs breaking into Croughton Post Office last
month. No, murder was something he wouldn't even
consider. An accident was what he had in mind. Some
sort of carelessness with the gas or a mixup over all
those pills and tablets Maud took.

A scheme for gassing Maud taking shape in his
mind, Stanley walked into the house whistling cheerfully.
He didn't kiss Vera but he said hallo to her and patted
her shoulder as he went to switch on television.

Thinking now of her days as numbered, Stanley had
been prepared to unbend a little with Maud. But as soon
as he saw her, sitting up straight at the table and already
on her second helping of eggs and chips, her face red
with determination and ill temper, he girded himself for
battle.

"Had a busy day, Ma?"

"Busier than yours, I daresay," said Maud. "I had
a chat over the fence with Mrs. Blackmore this afternoon and she said her husband went to get his petrol at
your garage but he couldn't get no service. He could see
you, though, and he reckoned you were asleep."

Stanley glared at her. "I don't want you gossiping
over the fence any more, is that clear? Walking all over
my garden and trampling down the plants."

"It's not your garden, it's Vera's."

She could scarcely have said anything more irritat-
ing to Stanley. Brought up in the country, on the bor-
ders of Essex and Suffolk where his father had a small
holding, he had loved gardening all his life and he called
it his only relaxation, forgetting for the time his crosswords and his medical books. But this passion of his was
out of character—gardening is generally associated with
the mild, the civilised and the law-abiding—and Maud
refused to take it seriously. She liked to think of Stanley
as among the outcast, the utterly lost, while gardening
was one of the pastimes she had respected all her life. So
she would watch him tending his heather garden or wa-

tering his gladioli and then, when he came in to wash his hands, tell him not to forget that the garden, along with the rest of the property, was Vera's and Vera could sell it over his head whenever the fancy took her.

Now, pleased that her retort had needled Stanley, she turned to Vera and asked if she had remembered to get her skein of wool.

"It went right out of my head, Mother. I *am* sorry."

"That puts paid to my knitting for tonight then," said Maud sourly. "If I'd known I'd have got it myself when I was in town."

"What were you doing in town?"

"I went," said Maud, shouting above the television, "to see my solicitor."

"Since when have you had a solicitor?" said Stanley.

"Since this morning, Mr. Clever. A poor old widow in my position needs a solicitor to protect her. He was very nice to me, I can tell you, a real gentleman. Great comfort he gave me. I told him, I'll be able to sleep in my bed now."

"I don't know what you're on about," said Stanley uneasily and he added, "for God's sake someone turn that T.V. down," as if Vera or her mother and not he had switched it on. "That's better. Now we can hear ourselves speak. Right, what's all this about?"

"My will. I made my will this morning and I got the solicitor to put it the way I want it. If Vera and me were living alone it'd be a different thing. All I've got is coming to her, I don't know how many times I've told you. But you listen, this is what I've done. If I die of a stroke you get the lot but if I die of anything else it all goes to Ethel Carpenter. And now you know."

Vera dropped her fork. "I don't know at all, Mother. I don't know what any of that's supposed to mean."

"It's clear enough," said Maud. "So just you think about it."

She gave them a grim smile, and hobbling rapidly to the television, turned up the volume.

"That," said Stanley in bed that night, "is the biggest bloody insult I've ever had said to me. Insinuating I'd put her out of the way! I reckon she's going cracked."

"If it's true," said Vera.

"It doesn't matter a damn whether it's *true*. Maybe she went and maybe she didn't, and maybe the solicitor put that in and maybe he never did. Whichever way you like to look at it, she's got us by the short hairs."

"No, she hasn't, love. It's not as if we'd have dreamt of harming her. Of course she'll die of a stroke. What hurts is that Mother should even think of such a thing."

"And if she doesn't die of a stroke, what then?"

"I don't believe any solictor'd put that in a will." Vera sighed heavily and turned over. "I must go to sleep now. I'm dead tired."

On the whole, Stanley thought Vera was right and no solicitor would have agreed to Maud's condition. It probably wasn't legal. But if Maud said it was and there was no one with the knowledge to argue. . . .

Vera worked all day Saturdays and Stanley and Maud were left alone together. On fine Saturdays Stanley spent hours in the garden and when it rained he went to the pictures.

March had been mild and the almond tree was already in flower. Daffodils were in bud but the ericas in his heather garden were just past their prime. It was time to nourish them with a bale of peat, for the soil of Croughton was London clay. Stanley fetched a new sackful from the shed, scattered peat around the established plants and dug a trench. This would be filled with peat for the new plants he had ordered.

Although he objected to Maud's gossiping over the fence with Mrs. Blackmore at number 59 or Mrs. Macdonald at number 63, Stanley wasn't averse to breaking off from his digging for an occasional chat. Today, when Mrs. Blackmore came out to peg a couple of shirts on her line, he would have like nothing better than to have catalogued, as was his usual habit, Maud's latest

solecisms and insults, but this would no longer do. He
must establish himself in his neighbour's estimation as a
tolerant and even affectionate son-in-law.

"She's all right," he said in answer to Mrs. Blackmore's enquiry. "As well as can be expected."

"I always say to John, Mrs. Kinaway's wonderful
really when you think what she's been through."

Mrs. Blackmore was a tiny birdlike woman who always wore her dyed blonde hair tied up in two bunches
like a little girl, although in other respects she seemed resigned to middle age. Her eyes were sharp and bright
and she had the disconcerting habit of staring hard into
the eyes of anyone with whom she happened to be talking. Stanley met those eyes boldly now, doing his best
not to blink.

"You can't help admiring her," he said with a little
smiling shake of his head.

"I know you really feel that." Mrs. Blackmore was
somewhat taken aback and temporarily her eyes wav-
ered. "Has she seen the doctor lately?"

"Old Dr. Blake retired and she won't have anything to do with the new one. She says he's too young."

"Dr. Moxley? He's thirty-five if he's a day. Still, I
daresay that seems young to her."

"You have to respect their funny ways, the old
folks," said Stanley piously. Their eyes engaged in a
hard tug-of-war which Stanley won. Mrs. Blackmore
dropped her gaze and, muttering something about getting the lunch, went into her house.

Stanley's own meal was of necessity a cold one. He
and Maud ate it in silence and afterwards, while Stanley
sat down with the *Daily Telegraph* crossword, his mother-in-law prepared to have her rest.

When she was alone she simply sat in an armchair
and dozed with her head against one of the wings, but
on Saturdays with Stanley in the room, she made a considerable fuss. First she gathered up every available
cushion, making a point of the pulling out of one behind
Stanley's head, and arranged them very slowly all over
the head and foot of the sofa. Then she made her way

upstairs, tapping her stick and humming, to return with an armful of blankets. The weight of the blankets made her breath laboured and she gave vent to groans. At last, having taken off her glasses and her shoes, she heaved herself up on to the sofa, pulled the blankets over her and lay gasping.

Her son-in-law took absolutely no notice of any of this. He filled in his crossword, smiling sometimes at the ingenuity of the man who had set it, and occasionally mouthing the words of a clue. When Maud could stand his indifference no longer, she said acidly:

"In my young days a gentleman took pride in helping an old lady."

"I'm no gentleman," said Stanley. "You have to have money to be a gentleman."

"Oh, no, you don't. Gentlemen are born, let me tell you. You'd be uncouth no matter what money you'd got."

"You could do with being a bit more couth yourself," said Stanley, and having triumphantly silenced his mother-in-law, he filled in 28 across which completed his puzzle.

Maud closed her eyes and set her mouth in a grim line. Doodling on the edge of his paper, Stanley watched her speculatively until those crinkled compressed lips relaxed, the hand which gripped the blanket went limp and he knew she was asleep. Then, folding his paper, he tiptoed out of the room and made his way to Maud's bedroom.

She had evidently spent the greater part of the morning writing to Ethel Carpenter, for the finished letter lay exposed on her bedside table. Stanley sat down on the edge of the bed to read it.

He had always suspected that he and his doings formed one of the favourite topics of the old women's discussions, but he had never supposed that Maud would devote three and a half sides of paper to nothing but a denigration of his character. He was outraged and he was also bitterly hurt. It was a favour he was doing

Maud, after all, letting her live in his house, and the ingratitude implicit in this letter made his blood boil.

Frowning angrily, he read through what Maud had to say about his laziness and his ill manners. She had even had the effrontery to tell Ethel that he had borrowed a fiver from Vera the day before which, Maud declared, he intended to put on a horse for the National. This had been Stanley's purpose but now he told himself he had wanted it to buy more peat and young heather plants. The old bitch! The evil-tongued old bitch! What was this next bit?

"Of course poor Vee will never see her money again," Maud had written. "He will see to that. She works like a slave but she wouldn't have a rag for her back, bar what I give her. Still, it is only a matter of time now before I shall get her away from him. She is too loyal to say yes mother I'll come, knowing no doubt what a scene *he* would make and perhaps even strike her. I wouldn't put anything past him, my dear. The other day I told her I would buy her whatever she liked to name on condition she would leave him and the tears came into her poor eyes. It went to my heart, I can tell you, seeing my only child in distress. But I tell myself I am being cruel only to be kind and she will thank me on her bended knees when she is rid of him at last and living with me in the lovely house I mean to buy her. I have got my eye on one I saw in an advertisement in the Sunday paper, a lovely place just built in Chigwell, and when Vee has her afternoon off I am thinking of hiring a car to take us both out to look at it. Without *him* of course. . . ."

Stanley nearly tore the letter up, he was so angry. Until then he had had no idea of Maud's plans, for Vera had been afraid to tell him about them, although he had guessed there was something afoot. If I'd only got money, he raged, I'd sue the old bitch for what-d'you-call-it? —enticement. That's what I'd do, have her up in court for trying to take a man's lawful wife away from him.

He sat staring moodily at the letter, suddenly aware

of the great danger he was in. Without Vera, he had no hope of ever getting his hands on that twenty thousand. It would be the breadline for him all the rest of his life while Vera lived in luxury. My God, he thought, even the house, the very roof over his head, belonged to her. And what a beanfeast those two would have, hired cars, perhaps even a car of their own, a modern house in snooty Chigwell, clothes, holidays, every convenience. The whole idea was unbearable to contemplate and suddenly he was seized with the urgency of what he must do and reminded too of his original purpose in coming up to Maud's room.

Leaving the letter as he had found it, he turned his attention to the three containers of pills which stood under the bedlamp. Those pale blue capsules were sleep-inducing; they didn't interest him. Next came the yellow vitamin things which, Stanley was sure, were responsible for Maud's abundant vitality and kept her tongue in sprightly working order. Nevertheless, he wouldn't mess about with them. These were the ones he wanted, the tiny anti-coagulant tablets called Mollanoid of which Maud took six a day and which, Stanley supposed, kept her blood from clotting as it coursed through those brittle arteries. He took one from the carton and folded it inside his handkerchief.

She was still asleep when he came downstairs and, generously, he would have let her have her rest without interruption on any other Saturday. But now, with the memory of the libellous letter uppermost in his mind, he switched on the television for "Sports Round-Up" and took a bitter pleasure in seeing her jerk awake.

Stanley wasn't allowed to leave his glass booth between nine and five, although he often did so and for this truancy had several times been threatened with the sack. But the chemist on the other side of the street would be closed when he knocked off and he couldn't afford to wait until the following Saturday before buying the substitute tablets he required.

He waited until one o'clock, the slackest time of

the day, and then he sneaked across the road. But instead of one of the girls being behind the counter, the pharmacist himself was on duty and showed such an interest in all this fumbling among the bottles and boxes that Stanley thought it wiser to try Boot's, although it was a quarter of a mile away.

There he found all the goods on display on self-service stands and he was able to study a variety of white pills without being observed. All the aspirin and codeine and phenacetin tablets were too big and the only thing he could find approximating in size to Maud's anti-coagulants were a saccharine compound for the use of slimmers.

These he thought would do. The tablets looked exactly like the one he had appropriated. He tried a single tablet on his tongue and it was very sweet, but Maud always swallowed her tablets down quickly in a sweet drink and very likely the taste would be disguised.

"D'you mind not eating the goods before you've paid for them?" said a girl assistant pertly.

"If you're accusing me of stealing I want to see the manager."

"All right, all right. There's no need to shout. That'll be five and six, please."

"And bloody daylight robbery," said Stanley. But he bought the phial of Shu-go-Sub and ran all the way back to the garage.

Three cars were drawn up by the pumps and Stanley's boss, holding the petrol nozzle delicately and furiously as far as possible from the lapels of his immaculate suit, was doing his best to serve the first customer. Stanley went into his booth and watched him through the glass. Presently, when the cars had gone, his boss marched into the booth, rubbing his oily hands.

"I've had about as much of this as I can stand, Manning," he said. "God knows how much custom we'd have lost if some enterprising motorist hadn't phoned me to ask what the hell was going on. I said I wouldn't tell you again and I won't. You can have your cards and get out on Friday."

"It'll be a pleasure," said Stanley. "I was going, anyway, before this dump goes bust."

The loss of his job didn't particularly dismay him. He was used to losing jobs and he enjoyed the freedom of several weeks out of work, during which he would draw ample untaxed unemployment benefit. Telling Vera, though, was something he didn't much look forward to and he was determined to prevent Maud finding out. That would be nice, something to cheer a man up, having his misfortunes shouted over the garden fences and sent winging in choice virulent phrases down over the river to Ethel Carpenter in Brixton.

But perhaps Maud wouldn't be able to gossip or write letters much longer. Stanley fingered the phial in his pocket. She often said it was only her tablets that kept her alive and maybe it wouldn't be more than a few days when her system reacted violently to a concentration of saccharine instead of its usual anticoagulant intake.

Stanley walked home slowly, stopping outside the Jaguar showrooms to eye speculatively a dark red E-type.

4

"These tablets," said Maud, "have a very funny taste. Sweetish. You're sure they made up the prescription right, Vee?"

"It's your regular prescription, Mother. The one old Dr. Blake wrote out before he retired. I took it to

the chemist like I always do." Vera picked up the carton
and looked at it just to make sure Maud wasn't taking
vitamins or diuretics by mistake. No, it was the Mollanoid all right. *Mrs. M. Kinaway,* the label said, *two to be
taken three times a day,* and there was the little smear the
chemist's thumb had made because he hadn't waited for
the ink to dry before handing it to her. "If you've got
any doubts," she said, "why don't you let me make you
an appointment with Dr. Moxley? They say he's ever so
nice."

"I don't want him. I don't want young boys messing me about." Maud sipped her breadfast tea and swallowed her second tablet. "I daresay I've made the tea
too sweet, that's what it is. Anyway, they're not doing
me any harm, whatever's in them. To tell you the truth,
I feel better than I have done for months, not so tired.
There's the postman now. Run down like a good girl
and see if there's anything from your auntie Ethel."

The telephone bill and a letter with the Brixton
postmark. Vera decided she wouldn't open the bill until
she got home. All right, that was being an ostrich, but
who not? Ostriches might stick their faces in the sand
but they did all right, galloping about in Australia or
wherever it was and they didn't get old before their
time. I wouldn't mind being an ostrich or anything come
to that, thought Vera as long as it was a change from
being me.

She grabbed her coat from the hook in the hall and
trailed up the stairs again, buttoning it as she went.
Maud was up, sitting on the side of her bed buffing her
fingernails with a silver-backed polisher.

"It's only ten to," said Maud. "You can spare the
time to hear what Auntie Ethel has to say. You never
know what news she's got."

What news did she ever have? Vera didn't want to
chance being late just to hear that Ethel Carpenter's cy-
clamen had got five flowers on it or her landlady's little
niece had the measles. But she waited just the same, tapping her feet impatiently. Anything to keep the peace,
she thought, anything to put Mother in a good mood.

"What d'you think?" said Maud. "Auntie Ethel's going to move. She's giving up her room and getting one near here. Listen to this: 'I heard of a nice room going in Green Lanes just half a mile from you, dear, and popped over to see it on Saturday.' Why didn't she call, I wonder? Oh, here it is, she says—yes, she says, 'I would have looked you up but I remembered you always have your rest in the afternoon and it seemed a shame to disturb you.' Ethel always was considerate."

"I must go, Mother."

"Wait just one minute . . . 'I wouldn't want to come when Vee was out and you say she works Saturdays.' Et cetera, et cetera . . . Oh, listen, Vee. 'My landlady has got a student to take my room from April 10th, a Friday, and as she has been so good to me and I don't want to put her out, and Mrs. Paterson in Green Lanes can't take me till the Monday, I was wondering if Vee could put me up for that weekend. It would be such a treat to see you and Vee and have a nice long chat about old times. . . .' I'll write back and say yes, shall I?"

"I don't know, Mother." Vera sighed and gave a hopeless shrug. "What will Stanley say? I wouldn't want you and Auntie Ethel getting at him all the time."

"It's your house," said Maud.

"That sort of thing now. That's the very thing I mean. I'll have to think about it. I must *go*."

"I'll have to let her know soon," Maud called after her. "You put your foot down. Stanley'll have to lump it."

He was bound to have heard that, she thought, lying in bed in the next room as he no doubt was. The prospect of the ensuing battle excited her and she felt a surge of well-being comparable to that she used to feel long ago on Sunday mornings when she was looking forward to her weekly walk with George.

It was wrong, of course, to *enjoy* quarrelling. George would have told her to keep the peace at any price. But George had never lived in the same house as Stanley Manning and if he had he would have approved of her tactics. He would have seen the importance of rescuing Vera.

Maud went over to the dressing table and took her framed photograph of George out of a drawer. The slight sentimentality which the sight of it aroused in her was mixed with that exasperation she had so often felt for her husband when he was alive. Without a doubt she missed him, and if he could have been resurrected, would have welcomed him back but still she had to admit that in some ways he had been a drag on her, too weak, too scrupulous and much too inclined to let things drift. Ethel now was a different person altogether. Ethel had had to fight for things all her life, just as she had.

Maud put the photograph away. Nothing could have pleased her more than the news contained in the letter. With Ethel just down the road, and very likely popping in every day, the conquest of Vera would be accomplished in a matter of weeks. Ethel had such a grasp on things, such bustling strength. She would talk to Vera and when Vera saw that an outsider, an uninvolved observer, agreed with her mother, she would surrender and bow to circumstances with all George's resignation.

Stanley would be left alone. It made Maud almost chuckle aloud to think of him dependent only on what he could earn for himself, cooking his own meals and sinking into the squalor which Maud felt was his natural habitat. Not that he would be allowed to occupy this house. He must find himself a room somewhere. But all that could be gone into once Vera was out of his influence. And then perhaps they could settle Ethel in here. Life had treated Ethel badly and it would be such a joy to give her a home of her own at last and see her smiling, maybe even weeping, with gratitude. Maud's heart swelled, full of the pleasure of philanthropy.

The unemployment benefit which the Labour Exchange paid out to Stanley was a good deal in excess of the sum he had mentioned to Vera. He needed the surplus for himself, for he was spending a fortune on Shugo-Sub as well as a fair amount on almost daily visits to the pictures to get out of Maud's way. Hoping to see a considerable decline in her health by this time, he was bitterly disappointed to notice that rather than enfeebled, she seemed actually stronger, more vital looking and younger than before he had begun emptying Shugo-Sub tubes into the Mollanoid carton. If only she would exert herself more, go for walks or carry heavy weights. Letter writing wasn't likely to raise her blood pressure.

Entering the house that evening after a pleasant three hours watching a double horror bill, he was sure there was something going on. Those two were hatching a plot between them, perhaps the very thing he most dreaded, the enticement of Vera. They had stopped talking the minute he walked in the back door and Vera looked as if she had been crying.

"I've been tramping the streets since one," he said, "looking for work."

"Work's not easy to come by when you've no qualifications," said Maud. "Can't they find you anything down at the Labour?"

Stanley took the cup of tea Vera handed him and shook his head gloomily.

"Something will turn up, dear."

"Doesn't matter to him one way or the other, does it?" said Maud. "He's got someone to keep him. Have you given Vee that money you owe her?"

Since he had been substituting saccharine for Maud's tablets, Stanley had moderated his attitude to her, calling her "Ma" and giving in over the television programmes, much as it went against the grain. But now his self-control snapped.

"You mind your own business, Maud Kinaway. That's a private matter between me and my wife."

"What concerns Vera concerns me. That's her money that she earned. Haven't you ever heard of the Married Women's Property Act? Eighteen seventy-something that went through Parliament. More than a hundred years a woman's had a right to her own money."

"I suppose you were sitting in the Ladies' Gallery when it was passed," said Stanley.

The blood rushed into Maud's face. "Are you going to sit there and let him speak to me like that, Vera?"

Vera wasn't sitting at all, but scuttling between the living room and the kitchen with plates of sausages and mashed potato. "I'm so used," she said not quite truthfully, "to hearing you two bicker that it goes right over my head. Come and sit down, do. We want to be finished and cleared away before 'Augusta Alley' comes on."

Prickly and resentful, Maud and Stanley sat down. Neither of them had done a stroke of work all day and their stored-up energy showed in their eyes and the zest with which they both fell on their food. Vera picked at a sausage and left half her mashed potato. It was no good, she hadn't any appetite these days and she began to wonder if Maud hadn't been right when she said she was heading for a nervous breakdown. Sleep didn't refresh her and she was as tired in the mornings as when she went to bed. Having Auntie Ethel here for a long weekend wouldn't help either, as Maud would want a great fuss made over her best friend's entertainment, a clean cloth on the table every day, homemade cakes and then, of course, there would be the spare room to get ready.

Maud must have read her thoughts or else she hadn't been thinking of anything else all day, for she said as she spooned up a second helping of potato, "Have you told Stanley yet?"

"I haven't had a chance, have I? I only got in half an hour ago."

"Told me what?" said Stanley.

Maud swallowed two tablets and made a face. "We're having my friend Ethel Carpenter to stay here."

"You what?" Stanley was much relieved, in fact, to hear that was all it was, for he had expected an announcement of Vera's imminent departure. But now that the greater evil was at least temporarily postponed, the lesser seemed outrageous and he got up, flinging back his chair, and drawing himself up to his full height of five feet five.

"Only for two or three days," said Vera.

"*Only*. Only two or three days. Here am I, up to my neck in trouble, no job, no peace in my own home, and you tell me I've got to have that old cow. . . ."

"Don't you dare! Don't you dare use that foul language in my presence!" Maud was on her feet as well now, clutching her stick. "Ethel's coming here and that's that. Vera and me, we've made up our minds. And you can't stop us. Vera could have you evicted tomorrow if she liked, turned out in the street with just the clothes you stand up in."

"And I," said Stanley, thrusting his face close up to hers, "could have you put in an old folks' home. I don't have to have you here, nobody can make me."

"Criminal!" Maud shouted. "Jailbird! Pig!"

"Two can play at that game, Maud Kinaway. Mean old hag! Poisonous bitch!"

"Lazy no-good wastrel!"

Watching them from the end of the table, Vera thought that any minute they would come to blows. She felt quite calm. If they did strike each other, if they killed each other, she thought she would feel just the same, just as enervated, disembodied and empty of everything but a cold despair. With a dignity neither of them had ever seen in her before, she got up and said in the steady emotionless voice of a High Court judge:

"Be quiet and sit down." They stopped and turned to look at her. "Thank you. It's quite a change for either of you to do anything I ask. Now I've got something to say to you. Either you learn to live together like decent people . . ." Maud tapped her stick. "Shut up, Mother. As I said, either you behave yourselves in future or I'm going." Vera turned away from the flash of triumph in Maud's eyes. "No, Mother, not with you, and not off somewhere with Stanley either. I shall go away by myself. This house doesn't mean a thing to me. I can earn my own living. God knows, I've had to do it long enough. So there you are. One more row and I pack my bags. I mean it."

"You wouldn't walk out on me, Vee?" Stanley whined.

"Oh, yes, I would. You don't love me. If I hadn't got a wage coming in and—and what I'll get from Mother one day, I wouldn't see you for dust. And you don't love me either, Mother. You just love power and playing God and being possessive. All your life you've got your own way but for the once, and you can't bear it that once somebody beat you at your own game."

Vera paused for breath and stared into the two flabbergasted faces. "Yes, I've shaken you both, haven't I? Well, don't forget what I said. One more row and off I go. And another thing. We'll have Auntie Ethel here but not because you want her, Mother. Because I do. She's my godmother and I'm fond of her, and as you're always pointing out, *this is my house*. Now we'll have the television on. 'Augusta Alley,' and you can watch it in peace, Mother. Stanley won't disturb you. He knows I mean what I say."

After that she went out into the kitchen and, although she had won and silenced them, although they were now sitting sullenly in front of the screen, she laid her head on the table and began to sob. Her strength wasn't like Maud's, constant, implacable, insensitive, but intermittent and brief as her father's had been. She doubted whether she had enough of it to make good her threat.

Presently, when she had stopped crying, she washed the tea things and went upstairs. There, in front of her dressing table, she had a good hard look at herself in the glass. Crying hadn't helped. Of course, her face wasn't usually as blotchy and patched with red, but the wrinkles were always there and the brown bruise shadows under her eyes, and the coarse white hairs among the sandy ones, dull pepper-coloured hair that had once been red-gold.

It was understandable that Stanley no longer loved

her, that he only kissed her now during the act of love and sometimes not even then. There came into her mind the memory of those afternoons they had spent in the country, London's country of commons and heaths, before they were married and when she had conceived the child that died before it could be born. It seemed like another life, and the man and the woman who had ached for each other and had clung together gasping in the long grass under the trees, other people.

Strange how important passion was to the young. Beside it, suitability and prudence and security went for nothing. How she and Stanley had laughed at James Horton with his bank account and his church membership and his modest ambition. He'd be a bank manager now, she thought, living in a fine house and married to a handsome woman in her early forties, while she and Stanley . . . She had wasted her life. If James saw her now he wouldn't even recognise her. Miserably she stared at her own worn and undesirable reflection.

Downstairs, Maud and Stanley watched "Augusta Alley," the old woman with a triumph that showed on her face in a perpetual smug smile, her son-in-law impassively, biding his time.

5

Everyone has his escape, his panacea, drugs, drink, tobacco or, more cheaply and innocently, the steady and almost mechanical habit of reading light fiction. Stanley liked a drink and a smoke when he could afford them and he had always been a reader, but the true and constant consolation of his life came from doing crossword puzzles.

Almost every paperback issue of crossword books as well as the fuller and fatter annuals reposed in his bedroom bookcase along with a much-thumbed copy of *Chambers' Twentieth Century Dictionary*. But the white squares in these books had long been filled in and, in any case, the solving of these problems afforded him less pleasure than completing a fresh puzzle each day, one which arrived virgin white on the back page of the *Daily Telegraph* and which, if the answers eluded him, could only be solved by waiting, sometimes almost breathlessly, for the following morning's issue.

He had been doing the *Telegraph* puzzle every day for twenty years and now there was no longer any question of not finishing it. He always finished it and always got it right. Once, some years back, he had found it necessary, like most crossword enthusiasts, to abandon the puzzle when it was half complete and take it up some hours later to find that the elusive clues had clarified during the interim. But even this small frustration had passed away. He would sit down with the paper—he never bothered to read the news—and generally every clue had been solved twenty minutes later. Then an immense satisfaction bathed Stanley. Self-esteem washed away his pressing problems, every worry was buried, sublimated in those interlocking words.

It was no sorrow to him that his wife and his mother-in-law showed not the slightest interest in this hobby of his. He preferred it that way. Nothing can be more irksome, more maddening, to the amateur of crosswords than the well-meaning idiot who, anxious to show off his etymological knowledge, demands from his armchair to be told how many letters in fifteen down or what makes you think four across is yelp and not bark.

Stanley had never forgotten George Kinaway's efforts in this direction, his feebly hearty, "Haven't you finished that puzzle yet?" and his groping determination to supply straightforward answers to clues whose fascination lay in their almost lunatic subtlety. How explain to such a fool as he that "One who is willing" (nine letters, five blanks, T, three blanks) is obviously Testatrix and not Volunteer? Or that "One way or the other, he is tops in the Moslem world" (three letters) is the palindrome Aga and not Bey?

No, those women knew their limitations. They thought it was a silly kid's game—or said they did because it was all Greek to them—but at least they didn't interfere. And these days Stanley needed his puzzles more than ever. The one high spot in his day was the half-hour, perhaps at lunch time, perhaps in the evening, when he could escape from his worries, and suddenly far away from Vera and her mother, lose himself in the intricacies or words and plays upon words.

The rest of the time, God knew, he had trouble enough. He saw very clearly that matters had come to a head, to a straight battle between Maud and himself. On his side he had youth, comparative youth, at any rate, but he couldn't see that he had much else. The dice were heavily loaded in Maud's favour. She wanted to get Vera away from him and it was hard to see how, in time, she could fail. Stanley couldn't understand how she hadn't already succeeded. If he had been in Vera's place, if his mother had come to him with bribes and offers of money and ease, he would have been off like a shot. Stanley felt quite sick when he thought of his fate if Maud were allowed to win. Why, the chances were that pair of bitches wouldn't even let him keep this house.

And now Maud had an ally rushing to her support. If that letter he had read was a typical example of the sort of effusions Maud sent weekly to Ethel Carpenter, her friend would arrive armed against him. He shuddered when he thought of Ethel taking Vera aside, whispering to her in corners, putting Maud's case far more forcefully than Maud could herself, because Ethel would appear as a detached observer, an impartial outsider, seeing the pros and cons without emotional involvement. There was nothing he could do about it. Ethel would come, put in three days' forceful persuasion, and if that wasn't enough to do the trick, would be just around the corner, dropping in two or three times a week, ready with arguments, wearing away Vera's opposition until, at last, beaten down by the pair of them, she would give in.

There was nothing he could do about it—except get rid of Maud first.

But the failure of the Shu-go-Sub had shaken Stanley badly. He read and re-read all his medical books and when he had digested every word reached the conclusion that there are basically no rules as to the incidence of stroke. Maud had had one: she might have another tomorrow; she might never have another. Worry could induce one, but on the other hand, it might not. And what worries did Maud have? Anti-coagulants might prevent one. Ease and quiet might prevent one. No one could say for sure that the absence of anti-coagulants and a life of anxiety would cause one. Stanley reflected disgustedly that what doctors didn't know about cerebral thromboses would fill more volumes than their knowledge. They couldn't even tell you when one was going to occur.

Then there was the question of the will. Stanley was almost certain that Maud couldn't have got any solicitor to agree to that condition. Why, she might quite accidentally fall under a bus. In that case was Vera not to inherit? No, it was an impossible, lunatic condition, but how was he to find out for sure whether or not it had been made? Of course, there was nothing to stop him walking into any solicitor's office and asking straight out. And then, if Maud died, accidentally or by his hand, you could be damn sure the first thing to happen would be that solicitor shooting his mouth off to the police. Clever Maud, Maud with the balance swinging down and throbbing heavily in her favour.

If only he could think of something. It was April now and in a week's time Ethel Carpenter would be here. Once let her arrive and he could say good-bye to everything he had ever hoped for, and look forward to a miserable poverty-stricken old age.

Meanwhile, Stanley continued to substitute Shu-go-Sub for Mollanoid, destroying the anti-coagulants as Vera fetched them on prescription from the chemist and dropping the saccharine into the labelled bottle while Maud was asleep. But it was a forlorn hope. Without his crossword puzzles, he sometimes thought he would go utterly to pieces.

"We can't let your auntie Ethel sleep in that room as it is," Maud said. "We'll have to get a new bedspread for one thing, and some sheets and towels."

"Well, don't look at me, Mother," said Vera. "I've just had the phone bill to pay."

"I wasn't intending you to pay for them, dear," Maud said hastily. "You get them and I'll give you a cheque." She smiled ingratiatingly at her daughter and stirred herself to help clear the table. The last thing she wanted at the moment was to antagonise Vera. Suppose she had really meant what she said and would be wicked enough to run away and leave her with Stanley? She would have to cook Stanley's meals and wait on him. "We'd better both have new dresses, too. When you have your afternoon off we'll go down to Lucette's and choose something really smart."

"Anyone would think it was the Queen coming," said Stanley.

Maud ignored him. "I'm getting quite excited. I think I'll have that girl in to give me a home perm and you must have your hair set in your lunch hour. And we'll need some flowers for Auntie's room. Auntie Ethel loves flowers."

She settled down contentedly with her knitting, repeating silently the words she had written to Ethel Carpenter that morning. ". . . You mustn't be too upset by the state of this house, dear. It's a poor old place and a crying shame that Vee should have had to live in it so long but we shall soon see some changes. When I see you I'll show you some of the details of new houses estate agents have sent me. The one I have my eye on has a fully fitted Wrighton kitchen and luxury sunken bath. Quite a change from the old days!! And I've been wondering if you would like to move in here. Of course, I would have it painted throughout for you and a sink unit put in. We can talk about it when you come. I know I can rely on you to help me in bringing Vee round to my point of view. . . ." Maud smiled and saw that Stanley had caught her smile. He frowned blackly. If only he knew!

"Time for 'Augusta Alley,' " she said confidently.

Stanley didn't say a word. He threw down his completed puzzle, flung open the french windows and went out into the darkening garden.

"We've got some old tab coming here," said Stanley to Mr. Blackmore. "Pal of my ma-in-law's. They couldn't make more fuss if it was royalty."

"I daresay Mrs. Kinaway doesn't see all that many people." Blackmore stuck his ladder against the house wall and mounted it, carrying with him brush and paint pot.

"Excitement's no good to her." Stanley stuck his fork in the soil. "Going on the way she is she'll have another one of those strokes."

"I sincerely hope not."

"Hmm," said Stanley and he turned away to concentrate on his trench. He had ordered a fresh bale of peat and it ought to arrive in a day or two. The next thing was to wheedle the money for some of that new variety of magenta heather out of Vera. If she had any. God knew how much she and the old girl together had blued on entertaining Ethel Carpenter.

For once, however, she'd done some of the work herself. Light work, of course, the kind of thing the ladies who had employed her wouldn't have been above undertaking. Stanley drew in his breath in an angry hiss when he looked at his ruined display of daffodils, every other one snapped off, not even cut, to make a fancy flower arrangement in Ethel Carpenter's bedroom.

The room itself had been transformed. Anxious about the sudden dissipation of his inheritance, Stanley had looked on gloomily while Maud wrote out cheques, one for Lucette's where her dress and Vera's had come from, one for all the special food they had to get in and another for the draper's who had sent up a pair of lemon nylon sheets, two matching frilled pillowcases and a pair of black and lemon towels. But it was Vera, of course, who had washed all the paintwork and turned the mattress and starched the little lace mats Maud wanted to see on Ethel's dressing table.

The depredations of his daffodil bed so depressed Stanley that he gave up gardening at eleven and trailed despondently into the house. He didn't go into the dining room. Maud was in there, having her hair permed by the dispirited young housewife who went out hairdressing to help make ends meet. The door was shut but didn't prevent a nasty smell of ammonia and rotten eggs from seeping into the rest of the house.

The second post had come, the one that brought local or near-local letters. A fortnight before Stanley had written to the editor of a national newspaper offering his services as a crossword puzzle setter, a job which he felt would really suit him and give outlet to his creative talents. But the editor hadn't replied and Stanley had almost given up hope. He picked up the letters from the mat and contemplated them gloomily. Nothing for him as usual. Just the gas bill and a long envelope addressed to Maud.

It wasn't stuck down. Stanley took it into the kitchen and wondered who could be writing to Maud and typing the address. Possibly her solicitor.

From the other side of the thin dividing wall he heard Maud say, "If that's the last curler in, dear, why don't you pop into the kitchen and make us a nice cup of coffee?" He grabbed the letter and took it upstairs.

In the privacy of his bedroom, his crossword annuals around him, he slid the single folded sheet out of the envelope. It wasn't from a solicitor. It wasn't a letter as such at all. Growing suddenly cold, Stanley read:

64, Rosebank Close, Chigwell, Essex.

This desirable bungalow property, freehold and overlooking the Green Belt, is moderately priced at
£7,600, and comprises a magnificent through lounge
with York stone fireplace, two double bedrooms, luxu-
rious air conditioned kitchen with waste disposal unit,
spacious bathroom and separate W.C. Details are as
follows: . . .

Stanley didn't read the details. He had seen
enough. Maud must be very confident if she had
reached the stage of actually approaching estate agents.
Like the commander of an army, she had decided on
her strategy and was marching ahead, overthrowing everything that obstructed her path. While he . . . He and
his poor forces were falling back on every hand, their
weapons impotent, their pathetic outflanking movement
ineffective. Soon he would be driven into what sanc-
tuary he could find for himself. And it wasn't going to
be any St. Helena but a furnished room or even—horror
of horrors!—a working man's hostel.

Here, at least, was one desirable property she
would never get her hands on. Stanley put a match to
the paper and burnt it in the grate. But destroying it afforded him small pleasure. It was about as satisfying as
burning the dispatch that tells the defeated general the
battle is over, his forces scattered and capitulation inevitable. As in such a case, another dispatch will come.
The destruction of the news does nothing to impair the
fact of defeat.

He went downstairs and indulged himself in the
only comfort left to him. But the crossword puzzle was
completed in fifteen minutes and Stanley found that
these days he was no longer able to derive his old pleasure from digesting and appreciating the clues after they
were solved, from chuckling silently over such witty efforts as: "Nutcracker Suite"—Tchaikovsky's interpreta-
tion of shelling, or "Wisdom Tooth"—Root cause of
biting wit? Nevertheless he repeated them slowly to himself and the very repetition of the words soothed him.

He rested his elbows on the kitchen table and whispered over and over again: "Underwear for barristers"—briefs. "Does this book tell of a terrible Tsar at Plymouth?"—Ivanhoe. A pity they didn't put two in every day instead of only one, he thought with a sigh. Maybe he'd write to them and suggest it. But what would be the use? They wouldn't answer. Nothing went his way these days.

The hairdresser girl was off now. He heard the front door close. Maud came out into the kitchen, her iron-grey hair in large fat curls all over her head. The curls reminded Stanley of those cushion-shaped pot scourers one buys in packets. They had the same hard, metallic and durable look. But he said nothing, only gave her a dismal stare.

Since Vera's threatening outburst they had been wary of each other in the evenings, distant rather than polite, scarcely ever provocative. But during the day war had been maintained with as much vitriol as ever and Stanley expected her to pull the paper away from him with some such accompanying insult as: "Why don't you take your lazy self out somewhere?" But Maud merely said, "She's made a nice job of my hair, hasn't she? I wouldn't want Ethel to think I'd let myself go."

Half a dozen apt and rude retorts came to Stanley's lips. He was deciding which one of them would have the most stinging effect, bring the blood rushing to Maud's face and spark off a bitter interchange, when, staring sourly at her, he saw it would be of no use. Maud hadn't made that innocent remark about her hair because she was weakening or softening with age or because it was a nice sunny day. She wasn't trying to establish a truce. She had spoken as she had because warfare was no longer necessary. Why bother to swat a fly when you have only to open a window and drive it outside? She had won and she knew it.

Speechless, Stanley watched her open the larder door and view with a blank, perhaps very faintly amused expression, the cold pie Vera had left for their lunch.

6

When Stanley was out of work, it was unusual for either him or Maud to appear downstairs before nine-thirty in the morning. Indeed, Maud often remained in her room until eleven, manicuring her nails, tidying her dressing table and her shelf of medicaments, writing another instalment of her weekly letter to Ethel Carpenter. But on Friday, April the tenth, the morning of Ethel's arrival —E-Day, as Stanley called it bitterly—both astonished Vera by appearing at the breakfast table.

Each had awakened early, Stanley because the gloom and actual dread occasioned by the imminence of Ethel's coming had made dozing in bed impossible, and Maud because she was too excited to sleep.

Taking her place at the table and filling her plate liberally with cornflakes, Maud thought how wonderfully and suddenly those two had begun to dance to her piping. It was a good fortnight since Stanley had spoken an insolent word to her. Defeat was implicit in every line of his body, hunched up as it was, elbows on the table, dull eyes staring disconsolately out into the garden. And as for Vera . . . Maud had hardly been able to stop herself from shouting with triumph at Vera's face when she had seen all those new towels and sheets arrive at the house, her wistful wonder at the blue and white spotted dress, a model, Maud had made her buy. One word from Auntie Ethel and she would yield utterly. Of course she would; it wasn't human nature to do otherwise.

"One egg or two, Mother?" Vera called from the kitchen.

Maud sighed with satisfaction. Her quick ears noted that Vera's voice had lost that querulous, martyred tone which used to annoy her so much. It was now reserved for Stanley.

"Two, please, dear." Maud swallowed her two tablets, washing them down with a big gulp of tea. Really strong and sweet it was, the way she liked it. Sugar was what she needed to keep her strength up for the long day ahead, sugar and plenty of protein.

Vera bustled in with the plate of eggs and bacon, stopping to saw off a thick slice of bread for Maud. Stanley sipped his tea slowly like an invalid.

"Try and get home early, won't you, Vee?"

"I'll see if I can make it by five. You said Auntie Ethel wouldn't be here till five, didn't you?"

Maud nodded complacently.

She went to work with a will as soon as Vera had gone, scouring the thin carpets with Vera's old vacuum cleaner, waxing the hall floor and lastly preparing the feast which was to gladden Ethel's heart. It was years since she had done a stroke of housework and in former days she would rather have seen the place turn into a slum about her than let Stanley Manning see her lift a duster. But now it no longer mattered. Stanley wandered about from room to room, watching her and saying nothing. Maud didn't care. She hummed her favourite old hymn tunes under her breath as she worked ("Lead Us, Heavenly Father, Lead Us" and "Love Divine, All Loves Excelling"), just as she used to do all those years ago in the big house before the master and mistress were up.

They had lunch at twelve.

"I'll clear away and do the dishes," she said when they had finished their cold rice pudding. "It wouldn't do to have Ethel come and find the place in a mess."

"I don't know why you and Vee can't act more natural."

"Cleanliness," said Maud, taking advantage of Vera's absence to have a prohibited dig at him, "*is* natural to some people." She rushed around, wiping surfaces, her limp hardly noticeable. "I shall put on my new dress and get myself all ready and then I'll have a lay-down on my bed."

"What's wrong with the couch in there?" Stanley cocked a thumb towards the dining room.

"That room is all tidied up ready for tea, and I can't go in the lounge on account of that's where we're going to receive Ethel."

"My God," said Stanley.

"Please don't blaspheme." She waited for the spirited rejoinder and when it didn't come, said sharply, "And you needn't go messing the place up. We don't want them crossword puzzles of yours laying about."

Stanley rose to that one but only with a shadow of his former verve. "You needn't worry about me. I'm going to take my lazy no-good self out. Maybe you'd like me to stay away the whole weekend." Maud sniffed. She rinsed her hands, dried them and moved majestically towards the door. Stanley tried a feeble parting shot. "Mind you don't oversleep. God knows what would happen if *Miss* Carpenter had to hang about waiting on the step."

"I'm a very light sleeper," Maud said gaily. "The least little thing wakes me."

Life wasn't going to be worth living for the next few days. Those women would be screaming at him morning, noon and night to wipe his feet and wash his hands and run around after Ethel Carpenter till he couldn't call his soul his own. She would go, of course, on Sunday or Monday, but only round the corner to Green Lanes, and how many times a week would he find her back here again, her feet under his table?

That in itself was a sufficiently gloomy prospect, Stanley thought, leaning forward on the table, his head in his hands. He could at a pinch put up with that, but one day he'd walk in from the pictures or from work—he'd have to get a job if only to get out of this house—to find the lot of them gone and a note on the table with a Chigwell phone number on it and a short sharp request for him to find other accommodation.

Once let Ethel arrive and the eventual outcome was inevitable. Stanley glanced up at the old kitchen clock. Half-past one. Three and a half hours and she would be here.

He wandered into the dining room to find himself a more comfortable chair but it was chilly in there and the excessive neatness had about it an almost funereal air. The laid and spread table was covered by a second cloth, as white as snow. Indeed, the whole arrangement, stiff and frigid-looking, gave the impression of a hillocky landscape blanketed by crisp fresh snow. Stanley approached the table and lifted the cloth, then pulled it away entirely.

In the centre of the table stood a pillar of red salmon, still keeping the cylindrical shape of the can from which it had come, and surrounded by circles of cucumber and radishes cut to look like flowers. This dish was flanked by one of beetroot swimming in vinegar, another of potato salad and a third of cole slaw. Three cut loaves of different varieties awaited Maud's attention when her guest arrived. The butter, standing in two glass dishes, had been cut about and decorated with a fork. Next Stanley saw a cold roast chicken wih a large canned tongue beside it, and on the perimeter of the table three large cakes, two iced and bound with paper frills and one Dundee. Chocolate biscuits and ginger nuts had been arranged in patterns on a doily and there were half a dozen little glass dishes containing fish paste, honey, lemon curd and three kinds of jam.

All that fuss, Stanley thought, for an old women who was no better than a common servant. Sausages or fish fingers were good enough for him. So this was the way they meant to live once they'd got all their sneaking underhand plans fixed up? He dropped the cloth back and wondered what to do with himself for the rest of the afternoon. He couldn't go out, except into the garden, for he hadn't a penny to bless himself with.

Then he remembered he'd seen Vera drop some loose change into the pocket of her raincoat the night before. She hadn't worn that coat this morning because the early part of the day had been bright and summery. Stanley went upstairs and opened his wife's wardrobe. Hoping for a windfall of five bob or so which would take him to the pictures, he felt in the pockets, but both were empty. He swore softly.

It had begun to rain, a light drizzle. Vera would get wet and serve her damn well right. Five past two. The whole grey empty afternoon stretched before him with an old women's tea party at the end of it. Might as well be dead, he thought, throwing himself on the bed.

He lay there, his hands behind his head, miserably contemplating the cracked and pock-marked ceiling which a fly traversed with slow determination like a single astronaut crossing the bleak surface of the moon. The *Telegraph* was on the bedside table where he had left it that morning, and he picked it up. He didn't intend to do the puzzle—that he was saving to alleviate the deeper gloom of the coming evening—but looked instead at the deaths column which ran parallel to the crossword clues.

How different his life would be if between the announcements of the departure of Keyes, Harold, and Konrad, Franz Wilhelm, there appeared Kinaway, Maud, beloved wife of the late George Kinaway and dear mother of Vera. . . . He scanned the column unhappily. Talk about threescore years and ten being man's alloted span! Why, to find a man or woman dying in their late eighties was commonplace, and Stanley counted three well over ninety. Maud might easily live another twenty years. In twenty years' time he'd be sixty-five. God, it didn't bear thinking of. . . .

Stanley was aroused from this dismal reverie by the front doorbell ringing. Only the girl come to read the gas meter, he supposed. Let her ring. By now Maud was snoring so loudly that he could hear her through the wall. So much for all that rubbish about being a light sleeper and hearing every sound.

She had overtired herself with all that unaccustomed work. A tiny shred of hope returned as Stanley wondered if the work and the excitement had perhaps been too much for her. All that polishing and bending down and reaching up . . .

The bell rang again.

It could be his new bale of peat arriving. Stanley got off the bed. The rain had stopped. He poked his head out of the window and, seeing no seedsman's van parked in the street, was about to withdraw it when a stout figure backed out on to the path from under the overhanging canopy of the porch.

Stanley hadn't seen Ethel Carpenter since his wedding but he had no doubt that this was she. The frizzy hair under the scarlet felt helmet she wore was greyish white now instead of greyish brown but otherwise she seemed unchanged.

She waved her umbrella at him and called out, "It's Stanley, isn't it? I thought for a minute there was nobody in."

Stanley made no reply to this. He banged down the window, cursing. His first thought was to go into the next room and shake Maud till she woke up, but that would put Maud into a furious temper, which she would assuage by abusing him violently in the presence of this fat old woman in the red hat. Better perhaps to let Ethel Carpenter in himself. Two or three hours' chatting alone with her was Stanley's idea of hell on earth, but on the other hand he might use the time profitably to put in some propaganda work.

On his way down, he peered in at Maud but she was still snoring with her mouth open. He trailed downstairs and opened the front door.

"I thought you were never coming," said Ethel.

"Bit early, aren't you? We didn't expect you till five."

"My landlady's new lodger came in a bit before

time, so I thought I might as well be on my way. I know Maud'll be sleeping, so you needn't wake her up. Well, aren't you going to ask me in?"

Stanley shrugged. This old woman had an even more shrewish and shrill manner than Maud and he could see he was in for a fine time. Ethel Carpenter trotted past him into the hall, leaving her two suitcases on the doorstep. Treating me like a bloody porter, thought Stanley, going to pick them up. God, they weighed a ton! What had she got in them? Gold bars?

"Heavy, aren't they? I reckon I've nearly broke my back lugging them all the way from the station. I'm not supposed to carry weights, not with my blood pressure, but seeing as you haven't got no car and couldn't put yourself out to meet me, I didn't have much option."

Stanley dumped the cases on the gleaming mosaic floor. "I was going to meet you," he lied. "Only you were coming at five."

"Well, we needn't have a ding-dong about it. By all accounts, you're fond of a row. There, I'm coming over dizzy again. The room's just going round and round."

Ethel Carpenter put one hand up to her head and made her way somewhat less briskly than before into the seldom used front room Vera and Maud called the lounge.

"I had a couple of dizzy spells on my way here," she said, adding proudly, " my blood pressure was two hundred and fifty last time I saw my doctor."

Another one, thought Stanley. Another one moaning about something no one could prove and using it to get out of doing a hand's turn. For his part, he was beginning to believe, despite all his reading, that there was no such thing as blood pressure.

"Don't you want to take your things off?" he said gloomily. Get her upstairs and maybe Maud would wake up. He saw that any anti-Maud propaganda he might have in mind would fall on stony ground. "D'you want to see your room?"

"May as well." Ethel took her hand from her head and shook herself. "The giddiness has passed off. Well,

that's a relief. I'll have my cases up at the same time.
Lead on, Macduff."

Stanley struggled up the stairs after her. Anybody
would think by the weight of them that she was coming
for a fortnight. Maybe she was. . . . Christ, he thought.

In the spare room Ethel took off her hat and coat
and laid them on the bed. Then she unpinned her scarf
to stand revealed in a wool dress of brilliant kingfisher
blue. She was about Maud's build but fatter and much
redder in the face. She surveyed the room and sniffed
the daffodils.

"I've been to this house before," she said. "There,
you didn't know that, did you? I came with Maud and
George when they were thinking of buying it for Vee."
Stanley clenched his teeth at this reminder, certainly in-
tentionally made, of the true ownership of the house. "I
thought you'd have bettered yourself by now."

"What's wrong with it? It suits me."

"Tastes differ, I daresay." Ethel patted her hair.
"I'll just have a peep at Maud and then we'll go down
again, shall we? We don't want to wake her up."

Grimly resigning himself to fate, Stanley said,
"You won't wake her. It'd take a bomb falling to wake
her. She always sleeps her three hours out."

A sentimental smile on her face, Ethel gazed at her
friend. Then, closing the door, she resumed a more truc-
ulent and severe expression.

"That's no way to talk about Vee's mother. Everything you've got you owe to her. I knew you'd be here
when I came, being as you're on the dole, and I thought
we might have a little talk, you and me."

"You did, did you? What about?"

"I don't want to stand about on the landing. The
giddiness is coming over me again. We'll go downstairs."

"It strikes me," said Stanley, "you'd be better lying
down if you feel queer. I've got to go out, anyway. I've
got things to see to."

Once in the lounge she sank heavily into a chair
and lay back in silence, her breath coming in rough

gasps. Stanley watched her, convinced she was putting on a show for his benefit. No doubt, she thought she'd get a cup of tea out of him this way.

Presently she sighed and, opening her large black handbag, took out a lace handkerchief with which she dabbed at her face. For the time being she seemed to have forgotten her plan to take him to task, for when she spoke her voice was mild and shaky and her attention caught by a framed photograph of Vera and Stanley which stood on the marble mantelpiece. It had been taken at their wedding and Vera, deriving no pleasure from looking at it, usually kept it in a drawer. But Maud, determined to brighten up this gloomy room, had got it out again along with a pair of green glass vases, a Toby jug and a statuette of a nude maiden, all of which were wedding presents.

"I've got that picture myself," said Ethel. "It stands by my bed. Or stood, I should say, seeing that it's packed in the trunk I'm having sent on with all my other little bits."

"Sent on to Green Lanes?" asked Stanley hopefully.

"That's it. Fifty-two Green Lanes, to Mrs. Paterson's." She stared at the picture. "No, I don't reckon that's the same as my one. My one's got the bridesmaids in, if I remember rightly. Let's have a closer look."

As soon as she got to her feet she became dizzy again. Although it went against the grain with him, Stanley got up to give her his arm. But Ethel made a little movement of independence, a gesture of waving him away. She took a step forward, and as she did so, her face contorted and she gave a hollow groan, an almost animal sound, the like of which Stanley had never heard before from a human being.

This time he started forward, both arms outstretched, but Ethel Carpenter, groaning again, staggered and fell heavily to the floor before he could catch her.

"My Christ," said Stanley, dropping to his knees. He took her wrist and felt for a pulse. The hand sank limply into his. Then he tried her heart. Her eyes were wide open and staring. Stanley got up. He had no doubt at all that she was dead.

It was twenty-five to three.

Stanley's first thought was to go for Mrs. Blackmore. He knocked at the front door of number 59 but there was no one in. There was no need to knock at Mrs. Macdonald's. Underneath the figures 63 a note had been pinned: "Gone to shops. Back 3:30." The street was deserted.

Back in the house a thought struck him. Who but he knew that Ethel Carpenter had ever arrived? And immediately this idea was followed by another, terrible, daring, wonderful and audacious.

Maud would sleep till four at least. He looked dispassionately at the body of Ethel Carpenter, speculatively, calculatingly, without pity. There was no doubt she had died of a stroke. She had overdone it. Her blood pressure had been dangerously high and carrying those cases three quarters of a mile had been the last straw. It was cruelly unfair. No one profited by her death, no one would be a scrap the happier, while Maud who had so much to leave behind her . . .

And of a stroke too, the one death Maud had to have if he was ever going to get his hands on that twenty thousand. Why couldn't it have been Maud lying there? Stanley clenched his hands. Why not do it? Why not? He had a good hour and a half.

Suppose it didn't work out? Suppose they rumbled him? There wasn't much they could do to him if one of them, Maud or Vera or some nosy neighbour, came in while he was in the middle of his arrangements. They might put him inside for a bit. But a couple of months in jail was better than the life he lived. And if it came off, if the hour and a half went well, he'd be rich and free and happy!

In his last term at school, when he was fifteen, Stanley had taken part in the school play. None of the boys had understood what it was all about; nor, come to that, had the audience. Stanley had forgotten all about it until now when some lines from it came back to him, returning not just as rubbish he had had to learn by heart, regardless of their meaning, but as highly significant advice, relevant to his own dilemma.

> *There is a tide in the affairs of men*
> *Which, taken at the flood, leads on to fortune.*
> *Omitted, all the voyage of their lives*
> *Is bound in shallows and in miseries.*
> *On such a full sea are we now afloat,*
> *And we must take the current while it serves*
> *Or lose our ventures.*

If ever a man was afloat on a full sea it was Stanley Manning. These iambic pentameters, hitherto meaningless, had come into his mind as a direct command. If he had been a religious man, he would have thought them from God.

The telephone was in the lounge where Ethel Carpenter lay. He ran upstairs two at a time to make sure Maud was still asleep and then he shut himself in the lounge, drew a deep breath and dialled the number of Dr. Moxley's surgery. Ten to one the doctor wouldn't be in and they'd tell him to phone for an ambulance and then it would all be over.

But Dr. Moxley was in, his last afternoon patient just gone. So far, so good, thought Stanley, trembling. The receptionist put him through and presently the doctor spoke.

"I'll come now before I make any of my other calls. Mr. Manning, you said? Sixty-one Lanchester Road? Who is it you think has died?"

"My mother-in-law," said Stanley firmly. "My wife's mother, Mrs. Maud Kinaway."

2. Across

7

When he put the phone down Stanley was shaking all over. He'd have to take the next step before the doctor came and his courage almost failed him. There was a half bottle of brandy, nearly full, in the sideboard and Stanley, sick and shivering, got it out and drank deep. It wouldn't matter if Dr. Moxley smelt it on his breath as it was only natural for a man to want a drink when his mother-in-law had fallen down dead in front of him.

Vee would have to see the body, *a* body. That meant he'd have to be careful about how he did it. God, he *couldn't* do it! He hadn't the strength, his hands weren't steady enough to swat a fly, let alone . . . But if Maud were to come down while the doctor was there . . .

Stanley drank some more brandy and wiped his mouth. He went out into the dark still passage and listened. Maud's snores throbbed through the house with the regularity of a great heart beating. Stanley's own had begun to pound.

The doorbell rang and he nearly fainted from the shock.

Dr. Moxley couldn't have got there already. It wasn't humanly possible. Christ, suppose it was Vee forgotten her key? He staggered to the door. This way he'd have a stroke himself. . . .

"Afternoon, sir. One bale of peat as ordered."

It was in a green plastic sack. Stanley looked from it to the man and back again, speechless with relief.

"You all right, mate? You look a bit under the weather."

"I'm all right," Stanley mumbled.

"Well, you know best. It's all paid for. Shall I shove it in your shed?"

"I'll do that. Thanks very much."

Dragging the sack through the side entrance, Stanley heard Mrs. Blackmore pass along the other side of the fence. He ducked his head. When he heard her door slam he tipped the peat out on to the shed floor and covered it with the empty sack.

Seeing two other people circumstanced very much like himself, the delivery man who lived, he knew, in a poky council flat, and Mrs. Blackmore, a tired drudge with a chronic inability to manage on her housekeeping, brought Stanley back to reality and hard fact. He must do it now, vacillate no longer. If he had been as familiar with *Hamlet* as he was with *Julius Caesar,* he would have told himself that his earlier hesitation, his moment of scruples, was only the native hue of resolution sicklied o'er with the pale cast of thought.

He closed the front door behind him and mounted the stairs, holding his hands clenched in front of him. Maud was quiet now. God, suppose she was up, dressed, ready to come down . . . ? Outside her door he knelt down and looked through the keyhole. She was still asleep.

It seemed to Stanley that never in his life had he been aware of such silence, the traffic in the street lulled, no birds singing, his own heart suspending its beats until the deed was done. The silence, heavy and unnatural, was like that which is said to precede an earthquake. It frightened him. He wanted to shout aloud and break it or hear, even in the distance, a human voice. He and Maud might be alone in an empty depopulated world.

The hinges of the door had been oiled a week before because Maud complained that they squeaked, and the door opened without a sound. He went to the bed and stood looking down at her. She slept like a contented child. His thoughts were so violent, so screwed to courage that he felt they must communicate themselves to her and wake her up. He drew a deep breath and put out his hand to seize the pillow from under her head.

Dr. Moxley didn't ring the bell. He used the knocker and it made a tumultuous metallic clatter through the house. Maud turned over, sighing, as if she knew she had been reprieved. For a moment, watching her, Stanley thought it was all up with him. His plan had failed. But still she slept and still her hand hung limp over the side of the bed. Holding his hand to his chest, as if he feared his lurching, actually painful, heart would burst through his rib cage, Stanley went down to admit the doctor.

He was a boyish-looking man with a shock of black hair, a stethoscope hanging round his neck.

"Where is she?"

"In here," said Stanely, his voice throaty. "I thought it better not to move her."

"Really? I'm not a policeman, you know."

Stanley didn't like that at all. He was beginning to feel sick. He shuffled into the room after the doctor, aware that his face was covered in sweat.

Dr. Moxley knelt down on the floor. He examined the body of Ethel Carpenter and felt the back of her neck.

"My mother-in-law," said Stanley, "had a stroke four years back and . . ."

"I know all that. I looked up Dr. Blake's notes before I came out. Help me to lift her on to the couch."

Together they got the body on to the couch and Dr. Moxley closed her eyes.

"Have you something to cover her with? A sheet?"

Stanley couldn't bear another moment's delay.

"Was it a stroke, Doctor?"

"Er—yes. A cerebral thrombosis. Seventy-four, wasn't she?"

Stanley nodded. Ethel Carpenter, he remembered, had been a bit younger than that, three or four years younger. But doctors couldn't tell, could they? They couldn't tell that precisely. Apparently they couldn't.

Now the doctor was doing what Stanley had longed for, getting a small pad out of his briefcase and a pen from his breast pocket.

"What about that sheet, then?"

"I'll get it," Stanley mumbled.

"While you're doing that I'll write out the death certificate for you."

The sheets were kept in the linen cupboard in the bathroom. Stanley pulled one out, but, before he could go downstairs again the sickness overcame him, accompanied by a fresh outbreak of sweat, and he vomited into the washbasin.

The first thing he saw when he came back into the lounge was Ethel Carpenter's ringless left hand dropping from the couch. Christ, she was supposed to be a married woman. . . . The doctor had his back to her and was writing busily. Stanley unfolded the sheet and draped it over the body, tucking the hand into its folds.

"That's right," said Dr. Moxley more pleasantly. "This is an unfortunate business for you, Mr. Manning. Where's your wife?"

"At work." Give me the certificate, Stanley prayed. For God's sake, give it to me and go.

"Just as well. You must tell yourselves that she'd had a long life, and certainly it was a quick and probably painless death."

"We can't any of us go on forever, can we?" said Stanley.

"Now you'll need these." Dr. Moxley handed him two sealed envelopes. "One is for the undertaker and the other you must take with you when you go to register the death. You follow all that?"

Stanley wanted to say, I'm not stupid just because I don't talk la-di-da like you, but instead he simply nodded and put the envelopes on the mantelpiece. Dr. Moxley gave a last inscrutable glance at the sheeted body and strode out, his stethoscope swinging. At the front door he stopped and said, "Oh, just one thing . . ."

His voice was terribly loud, ringing as if he were addressing an audience instead of just one man. A cold shiver ran through Stanley, for the doctor's expression was suddenly thoughtful. He looked like a man who has recalled some vital step he has omitted to take. Holding the door ajar, he said, "I didn't ask whether you wanted burial or cremation."

Was that all? Stanley hadn't thought of it either. He wished he dared ask the doctor to keep his voice down. In a tone so low that it was almost a whisper, he said, "Cremation. That was her wish. Definitely cremation." Burn Ethel, destroy her utterly, and then there could never be any questions. "Why d'you want to know?" he asked.

"In cases of cremation," said Dr. Moxley, "two doctors are required to certify death. It's the law. Leave it to me. I imagine you'll be having Woods's, the undertakers, and I'll ask my partner. . . ."

"Dr. Blake?" Stanley said before he could stop himself.

"Dr. Blake has retired from practice," said Moxley a shade coldly. He gave Stanley a penetrating look, reminiscent of Mrs. Blackmore, and then he banged out of the house, crashing the front door.

Enough to wake the dead, Stanley thought. It was a quarter to four. Time enough to get on to the undertakers when he had hidden Ethel's body and dealt with Maud. . . . The corpse under the sheet might get by a doctor who had never seen Maud before, but it wouldn't get by Vera. Vera must see Maud and, needless to say, she must see Maud dead.

He pulled back the sheet and rolled it up. Then he put his hands under Ethel Carpenter's arms and dragged her half on to the floor. He was a small thin man and her weight was almost too much for him. He stood up, gasping, and his eye lighted on the black handbag which stood beside the chair she had been sitting in. That would have to be hidden too.

He opened the bag and a wave of something sweet and sickly tickled his nostrils. The scent came from a half-empty packet of violet cachous. Stanley vaguely remembered seeing these things, sweets used as breath fresheners, in glass bottles in sweetshops before the war when he had been a boy. Sometimes his mother used to buy them at the village shop or when they went into Bures for a day out. He thought they had long elapsed into disuse along with aniseed balls and Edinburgh rock and now their scent, assailing him unexpectedly, brought back his old home to him, the green river Stour where he had fished for loaches and miller's thumbs, the village between a fold in the shadow hills, an ancient peace.

He took out a violet cachou and held it between finger and thumb. A powerful perfume of violets and strong sugar came to him and he held it to his nose. Seventeen he'd been when he'd run away from them all, his parents, his brothers, the river and the fishing. Off to make his fortune, he'd told them, sick with envy and resentment of his two brothers, one halfway through a good apprenticeship, the other off to college. I'll be back, he'd said, and I'll be worth more than the lot of you. But he never had gone back and the last time he'd seen his father was at the Old Bailey where they'd sent for him to be present at his son's trial.

Things were different now. That fortune had taken nearly thirty years to make but now it was almost made. Just one more little step to take . . . And when he'd got the money, maybe next week, he'd go up to Bures in his car and surprise them all. "How about a spot of fishing?" he'd say to his brother, the master printer, and he'd bring out his shining new tackle. "Put it away," he'd say to his brother, the secondary school teacher, when he felt in his pocket for a handful of silver. The envy and the resentment would be theirs then when his mother took him about to the neighbours boasting of her most successful son. . . .

Stanley put the cachou back in the packet and the vision dimmed. The only other thing of interest in the bag was a fairly thick wad of pound notes, bound with an elastic band. Ethel's savings, he supposed, money to pay her new landlady advance rent.

No need to destroy those with their dead owner.

He was counting the notes when he heard a very faint sound above him, a stair creaking. His fantasies had temporarily calmed him but now the sweat started again all over his face. He took a step backwards to stand trembling like a small animal guarding its kill in the face of a larger advancing predator.

The door opened and Maud came in, leaning on her stick.

8

Maud screamed.

She didn't stop to argue with Stanley or question him. What she saw before her told her exactly what had happened. For twenty years she had been expecting her son-in-law to repeat the violence for which he had been sent to prison. It had been an elderly woman then; it was an elderly woman now. As before, Stanley had attacked an old woman for her money but this time he had gone further and had killed her.

She raised her stick and advanced upon him. Stanley dropped the wad of notes and backed against the open piano. His hands, crashing down on the keys, struck a deep resounding chord. Maud made for his face, but Stanley ducked and the blow caught him agonisingly between his neck and his shoulder blade. He fell to his knees but staggered up again almost at once and hurled one of the green glass vases at her.

It struck the wall behind Maud's head and sent a

shower of emerald slivers spraying across the room.

"I'll kill you for this!" Maud screamed. "I'll kill you with my own hands."

Stanley looked around for more missiles, edging between the couch and the piano, but before he could snatch up the second vase, Maud struck him again, this time on the top of his head, and caught him as he staggered with a series of violent blows to the body. For a moment the room went black and he saw shapes whirling against the blackness, red squares and triangles and cascading stars.

Maud would beat him to death. Horror and rage had given her an unexpected strength. Sobbing now, crouched in a corner, he turned his shoulder to receive the coming blow and as it struck him he seized the tip of the stick.

It struggled in his grasp like something alive. Stanley pulled himself up on it, hand over hand. He was stronger than she, for he was male and thirty years younger, and he pulled himself to his feet until he was face to face with Maud.

Still they didn't speak. There was nothing to say. They had said it all in those four years and now all that was left was a crystallisation of mutual loathing. It throbbed in Maud's breathless grunts and in Stanley's hiss. Once again they might have been alone in the world or outside the world, on some unpeopled unfurnished plane where there was no emotion but hatred and no instinct but self-preservation.

For each of them there was one desire, possession of the stick, and they concentrated on it in a savage, but for some moments, equal tug-of-war. Then Stanley, seeming to retreat from a very slightly advantageous position, kicked hard at Maud's shins and with a cry she let the stick fall and rattle to the floor.

Stanley picked it up and hurled it across the room. He made a leap for her throat, seizing her neck in both hands. Maud gave a hoarse gasp. As Stanley's hard fingers dug into her carotid artery, she kneed him in the groin. They both cried out simultaneously, Stanley sobbing with pain, and fell apart.

He jerked back on his heels, ready to spring again, but Maud was enfeebled without the stick she had depended on for years. Her arms flailing, she had nothing to break her fall, and as she toppled her head struck the jutting edge of the marble mantelpiece.

Stanley crept over to her on all fours and looked down, his heart drumming, at the consummation of all his wishes.

Vera didn't cry or even speak at all when he broke the news to her but her face went very white. She nodded her head, accepting, as he told her how Maud had been in the lounge, just standing by the mantelpiece and looking at the wedding photograph, when suddenly she had felt bad, touched her forehead and fallen to the floor.

"It was bound to happen sooner or later," he ended.

"I'll go up and see her," said Vera.

"As long as it won't upset you." He had expected this, after all, and provided for it. He followed her up the stairs.

Vera cried a little when she saw Maud.

"She looks very peaceful."

"I thought that myself," Stanley said eagerly. "She's at peace now, I thought."

They spoke in whispers as if Maud could hear them.

"I wish you'd rung me at the shop."

"I didn't see any point in upsetting you. It wasn't as if there was anything you could do."

"I wish I'd been here." Vera bent over and kissed Maud's cold forehead.

"Come on," said Stanley. "I'll make you a cup of tea."

He wanted to get her out of there as quickly as possible. The curtains were drawn and the room dim, only a wan filtered light playing on Maud's features and the medicine store by the bed. But let Vera shift that pillow an inch and she'd see the gash on Maud's head under the grey curls.

"I suppose I ought to watch by the bed all night."

"You what?" said Stanley, alarmed, forgetting to whisper. "I never heard such rubbish."

"It used to be the custom. Poor mother. She loved me really. She meant things for the best. The doctor said it was another stroke?"

Stanley nodded. "Come on down, Vee. You can't do any good hanging about in here."

He made a pot of tea. Vera watched him, murmuring the same things over and over again as recently bereaved people do, how unbelievable it was but really only to be expected; how we must all die but still death came as a shock; how glad she was that her mother had had a peaceful end.

"Let's go into the other room. It's cold out here."

"All right," said Stanley. As soon as she saw the table she'd remember and start asking questions, but he was ready for her. He picked up their two cups and followed her.

"My God," said Vera, opening the dining room door, "Auntie Ethel! I forgot all about Auntie Ethel." She looked at her watch and sat down heavily. "It's nearly six. She's late. She was coming at five. Not like Auntie Ethel to be late."

"I don't reckon she'll come now."

"Of course she'll come. She wrote and said definitely she was coming. Oh, Stan, I'll have to break it to her. She'll take it hard, she was ever so fond of Mother."

"Maybe she won't come."

"What's the good of saying that?" said Vera. "She's late, that's all. I couldn't eat a thing, could you?"

Stanley was famished. The mingled scents of the salmon and the chicken were working on his salivary glands and he felt sick with hunger, but he shook his head, puting on a maudlin expression.

As well as hungry, he felt utterly exhausted and he couldn't relax until he was out of danger. Vera had seen her mother and hadn't been suspicious; there was no reason why she should go into the spare room where the body of Ethel Carpenter lay under the bed, concealed by the overhanging bedspread. So far so good.

"I can't think what's happened to Auntie," said Vera fretfully. "D'you think I ought to ring her landlady in Brixton?"

"She's not on the phone."

"No, but I could get on to the café on the corner and ask them to take a message."

"I wouldn't worry," said Stanley. "You've got enough on your plate without bothering about Ethel Carpenter."

"No harm in waiting a bit longer, I suppose. What time are the undertakers coming in the morning?"

"Half ten."

"I'll have to ring Doris and say I shan't be in to work. Though God knows how they'll manage with the other girl away on holiday."

Stanley almost choked over his tea. "I can see to the undertakers, Vee. You don't want to be here when they come."

"I don't want to . . . But my own mother, Stan!"

"If you want to go in, you go in. You leave everything to me."

Further discussion was prevented by the doorbell ringing. Vera came back with Mrs. Blackmore who, though Stanley had imparted the news to no one, was by this time in full possession of the facts. Perhaps the doctor's doorstep speech had been overheard by her. Whatever her source, she had, she told Vera, already passed on what she called the "sad tidings" to Mrs. Macdonald and various other cronies in the neighbourhood. So confident was she of her intuition in matters of this kind that she had not thought it necessary to wait for confirmation. A black coat thrown hastily over her floral overall, she announced that she had come to pay her last respects to Mrs. Kinaway. In other words, she wanted to view the body.

"Only yesterday I was having such a lovely talk with her over the fence," she said. "Well, we're all cut down like flowers, aren't we?"

Distastefully eyeing Mrs. Blackmore's inquisitive rabbity face and her bunched hair, Stanley reflected that the only flower she reminded him of was the deadly nightshade. Still, better let them all come and gawp at Maud now than sneak in on her substitute at the Undertakers'. A watchful guardian of his dead, ready to intercept any tender hand which might try to smooth back Maud's hair, he went upstairs with the two women.

Five minutes after Mrs. Blackmore, loudly declaring her willingness to do "anything I can, dear. Don't hesitate to ask," had gone, both Macdonalds arrived with a bunch of violets for Vera.

"Sweet violets for mourning," said Mrs. Macdonald sentimentally. Their scent reminded Stanley of Ethel Carpenter's handbag. "We don't want to see her, Mrs. Manning. We want to remember her as she was."

After that Vera and Stanley were left alone. It unnerved Stanley to realise that his wife was waiting for Ethel Carpenter but he could do nothing about that. Presently, without a word, Vera took away the cutlery that had been laid by her mother.

"You'd better eat something," she said.

At ten o'clock when Ethel Carpenter still hadn't come, she cleared the table and they went to bed. She had a last look at Maud from the doorway but she didn't go in again. They put the light out and lay side by side, not touching, each wide awake.

Vera fell asleep first. Every nerve in Stanley's body was tingling. What was he going to do if Vera didn't go into work in the morning? He'd have to make her go out. Perhaps he could get her to go and register the death. . . . That wouldn't leave him much time for all he had to do.

Soon after midnight he too slept and immediately,

or so it seemed to him, began to dream. He was walking
by the river, going home, and he had walked all the way
from London like a tramp, his possessions in a bundle
on his back. It seemed that he had been walking for
years, but he was nearly there now. Soon he would
reach the point where the river described a great meander and at this point his village would come into view,
the church spire first and then the trees and the houses.
He could see them now and he quickened his pace. For
all his apparent poverty, the pack on his back and his
worn-out shoes, he knew they would be glad to see him
and welcome him home with congratulations and tears
of joy.

The sun was coming up, for it was very early morning, and Stanley struck across the meadow, soaking his
trousers in dew up to his knees. In the village no one
was up yet. But his mother would be up. She had always been an early riser. The cottage door opened when
he pushed it in and he went in, calling her.

He heard her coming down the stairs and went to
the foot of them, looking up. His mother came down.
She had grown old and she used a stick. First he saw her
legs and her skirt, for the stairs had become long and
steep in his long absence, and at last her face. He started
back, crying something aloud. It wasn't his mother's
face, but Maud's, waxen yellow, the teeth bared, blood
running from a wound in her scalp. . . .

He awoke screaming, only the screams came out as
a strangled groan. It took him several minutes to re-
orientate himself, to realize it had been a dream and that
Maud was dead. After that he couldn't sleep again. He
got up and walked about the house, looking first in on
Maud and then into the spare room. The daffodils
Maud had picked for Ethel gleamed whitely at him in
the thin moonlight.

He went downstairs where he felt it was safe to put
a light on. The house smelt of food, tinned fish and cold
meats which wouldn't keep long because there was nothing to preserve them. Now that he had come to himself
and the dream was fading, he was struck by a sudden

anxiety that he had failed to take some important step. He had forgotten to do something but he couldn't think what that something was. He sat down and put his head in his hands.

Then he remembered. Nothing so very important after all. For the first time in twenty years he had passed a day without doing the crossword puzzle.

He found the *Daily Telegraph* and a ballpoint pen. The sight of the virgin puzzle sent a little thrill of pleasure through him. Funny how just looking at the empty puzzle frame, the exquisitely symmetrical mosaic, brought him peace and steadied his shaking hands. He must have done thousands of them, he thought. Six a week times fifty-two times twenty. God, that was six thousand, two hundred and forty puzzles, not counting all the ones in his crossword paperbacks and annuals.

Stanley picked up the pen.

One across: "Calf-love may decide one to take this German language course" (two words, six, eight). Stanley pondered only for a moment before filling in "Wiener Schnitzel." His body relaxed as if it was immersed in a warm bath and he smiled.

9

The alarm went off at seven.

Vera was out of bed and halfway to the bathroom before she remembered. She came back, wondering whether there was any point in waking Stanley, but he was awake and staring wide-eyed at the ceiling.

"I'm up now," she said. "I may as well go to work."

"I should. It'll take your mind off things."

But he couldn't be sure she really would, she dithered and hesitated so much, until he saw her actually going down the path. As soon as she was out of sight he fetched in the empty peat sack and took it upstairs. Better remove Maud's wedding ring and slip it on Ethel's finger. Funny, the way it made him feel so squeamish. He was glad he hadn't eaten the eggs and bacon Vera had offered him for breakfast.

Ethel had a ring of her own which she wore on the little finger of her right hand. His own hands shaking, Stanley pulled it off. It was an odd little ring, a thin circle of gold with two clasped hands, tiny gold hands, where there might have been a stone. Stanley put it on Maud's finger and then he bundled her body into the sack.

There was no one about in Blackmore's garden—they lay in bed till all hours on Saturdays and their bedroom was in the front. Gasping with the weight of it, Stanley dragged the sack across the narrow strip of concrete outside the back door and humped it into the shed. Next Ethel's suitcases. They were of the expanding kind and not fully expanded, although they were so heavy. Stanley opened the lighter of the two and crammed in Ethel's coat and hat and the umbrella which, to his relief, he found was of the telescopic variety. He lugged them downstairs and put them in the shed beside the sack. Nobody but he ever went to the shed, but just to be on the safe side, he shovelled peat all over the sack and the cases. Anyone going in and just giving things a cursory glance would think Stanley Manning had a ton of peat in there instead of a couple of hundredweight.

Things were going well.

By half-past nine he had got Ethel lying where Maud had been, on the back room bed, covered by a sheet. It would be a nice touch, he thought, and one likely to impress the undertakers if the corpse they came for had flowers by it so he fetched the vase of daffodils and put it among Maud's pills.

On the dot of ten the undertakers arrived, and having given Stanley a form to fill in, applying for permission to cremate, took away the body of Ethel Carpenter.

When she had registered Maud's death during her lunch hour, Vera telephoned the Brixton café next door to Ethel's former landlady.

"I'm ever so sorry to bother you. My dad was in business and I know you're busy, but could you ask Mrs. Huntley to ring me back?"

It was ten minutes before the phone rang and when it did Vera was filling in time by placing newly cleaned blankets into polythene bags.

"I just wondered," she said to Mrs. Huntley, "if Miss Carpenter's still with you. She never turned up at our place yesterday."

"Never turned up? She left here—let's see—it would have been about twenty to one. She had her two cases with her and she left a trunk for me to send on to her new address in Green Lanes, 52, Green Lanes, Croughton. The men came for it just now."

Vera had to sit down, she felt so weak at the knees.

"Did she say anything about coming to us?"

"The last thing she said to me was, 'They won't be expecting me so early, Mrs. Huntley, but I may as well go. Mr. Manning's bound to be in,' she said, 'and I can have a chat with him.' She said she'd take it slow on account of her cases being so heavy."

"Did you say *twenty to one?*"

"Might have been a quarter to," said Mrs. Huntley.

"Then she should have been here by two!"

"Maybe she changed her mind. Maybe she went straight to Green Lanes after all."

"I suppose she must have done," said Vera.

But it wasn't like Ethel. To arrange to come to stay, arrange it by letter, putting everyone out, and then just not turn up would be a churlish way to behave. And

Ethel, though sometimes sharp and malicious and difficult, wasn't churlish or unpunctual or casual at all. She
belonged to the old school. Vera couldn't understand it.

At five, when things were slack and the High Street
shops emptying, Vera left the cleaners in charge of Doris, her assistant, and caught the bus that went down
Green Lanes.

Number 52 was a much nicer house than her own
in Lanchester Road. Although semi-detached, it had a
double front with imposing gables, a big front garden
that was mostly elaborate rockery and a half-timbered
garage. A thin middle-aged woman came to the door
with a boy and a girl tagging along behind her who
might have been either her children or her grand-
children.

"Won't you come in?" she said when Vera had introduced herself.

"I mustn't. My husband will worry if I'm late."
Stanley had never worried in the past when she was late
but he had been so nice to her since Maud died, so considerate, that the possibility didn't seem so fantastic as it
might have been once. "I only wanted to know if Miss
Carpenter was here."

"I'm not expecting her till Monday," said Mrs. Paterson in a breathless harassed voice. "Monday she said
definitely. I couldn't cope with anything extra *now*."
The hall behind her was cluttered with toys and from
the depths of the house came sounds suggestive of a
hungry bitch with a litter of puppies. "My daughter's
had to go into hospital and left the children with me,
and my dog's just whelped. . . . Really, if I'd known
there was going to be all this trouble, I wouldn't have
considered letting the room at all."

Vera looked at her helplessly. "I thought she must
be here," she said. "She's disappeared."

"I expect she'll turn up," said Mrs. Paterson.
"Well, if you won't come in, perhaps you'll excuse me
while I go and get all this lot fed."

Stanley was waiting on the doorstep for her, the
anxious husband she had never quite believed in even

when she was boasting of his concern for her to Mrs. Paterson.

"Where have you been? I was worried about you."

Vera took off her coat. That he should have worried about her brought her such intense pleasure that it was all she could do not to throw her arms around him.

"The undertakers came," he said. "I've fixed up the cremation for Thursday. We'll have to get cracking asking all the family along. Leave getting the tea for a bit. I've got a form here I want you to sign." Completing it had been interesting but somewhat frightening as well. Stanley had not much cared for that bit where the applicant was asked if he had any reason to suspect foul play or negligence. Nor had he enjoyed telephoning Dr. Moxley to ask for the name of the second certifying doctor, although it had been a relief when Moxley had called him back to say all was done and that the other doctor was some character called Diplock. Blake's name hadn't been mentioned.

"Just sign here," he said, putting the pen into Vera's hand.

Vera signed.

"Oh, Stan, you've been so marvellous in all this. I can't tell you what a comfort you've been, taking everything off my hands."

"That's O.K.," said Stanley.

"Now the only real worry I've got is Auntie Ethel." Briefly Vera told him about her phone call and her visit to Mrs. Paterson. "D'you think we ought to go to the police?"

Every scrap of colour left Stanley's face. *"Police?"*

"Stan, I'll have to. She may be lying dead somewhere."

Stanley couldn't speak properly. He cleared his throat. "The police aren't interested when women go missing."

"That's only when it's young girls, when it's women who may have gone off with men. Auntie Ethel's seventy."

"Yeah. I can see that." Stanley thought quickly, wishing he didn't have to think at all. And now, just when everything was going so well. . . . "Look, don't you do anything till Monday. Wait and see if she turns up at Mrs. Paterson's. Then if you don't hear from her we'll get on to the police. Right?"

"Right," said Vera doubtfully.

All day long John Blackmore had been stuck on a ladder outside his back door painting his house. And as soon as he had gone in for tea Vera had come home. Stanley peeped into his shed, noting that the pile of peat was just as he had left it. He locked the door and put the key in his trousers pocket. Then he went over to the heather garden where the deep trench was still unfilled. In the cool May twilight the heathers stood brilliant white against the soft chestnut-coloured peat. White heather, he thought, white heather for luck. . . .

The following day, Sunday, was bright and hot. Vera got the piece of beef topside out of the larder and sniffed it. Just on the turn again. It was always the same. Every hot weekend the Sunday joint was high before she could cook it and she had to soak it in salt water to try and take away the sweetish fetid taint.

"You'll be able to buy a fridge now," said Stanley. He could see she didn't quite know what reply to make to this. Casually he gave her arm a light pat. Tears came into Vera's eyes. "I'll just walk up the road and get myself a paper," he said. "I miss the crossword on Sundays."

It was years since he had felt so happy and light-hearted. Everything had gone perfectly. And what had he done wrong? Nothing. It would have been unpleasant if he had actually had to—well, smother Maud, but that hadn't been necessary. Maud had died through her own fault. Now all that remained to stop any awkward questions being asked was to pay a visit to Mrs. Paterson.

He jumped on the Green Lanes bus. It stopped right outside the house and within two minutes Stanley was smiling ingratiatingly at Mrs. Paterson whom he quickly summed up as a tired grandma, a busy woman who would be only too glad to have one of her problems taken off her shoulders.

"Name of Smith," he said. A dog was howling and he raised his voice to a shout. "Miss Ethel Carpenter asked me to call."

"Oh, yes?" Over her shoulder, Mrs. Paterson bellowed, "Shut the dog in the garden, Gary. I can't hear myself speak. There was a lady here," she said to Stanley, "asking after her."

"Well, it's like this. She's stopping with me. I've got this room going, you see, and she looked at it last week. Couldn't make up her mind between this place and mine."

"These old dears!" said Mrs. Paterson, clearly relieved.

"Yeah. It's good of you to take it this way. Fact is, she came round Friday afternoon and said she'd settled for my place, after all. I reckon she didn't like to tell you herself." With some reluctance, Stanley felt in his pocket for the wad of notes he had taken from Ethel's handbag. "She wouldn't want you to be out of pocket. She reckoned five quid would make it all right."

"You don't want to bother," said Mrs. Paterson, taking the notes just the same. "I'm not sorry things have turned out this way, I can tell you. Now I can let my grandson have her room."

"There'll be a trunk coming," said Stanley. "Being sent on it is. I'll call round for that." Was she going to ask for his address? She wasn't.

"You can leave that to me. I'll take it in. It was good of you to come."

"My pleasure," said Stanley.

He bought a paper from the kiosk on the corner and by the time the bus got to the top end of the Lanchester Road he had done half the clues in his head. "Frank takes a well-known stage part." Candida, thought Stanley, wishing he had brought a pen with him. Marvellous, really. Whatever would they think of next? Good training for the mind, crossword puzzles. He marched up the path, whistling.

10

Throughout that Sunday John Blackmore stood on his ladder, painting the side of his house, and every time Stanley put his nose outside the back door, Blackmore acknowledged him with a wave of his brush or a remark to the effect that it was all right for some. It was still light at eight and Blackmore was still painting.

"Don't you worry about me if I'm late home tomorrow," said Vera as they went to bed. "I'm going straight round to Mrs. Paterson when I've finished work to see if Auntie Ethel's turned up."

"Sometime," said Stanley casually, "I suppose we'd better have a word with your mother's solicitor."

"That can wait until after the funeral."

"Oh, sure. Sure it can," said Stanley.

He slept well that night and when he got up Vera had gone. Everything was clean and tidy downstairs and Vera had left his breakfast on a tray as usual, cornflakes poured out for him, milk already in his teacup and water in the kettle. Blackmore's car was gone; he had left for work. Stanley felt considerable relief. He was beginning to be afraid his neighbour might be taking his summer holiday and intended to devote an unbroken fortnight to house painting.

Mr. Blackmore's Monday wash was flapping on the line, but she was still coming and going with pegs and odds and ends of small linen, adjusting the clothes prop and disentangling sheets which had wound themselves round the line in the stiff breeze.

"Lovely drying day!"

"Uh-huh," said Stanley.

"Things are getting back to normal with you, I daresay. Mrs. Manning bearing up all right?"

Stanley nodded, trying not to look at the shed.

"Well, I'll get these last few bits out and then I'm off to my sister's."

Feeling more cheerful, Stanley pottered about the garden. He pulled a couple of groundsel plants and a sow thistle out of the rose bed but he wasn't in the mood for weeding this morning and his attention kept wandering back to the heather bed with its blanket of peat and the yawning trench in the middle of it. Mrs. Blackmore's voice made him jump.

"What are you going to put in that great hole?"

A light sweat broke out on Stanley's forehead.

"I'm going to fill it up with peat. I'm putting a whole sack of peat in there."

"That's what I said it was for," said Mrs. Blackmore. "John and me, we noticed it, you see, and John said . . ." She giggled embarrassedly and bit her lip. "Well, never mind what he said. I wondered if you were going to bury some new potatoes in a tin. They say if you do that you have them all fresh for Christmas."

"It's for peat," said Stanley doggedly. He knew what Blackmore had said all right. He could just picture the two of them gossiping and sniggering and Blackmore saying, "Maybe that's for Mrs. Kinaway, save him paying out for the funeral."

He moved over in the direction of the Macdonalds' garden. Mrs. Macdonald, whose husband had a better job than Blackmore, was hanging her wash on a metal whirl line with plastic strings. She, too, glanced up in happy anticipation of a chat but Stanley only nodded to her.

The two women began shouting amicably to one another across his intervening lawn. Stanley went back into the house and did the crossword puzzle.

In the end, by a stroke of luck, the two women set off out together. From his vantage point behind the piano in the lounge, Stanley watched Mrs. Macdonald come out of her own house with her basket on wheels and wait at Mrs. Blackmore's gate. The Blackmores' door closed with a crash and then Mrs. Blackmore, dressed for a day out in a summery pink coat and floral hat, trotted up to her friend and whispered something to her. They both looked hard at Stanley's house. Blackening my character again, he thought. He watched them move off towards the bus stop.

When they were out of sight, he went upstairs and from the bedroom that had been Maud's, scanned the surrounding gardens. Everywhere washing waved and bellied and streamed in the wind. The linen was brilliant white, whiter and tidier than the ragged clouds which tossed above the tossing lines, and all this eddying whiteness had an almost hypnotic effect on Stanley so that he felt he could stand there forever, staring himself to sleep. His limbs seemed weighted down by a great reluctance for the task ahead of him. So far everything had been done secretly and covertly. Now he must do something in the open air, publicly (although he couldn't see a soul in all those gardens who might observe him), and perhaps what he was about to do was the first truly illegal and punishable thing. But it must be done, and now before Mrs. Macdonald returned from shopping.

Both his neighbours' houses were empty. Stanley was sure of that. The Blackmores had no children and the Macdonalds' two teenagers were at school. It was unnerving, though, to have to start work with that blank bedroom window of the Macdonalds' staring down at him. Who did those Macdonalds think they were, anyway, having an extension built on the back of their house, jutting right out and overlooking his garden? He'd have had the law on them for that, infringing his right to ancient lights or whatever it was, only he'd never been able to afford a solicitor. . . . Damn that sightless, closed, uncurtained window! There's no one

at home, no one at home, he assured himself as he unlocked the shed and scraped away peat with his hands.

The wind blew the light feathery stuff about, pow-
dering Stanley's clothes and hands with brown dust. He
lugged the suitcases out first and, having peeped out
cautiously to make sure he was still unobserved, dragged
them towards the trench and lowered them in. They
took up more room than he had bargained for, leaving
only about a foot to accommodate the sack which contained Maud's body.

Maud's body . . . Up till then Stanley had felt a
little weary, a little mesmerized and considerably appre-
hensive, but he hadn't felt sick. Now a lump of nausea
came up into his throat. He kicked some peat over the
suitcases and breathed deeply. The nausea receded
slightly.

Screwing himself to a pitch of determination, Stanley went back into the shed and grasped the neck of the
sack. His fingers, slippery now with sweat, slid about on
the thick green plastic. No one watching him would imagine that sack contained anything as soft and amor-
phous as peat. But no one *was* watching him. He was
observed only by a bird which sat on the spiraea branch
and by the black, pupilless eye of Macdonalds' window.

If only it was quiet . . . The thrashing linen made
slapping, cracking sounds as it filled with air and the
wind drove the air out of it. Stanley was surrounded by
a chorus of busy disembodied noise, but the linen didn't
seem disembodied to him. Rather it was as if he was at-
tended and observed by a crowd of crackling idiots,
white watchers that cackled and sniggered at each fresh
move he made.

Cocooned in gleaming slippery green, Maud's body
slithered and bumped over the concrete. Stanley had to
drag it, for it was too heavy for him to lift. A dead
weight, he thought, a dead weight. . . . He mustn't be
sick.

Pushing the body into the cavity above the cases
was the worst part of all. He had thought he would be
able to avoid actually touching Maud, but now he

couldn't. Her dead flesh felt icy and stiff through the cold damp folds of plastic. Stanley heard himself give a sob of horror. The top of the sack lay almost level with the surrounding earth. Stanley crouched over it, pressing at it with his hands. He didn't think he had the strength to get up, but he managed it at last, staggering. With heavy hands from which the sweat streamed just as if they had been dipped in water, he got his shovel and filled bucket after bucket with peat.

When the operation was completed, the resulting heap looked just what it was—a grave. He began leveling the soil which abutted on to it, pulling heather fronds and flowers above the dusty brown mass, until finally the sickness overcame him. He lay spreadeagled, face downwards on the ground and retched.

"Whatever's the matter, Mr. Manning? Are you all right?"

It sounded to Stanley as if Mrs. Macdonald must be standing right behind him. He jerked up, half-rolling on to the peat heap. She was ten yards away, staring curiously at him from the other side of her fence, the washing on her whirl line streaming out and crackling as the metal shaft squeaked. Ghosts on a crazy roundabout, Stanley thought wildly.

"I came back from shopping and I saw you lying on the ground. Whatever came over you?"

He muttered, "Something disagreed with me. . . ." And then, his face and hands streaked with peat dust, he lurched unsteadily to his feet and staggered into the house.

When Vera came away from Mrs. Paterson's, she felt as if a load had been lifted from her shoulders. But her relief was mixed with annoyance. How could Auntie Ethel be so inconsiderate? To write to Maud promising to come for the weekend, even to fix a definite time of arrival, and then just not turn up; worse even, to take Mrs. Paterson's room only to throw her over for someone else. Well, she was very lucky, Vera thought, in encountering someone as tolerant and easy-going as Mrs. Paterson. Not many landladies would take that sort of treatment and be content with a mere five pounds as recompense. It was a pity, though, that she hadn't had the presence of mind to ask this Mr. Smith for his address.

Still, if Ethel was going to behave in this cavalier way, they were well rid of her. Let her make a fuss because no one told her Maud was dead or asked her to the funeral. How was anyone supposed to get in touch with her when she hid herself in this stupid mysterious way?

As Vera was unlatching her front gate, Mrs. Macdonald came out.

"Has your husband got over his bad turn?"

"Bad turn?"

"Oh, haven't you seen him yet? I never meant to upset you, really I didn't."

"Just tell me what's happened, Mrs. Macdonald."

"Well, nothing really. Only when I got in from the shops this morning there was poor Mr. Manning laying, actually laying, on the ground out among those heather plants of his. Been sick, he had."

"But what was it?"

"Something that disagreed with him, he said. My boy Michael was home from school with a sore throat and he said he'd been watching Mr. Manning at his gardening, watching him through the back bedroom window, and he saw him collapse."

Vera hurried indoors, expecting to see Stanley prone on the sofa, but he was sitting in a chair, intent on his crossword annual, and he had his usual healthy, though sallow, colour. Better say nothing of what she had seen. Stanley hated being spied on by the neighbours. Instead she told him of her interview with Mrs. Paterson.

"I said it'd be all right," said Stanley.

"I know, dear. I've been very silly. The best thing will be to forget all about Auntie Ethel and her nonsense. Could you eat a bit of steak?"

"Uh-huh," said Stanley, taking no further notice of her. Vera sighed. Of course he'd been under a strain, what with Mother dying like that before his eyes, but if only he would sometimes, just sometimes, speak nicely to her or thank her for what she did for him or show by a glance or a smile that he still loved her. Perhaps you couldn't expect it after twenty years. Vera ate her meal in silence. There was a lot she would have liked to discuss with her husband but you cannot have much of a conversation with a man whose face is concealed behind a large book. She cleared the table, Stanley moving impatiently but not looking up while she removed his plate, and then she went up to the room that had been Maud's.

She sat down in front of the dressing table, but before she opened the drawer where Maud had kept her papers she caught a glimpse of herself in the glass and sighed afresh at her reflection. It wasn't only lack of money but lack of time. . . . She wondered apprehensively what Stanley would say if she spoke to him of giving up her job. Then, averting her eyes, she opened the middle drawer and lifted its contents out on to the bed.

On top was a bundle of letters from Ethel Carpenter. Beneath these Maud's cheque book, her birth certificate, her marriage lines, Vera's own certificate of baptism. How painful it all was, a job that had to be done and as quickly as possible. The light was fading fast now and the room growing dim, but the papers in her hands still showed white with the last brilliant whiteness that comes before dark.

Here was a letter from a firm of solicitors: Finbow and Craig, of High street, Croughton. "Dear Madam, An appointment has been made for you with our Mr. Finbow to discuss the question of your testamentory dispositions. . . ." After the funeral, Vera decided, she too would make an appointment with Mr. Finbow.

Next, sandwiched among the papers, she found a flat jewel box full of little brooches and chains and souvenir trinkets. There was nothing she really fancied for herself—perhaps she might keep that cameo pendant with the picture of Mother and Dad inside it, and most of it would be given away to the relatives coming on Thursday.

Vera came next to Maud's red leather photograph album. On the first page was her parents' wedding picture. George tall and awkward in his hired morning coat, Maud in a knee-length dress of white crepe-dechine, clutching his arm determinedly. Then there were photographs of herself as a baby. Maud had put captions to them all in careful copperplate: Vera aged one; Vera takes her first steps; then, when she was older, a child of five or six: Vera gets to know her auntie Ethel; Vera on the sands at Brayminster-on-Sea.

Dear old Bray! That was the heading written across the next double page. Maud had always called the seaside resort that, loving it and making it her own. Dear old Bray! On a postcard photograph, taken by a beach photographer, Ethel Carpenter in 1938 hat and Macclesfield silk dress walked along the sands, holding the hand of ten-year-old Vera. Maud wore sunglasses in the next snapshot and George had a handkerchief with knots in its four corners stuck on his balding head to protect it from the sun.

More and more snaps of Bray . . . 1946 and the war over. Vera grown up now, a pretty eighteen with long curls and a crimson mouth that looked black and shiny in the snap.

Two years later the New Look. Little cotton jacket with a peplum, long skirt with a flare at the hem. Had she really worn shoes with ankle straps and heels four inches high? James Horton holding her hand, whispering something to her in the sunshine, the bright sea behind them. James Horton. Suppose it had been he downstairs, he her husband who had been ill and on whom she had tended, would he have smiled and thanked her and held up his face for a kiss?

There were no pictures of Stanley in the album, not even a wedding photograph. Vera closed it because it was too dark now to see any more. She bent her head and wept softly, the tears falling on to the old red leather binding.

"What are you doing up here in the dark?"

She turned as Stanley came into the room, and thinking she heard in his voice a tiny hint of tenderness or concern, she reached for his hand and held it against her cheek.

11

Standing with bowed head between George Kinaway's brother Walter and Maud's sister Louisa, Stanley watched the coffin slowly drawn away from behind the gilt screen towards the waiting fire. The vicar exhorted them to pray for the last time and while Vera wept quietly, Stanley looked down even further, studying his shoes.

"Nothing from Ethel Carpenter, I see," said Aunt Louisa when they were outside the paved courtyard looking at the flowers. "I must say I expected to see her here. These are from Uncle Tom and me, Stanley. Wreaths are so dear these days and they all go to waste, don't they? So we thought a sheath would be nice."

"Sheaf," said Stanley coldly. It was just like those Macdonalds to send an enormous great cross of lilies. Done on purpose to make the relatives' flowers look mean, he had no doubt.

The got into the hired cars and went back to Lanchester Road. It was all Stanley could do to keep his temper at the sight of Mrs. Blackmore getting stuck into the sherry and the ham sandwiches. They hadn't even had the decency to send flowers either. With a long pious

face he brushed off Mrs. Blackmore's attempts to find
out how much Maud had left but as soon as they had all
gone he telephoned Finbow and Craig.

"It seems a bit soon," said Vera when he told her
an appointment had been made for the following day.

"Tomorrow or next week, what's the odds?"

"I'll be glad to get it over. It was a nice funeral."

"Lovely," said Stanley with sincerity. He couldn't,
in fact, recall any clan gathering he had ever enjoyed so
much. If only he hadn't got to solve the problem of collecting that trunk . . .

"You know, love," Vera said, "it's years since we
had a holiday. When we've got everything settled, why
don't we go down to dear old Bray for a week?"

"You go," said Stanley. "I've got business to see
to."

"You mean you've got a job?"

"Something in the offing."

Stanley looked away coldly. He didn't care for that
wistful encouraging look Vera had given him. A job indeed. She couldn't think big, that was her trouble. He
poured himself the dregs of the sherry and began to
think about Pilbeam.

In telling his wife he had a job in the offing Stanley
hadn't been strictly truthful. It was not in the offing, it
was in the bag but it was also nothing to be proud of.
He had only taken it because it allowed him more or
less unrestricted use of a van.

A florist in Croughton Old Village wanted a driver
and delivery man and on the day before the funeral
Stanley had walked down to the old village, the vestigial
remains of a hamlet that had been there before London
spread across the green fields, applied for the job and
was told to start on the following Monday.

Delighted with the way things were working out for
him, he wandered across the village green and, sitting
down on the steps of the war memorial *(Dulce et deco-
rum est pro patria mori)*, lit a cigarette.

There is perhaps no more pleasant occupation for a

man whose expectations have almost come to fruition as that of speculating what he will do with the money when he gets it. His thoughts toyed happily with visions of cars, clothes, abundant liquor and the general appurtenances of making a splash, but Stanley was under no illusion that he could live for the rest of his life on twenty thousand pounds. He was too big a man now to consider working for anyone else, unless it was as a setter of crossword puzzles. That might come later as a sideline. First, he thought, he would rather like to go into business and what he saw before him as he crossed the road and stepped on to the pavement gave him the idea that it might be profitable and consistent with his new dignity as a man of private means to keep a shop. After all, dreary old George Kinaway had made a good thing out of it, a very good thing, and what George Kinaway could do he could do standing on his head.

In front of him was a row of shops with crazily sagging Tudor gables above them and a row of aged trees to give them an old-world expensive look. There was a chi-chi-looking art place with abstract paintings in its window, a dolly girl's boutique, a treasure house of Indian jewellery and between this and a place selling old books a vacant shop, its door boarded up and a notice over its window: *These desirable premises to let.*

Standing with his nose pressed against the dirty fingermarked glass of the shop window was a short stout man. Still whistling, Stanley too stopped and stared inside at a dim dusty interior cluttered with cardboard boxes. The other man gave a heavy sigh.

"Lovely day," said Stanley cheerfully.

"Is it?" His companion turned to face him and Stanley saw a snub-nosed baby face topped by sparse colourless hair. He was smoking a cigarette he had obviously rolled himself and as he raised his hand to his mouth Stanley noticed that the top of the forefinger was missing and this finger ended in a blob of calloused flesh instead of a nail. It reminded him of a chipolata sausage. "All right for some, I daresay." Stanley grinned. "What's with you, friend? Won the pools, have you?"

"As good as," said Stanley modestly.

The other man was silent for a moment. Then he said somewhat less lugubriously, "I'm a joiner by trade, a joiner and cabinet-maker. Thirty years I've been in the trade and then the firm goes bust."

"Hard cheese."

"This place . . ." He banged on the glass. "This place could be a little gold-mine in the right hands."

"What sort of a gold-mine?" Stanley asked cautiously.

"Antiques." The other man bit off the dental with a short sharp explosion and a spot of saliva struck Stanley's cheek. "What I don't know about the antique . . ." Spit, splutter, bite . . . "business you could write down on a postage stamp." He backed away from Stanley slightly and assumed the attitude of an orator. "It's like this," he said. "You buy up a couple of chairs, genuine Hepplewhite, say, and make—or I make —a dozen more, incorporating bits of the genuine two in each chair. D'you get the picture? Then you can sell the lot as Hepplewhite. Who's to know? It'd take a top expert, I can tell you. Or a table. An inlaid table top, circa eighteen ten—put legs on it, Bob's your uncle."

"Where d'you get the table top?"

"Knocking. Going on the knock. Up Barnet way and further out, Much Hadham and the villages. Some of those old girls have got treasure trove hidden away in their lofts."

"Who'd buy it?"

"You're joking. There's not an antique shop in Croughton as yet, but there's folks with so much lolly they don't know what to do with it. Antiques are the thing. Didn't you know? All you need is capital."

"I might be able to lay my hands on some capital," said Stanley carefully.

The snub nose wrinkled. "Come and have a drink, my old love. Name of Pilbeam, Harry Pilbeam."

"Stanley Manning."

Pilbeam bought the first round and they discussed

it. When it came to Stanley's turn he excused himself, saying he had to see a man, but they arranged to meet on the following Wednesday when Stanley said he would have more idea of how the land lay.

He didn't want to waste his money on Pilbeam yet, and whisky was a diabolical price these days. Of course, he'd still got most of the money he'd taken from Ethel Carpenter's handbag but he was reluctant to break into that.

Alone in the house the morning after the funeral, he took the notes out of his pocket and looked at them. They smelt strongly of violet cachous. Compared to what was coming to him, they were a drop in the ocean. The smell slightly disquieted him and he knew the wisest thing would be to burn them but he couldn't bring himself actually to destroy money. No harm could come of keeping them for a week or so. He went upstairs and from the bedroom bookcase took out the crossword annual of 1954. Then he distributed Ethel's money evenly among its pages before replacing it in the bookcase.

At this moment, he thought, looking at the old metal alarm clock, Vera would be at the solicitor's. He had almost made up his mind to enter into partnership with Harry Pilbeam but it would be nicer if he could go to the Lockkeeper's Arms next Wednesday a rich man instead of just an heir apparent.

"Your mother's will is quite straightforward, Mrs. Manning," said Mr. Finbow. "I don't understand what you mean about a condition."

Vera didn't know how to put it. It sounded so strange.

She floundered. "My mother . . . er, my mother said she'd altered her will—well, way back in March. She said her money would only come to me if— Oh, dear, it does sound so awful—if she died of a stroke and not of anything else."

Mr. Finbow's eyebrows went up at that as Vera had known they would. "There was nothing like that.

Mrs. Kinaway made her will on March fourteenth and, as far as I know, that was the only will she had ever made."

"Oh, I see. She must have been—well, joking, I suppose. She really led us to believe . . . It was rather awful."

"Such a condition would have been most irregular, Mrs. Manning, and hardly legally binding." What must he think of her? Vera wondered. That Maud had gone in terror of her life while she lived with her only daughter? It was cruel of Maud to have exposed her to such embarrassment.

"Anyway, I have the will here," said Mr. Finbow. He opened a drawer in his cabinet and withdrew an envelope. "All the late Mrs. Kinaway's estate passes unconditionally to you as her sole heir. Indeed, there was no real need for her to have made a will under the circumstances, except that it avoids intestacy problems, probate and so on. Had you predeceased her, the estate was have been divided equally between Mrs. Louisa Bliss, her sister, and a Miss Ethel Carpenter. The property amounts to—let me see—approximately twenty-two thousand pounds, at present mostly invested in stock."

"When can I . . . ?"

"Quite soon, Mrs. Manning. In a week or two. If you wish the stock to be sold, I will personally hand you a cheque. Of course, should you require any cash at present, a hundred or two can easily be made available to you."

"No, thank you," said Vera.

"A week or two?" said Stanley thoughtfully when she got home. "Just what I thought, all plain sailing." He smiled wryly to himself when he thought how Maud had fooled them, or half-fooled them, over that condition. Not that it mattered. Taken all in all, things were working out beautifully.

12

The van was a green one, plain on one side and painted with a wreath of roses on the other. Stanley parked it at the kerb, the plain side towards Mrs. Paterson's house, and tossing the bouquets of flowers on to the van floor so that they wouldn't be visible through the window, knocked at the front door.

As soon as Mrs. Paterson opened the door, he saw the trunk behind her in the hall.

"Oh, Mr. Smith, I'd just about given you up."

"Couldn't make it before," said Stanley.

"Would you like my son-in-law to give you a hand with it?"

And see the flowers he was supposed to be delivering?

"I'll manage," said Stanley. The heavy weights he had to carry these days! He'd rupture himself at this rate.

"Here, why don't you put it on my grandson's push-chair and wheel it out."

To Stanley's relief she didn't come down the path with him as he trundled the wobbly trunk to the van. Nor did she seem sufficiently curious about him as to ask his address or keep the door open after he had started the van.

He drove the van down the narrow cobbled lane that led from the old village into Croughton High Street and parked it half on the pavement and half in the street. Then, making sure no one was watching him, he clambered into the back of the van and contemplated Ethel Carpenter's trunk.

It was made of wood and painted black. Stanley thought it must be very old, probably the "box" Ethel had taken with her from situation to situation when she was in service. Of course, it *would* be locked. He wasn't at all anxious to dispose of it without making himself aware of its contents, so he got a hammer and a wrench out of the van's tool kit and got to work on the lock.

After about ten minutes straining and hammering the lock finally gave. Stanley lifted the lid and looked inside. On top of the winter clothes was a cardboard box made to contain writing paper. It still contained writing paper only this paper had been written on. His eyes narrowing, Stanley read the letters Maud had written to her best friend. As he had suspected, they were full of derogatory allusions to himself. Fine thing if they fell into the wrong hands. The best thing would be to burn them. Stanley rolled them up and stuffed them in his pocket.

There didn't seem much else of any interest apart from a wedding photograph of himself and Vera and one of George Kinaway. Someone had written on the back of it. *This and your ring, all I have of you.* Stanley put it in his pocket with the letters and then he looked to see if any of the clothes were marked with Ethel's name. They weren't, but rummaging among camphor-smelling wool, his hand encountered something hard and cold.

The bottom of the trunk contained several small parcels wrapped in tissue paper. The cold thing his hand had touched was the elbow of a china figurine protruding from the paper. He unwrapped it and saw a shepherdess with a crook and a black lamb. Tearing off paper excitedly, he brought to light next a carriage clock, a pot pourri bowl and a silver cream jug. With a thoughtful backward glance at the vacant shop, Stanley wrapped all these things in the *Daily Telegraph*.

The canal banks were shored up with walls of yellow brick beneath which the duller yellow water flowed sluggishly. A couple of barges waited at the lock gates and a woman was walking a corgi along the towpath. Two children were at play in the garden of the lock-keeper's house and Stanley quickly realised he had no opportunity of disposing of the trunk at present.

He drove back to the shop and gave a fictitious order to the florist to have a bouquet of spring flowers made up for delivery to the other side of Croughton at 10 P.M. The florist grumbled a good deal but cheered up when Stanley said he would take the flowers himself. Stanley didn't want any bills sent out to people who didn't exist and he decided reluctantly to pay for the order himself with what remained of his dole money.

While he had his tea he left the van parked outside the house with the trunk still in it but he brought the newspaper parcel indoors. He hid Ethel Carpenter's treasures in the back of his wardrobe and burnt the letters and the photograph in the bedroom fire grate.

It had been raining intermittently all day but now the rain fell heavily, drumming against the windows. Vera drew the curtains, put the light on and fetched writing paper and envelopes. Then she sat down and stared helplessly at the paper. What a fool she was! All day long she'd been thinking about this holiday of hers without ever considering how to set about finding a hotel in Brayminster. How did you find out about hotels, anyway? Vera had never stayed in one.

This, she reflected miserably, was something everyone knew about, everyone but her. Her life had been hard but it had also been sheltered and now she realised that, though forty-two years old, she couldn't begin to do any of the things other people seemed to take in their stride. Suppose I had to book a restaurant for a dinner or buy theatre tickets or make a plane reservation or buy a car, she thought. I wouldn't know how to set about it. I'm like a child.

Other people had guidebooks and holiday brochures. You wrote to the address or rang them up. Vera knew she would never have the courage to telephone an hotel. Oh, it was all hopeless, she was too tired and too old to learn now.

Unless . . . of course! Why hadn't she thought of it before? She knew one boarding-house in Bray, Mrs. Horton's in Seaview Crescent.

It was more than twenty years since she had last stayed there. Mrs. Horton had seemed old to her then but probably she had really been younger than Vera was now. That meant she'd be under sixty. Certainly James wouldn't still be living with his aunt, so she needn't be afraid of running into him, of seeing his face fall at the sight of the change in her. But James would have moved far away. . . .

More at ease than she had been all day, Vera began to write her letter.

The rain had driven much of the traffic off the roads but Stanley drove on doggedly, the wheels of the van sending fountains spraying over the pavements. He kept to a snail's pace, though, for the windscreen wipers were inadequate to deal with the torrents that poured down the glass and he could hardly see.

A deluge, he thought, that's what it is. A nice word for a crossword puzzle. How would you set about making up a clue for it? "A pull in the river causes this flood?" Not bad that. "Lug in Dee," he said aloud, as if explaining to some novice. Now that would be a job he'd really like, setting crosswords, and maybe, after the business had got going and he had ample time on his hands, he would be able to get himself such a job, for money talked and influenced and opened doors. With money you could do anything.

This was just the weather he would have ordered if he'd had any choice in the matter. You'd think the end of the world was coming the way everybody was shut up indoors. He drove slowly up the approach road to the lock and saw that the windows in the lockkeeper's house were curtained. The rain, though savage enough close to, had the appearance in the distance of a thick swirling mist.

No silly old bags giving their dogs an airing to-night. Two empty barges were moored this side of the lock, their hulls rapidly filling with water. The canal had already begun to rise. Its yellow frothing waters seemed to reach up and meet the rain which crashed on to it like a quivering sheet of steel.

Stanley had never seen the canal quite like this be-fore. Usually, at any rate by day, it was busy with barges and kids fishing and the eternal procession of dog walk-ers. And although it wound among fields of a sort, litter-covered waste ground really, dotted about with sick-looking trees, it was a hideous mockery of what a water-way should be. Instead of woods and unspoilt countryside, all you could see were the slummy backs of two or three converging suburbs, half-built factories and tumbled warehouses.

But tonight the rain obscured all this. No houses were discernible in clear silhouette, only lights visible in clusters and separated from each other by the black un-lit masses of factory buildings. And suddenly, because of the rain and the sparse scattered lights, the whole place took on an almost rural aspect so that Stanley was again reminded strongly of his old home where, as you walked along the river bank by night, a mist rose thickly from the water and the villages could be seen as knots of light gleaming between the shallow folded hills.

A faint nostalgia took hold of him, a nostalgia that was mixed with irritation as he drove very slowly along the towpath, wincing each time his tyres sank into ruts filled with muddy water.

When he was well out of sight of the lockkeeper's house, he switched off his own feeble sidelights and drove on for a few yards in darkness, very conscious of the canal—briefly and foolishly he had thought of it for a moment as the river—lapping and gurgling to the left of him. Now if it *had* been his river, there'd be a bend here where you had to turn sharply to the left. When you got along a few yards the hills divided and you could see the village lights winking over there. Well, this wasn't the Stour but Croughton canal and now was no time for fantasies of that sort. A fine thing if he and the van went into the water with Ethel's trunk.

When he had reversed it almost to the brink, he opened the van's rear doors. Cursing the blinding rain, he clambered over the driver's seat and began to shove the trunk from behind. It slid slowly along the rubber mat. Stanley grabbed the bouquet of flowers and tossed them on to the passenger seat. Another final heave . . . He pushed, bracing his feet against the dashboard.

Suddenly the trunk shot out, bounced once on the canal wall and fell into the water with a tremendous splash. Kneeling between the open doors, Stanley started back on to his heels but the water broke against him in a huge wave, drenching him from head to foot. He swore luridly.

Great eddies wheeled away across the canal. Too wet now to bother with a raincoat, Stanley crouched on the parapet of the wall and looked down into the depths. Then, rolling up his soaked sleeves, he thrust his arm into the water. But he couldn't touch the top of the trunk, although he reached down as far as he could without actually toppling in. Right, he though, getting up, another job jobbed.

After she had sent the letter Vera thought she had been rather silly. Twenty years were a long time and Mrs. Horton would have moved away. But in the middle of the week a letter arrived with the Brayminster postmark. When she had allowed herself to hope at all, Vera had looked forward to a long chatty letter full of reminiscences and news, but Mrs. Horton wrote formally, simply saying she would be pleased to see Mrs. Manning and would reserve a nice room for her with a view of the sea.

The price quoted was well within Vera's means. She would have her holiday money and the small bonus the dry-cleaners gave their manageresses in the summer. Nor was there any need to worry about Stanley who had settled down quite marvelously in his new job and would have his own wages to live on while she was away.

"You won't be here to collect the cheque from Finbow and Craig," he grumbled when she told him her holiday was fixed.

"Mr. Finbow said a week or two, dear, and two weeks will only just be up when I get back." She smiled lovingly at him, remembering the beautiful and totally unexpected gift of flowers he had brought her that wet night when he had had to work late. If only he was coming with her . . .

"I'll drive you to the station in the morning if you like."

"That's sweet of you, dear."

"The week after you come back I'll have my own car."

"Whatever you like, Stan, and I'll have an automatic washer, I think, and a fridge."

"There's no need to go mad," said Stanley coldly and he pencilled in the word which completed his crossword, "onyx." "Only a pound left out and with ten to come it's turned to stone."

"I only hope you'll be all right on your own."

"I'll be fine," said Stanley.

13

Alone in the house, Stanley took stock of his life, congratulating himself on his excellent management. Nothing had gone wrong. Maud was safely buried and the heathers were beginning to flourish on her grave. Perhaps in a few months' time he'd have a garage built just on that spot. He'd need somewhere to keep his Jaguar. Ethel Carpenter was a handful of grey ashes, or rather an urnful, the mere powdery contents of a casket now reposing on the lounge mantelpiece between the wedding photograph and the nude statuette. Her trunk and clothes were at the bottom of the canal, the *objets d'art* which he had retrieved stowed in his wardrobe and waiting to be sold over the counter as soon as he and Pilbeam had opened their shop.

He had met Pilbeam as arranged and they had celebrated their new partnership in the Lockkeeper's Arms. Pilbeam had been less affable when Stanley had admitted his capital was at present tied up but Stanley thought he had been able to allay his doubts. Once Vera had returned and Finbow come up with the loot, a matter of ten days or so, he would be able to show Pilbeam concrete proof of his affluence.

Yes, things had gone admirably.

Stanley went down to the old village, told the florist that the job didn't suit him, after all, and, turning a deaf ear to the reproaches and indeed abuse which ensued, collected his week's money. He walked across the green and smoked a cigarette, siting on the steps of the war memorial and gazed in the direction of the shop which would soon be his. His vivid imagination presented it to him not as it now was but as it would be when Gothic gilt lettering ornamented the blank space above the window, when the door was a mullioned affair with a chased brass knob, the window was full of apparently authentic collector's pieces and the interior thronged with customers all desperate to part with their money.

Life was glorious.

He went into the Lockkeeper's off-licence and bought himself a half-bottle of whisky and six cans of beer. Then, armed with the materials for a liquid lunch, he returned home where he settled himself on the dining room sofa, a spot for four years sacrosanct and reserved to Maud.

Stanley poured himself a tumbler of whisky and raised it at the framed photograph of her mother Vera

had hung on the wall. "Absent friends!" he said. He
smiled and switched on the television for "Sports
Round-up," recalling how in the past he had almost always had to miss it because the noise disturbed Maud's
afternoon rest.

Vera only had one case and she meant to go from
the station to Mrs. Horton's by bus. The bus came and
it was a single-decker green one, not very different from
the buses she and James used to travel in down to the
sea. They hadn't changed the sea-front at all. There was
the old bandstand, the pretty little pier, there the cliffs
where thrift grew and the orange daisies with the long
Latin name Vera could never remember.

She couldn't see a single amusement arcade or fish
and chip shop but the old stall selling rock and candy
floss was still there and she saw a child go up to it with a
bucket and spade, a fair-haired child who might have
been herself all those many years ago.

Vera got off at the bottom of Seaview Crescent,
feeling she must be in a dream. It wasn't possible that
progress and the current mad craze for pulling things
down and putting new things up had passed Brayminster
by. It wasn't possible but it had happened. It was a Saturday afternoon in summer on the South Coast and
there was no canned music, no screaming mobs, no
coach parties and no strings of exhausted donkeys carrying screaming children along the sands. Vera listened to
the quiet. In the copper beech tree, which still stood in
the garden of the big house on the corner, a bird was
singing. She was at the seaside in the South of England
in spring and the only sound was a singing bird.

She walked slowly up the street and rang the bell of
Crescent Guest House and when Mrs. Horton herself
opened the door, Vera was almost too moved to speak.
Inside, the house looked just the same. Vera looked
wonderingly at the beach ball and the spade a child had
left by the umbrella stand, just where she had left hers.

"Brings back the past a bit, doesn't it?" said Mrs.

Horton kindly. "You look all in. Would you like to go up to your room and have a lie-down?"

"I'm not tired," said Vera, smiling. "I was just thinking how nothing's changed."

"We don't like changes in Bray."

"No, but how do you avoid them? I mean, everywhere else has changed utterly since the war."

Mrs. Horton led the way upstairs. "Well, down here, you see, we like to keep ourselves to ourselves. We're a bit like Frinton in Essex. Other places want the money, but we don't care so much about that. We don't let the coach parties in and our preservation society sees to it that the place doesn't get all built up. And we've got a good council. I only hope things stay this way."

"So do I," said Vera as Mrs. Horton showed her into the room Maud and George used to share.

"Your mother was so fond of this room. How is your mother, Mrs. Manning?"

"Dead," said Vera.

"Oh dear, I'm sorry to hear that." Mrs. Horton looked searchingly at Vera and then she said, before she went downstairs, "You have had a bad time, one loss after another."

Stanley lay on the sofa all Saturday afternoon. He wasn't used to whiskey and it made him sleep heavily. The phone ringing awakened him but before he could get to it it had stopped. Ten minutes later it rang again. Pilbeam. Would Stanley meet him for what he called a short snort in the Lockkeeper's Arms at eight and discuss business? Stanley said he would and had Pilbeam phoned him before?

"Not me, my old love. Maybe it was your stockbroker."

Well, suppose it had been? The solicitor, that is, to say the money had come through. But he wouldn't be working on a Saturday, would he? Stanley considered calling the number of Finbow and Craig but then thought better of it. Early days yet.

He opened a can of beans for his tea and he was

making himself a piece of toast to go with them when the phone rang again. Vera, he supposed, to tell him she'd arrived safely just as if he'd be worrying himself in case the train had crashed.

He gave the number and it was a girl's voice he heard.

"Mr. Manning? Mr. Stanley Manning?"

Finbow's secretary. Bound to be. "Speaking," Stanley said smoothly.

"You won't know me, Mr. Manning. My name's Caroline Snow. I was given your phone number by a Mrs. Huntley."

Mrs. Huntley? Mrs. Huntley? Where had he heard that name before? In some unpleasant connection, he was sure. Stanley felt a very faint disquiet, nothing amounting to a shiver, but a kind of sense of coming events casting their shadows before them. He cleared his throat. "What were you wanting?"

"Well, to talk to you or your wife, actually. I'm making some enquiries about a Miss Ethel Carpenter."

Stanley lowered himself gingerly into the chair Ethel Carpenter had occupied a few minutes before her death. His mind was curiously blank and he found himself temporarily quite unable to speak.

The girl's voice said, "Could I come over and see you? Would you be very kind and let me come tomorrow evening?"

A faint squeak that Stanley hardly recognised as coming from himself said, "No, but . . . look, what exactly . . . ?"

"Then, may I come at eight? That's marvellous. I'll be over at eight and I'll explain everything. Thank you so much."

"Look, don't ring off. I mean, could you give me some idea . . . ?" The phone clicked and went dead in his hand.

He found that he was trembling very much as he had done when, sitting in this very chair, he had held the receiver in his hand after Dr. Moxley had promised to come. Then he had been at the height, the very zenith of his troubles, but now they were all over. Or were they? He found that the palms of his hands were sweating and he wiped them on the knees of his trousers.

This was trouble from the least expected quarter. The beauty of making use of Ethel Carpenter in his plan had been her solitary state, her lack of any friends in the world but Maud and the extreme unlikelihood of anyone ever enquiring about her. This was the last thing he had anticipated. He went back into the dining room and finished off the whisky, but he had no appetite for his beans and he dropped the can into the pedal bin.

The whiskey comforted him a little but it also made him feel slightly sick. Suppose that girl had been a policewoman? Unlikely. She had sounded young, nervous and eager. Who the hell could she be, this Caroline Snow? She didn't sound more than twenty-five, if that. Not one of Mrs. Huntley's friends or she wouldn't have said "a Mrs. Huntley" like that. Some child, now grown up, whose family Ethel had worked for?

That would be it. He wished he had bothered to listen when Maud had told all those interminable stories about where Ethel had worked and whom she had worked for and the names of their kids. But he hadn't and it was too late now. Still, the more he thought about it the more likely it appeared that this was who she was, some upper-class little madam looking up her old nanny. In London on holiday from the provinces, no doubt, and taking it into her head to go and be patronising to the family retainer. Mrs. Huntley would simply have told her the Mannings were Ethel's friends and their house the best place to root her out. In that case, why hadn't Mrs. Huntley sent her along to Green Lanes?

There would be, no doubt, a perfectly simple explanation. Feeling a good deal better, Stanley decided to tell her Ethel was lodging with some people called Smith but that he didn't know where they lived. A girl like that, spoilt and used to having everything done for her, would soon get fed-up. He belched loudly, looked around for his crossword and then remembered he had already done it.

Still rather queasy, Stanley made his way down to the Lockkeeper's Arms at eight o'clock. He took a single pound note with him for, since Vera wasn't about to borrow from, he'd have to make his pay last him a week.

Pilbeam was already there and he looked as if he had been drinking steadily for several hours. The whisky he was putting away had put him in an aggressive, prickly mood.

"Your round, I think," he said to Stanley. Evidently he had a long memory. Reluctantly Stanley bought two double whiskies.

"Well, old man, when can I expect the first instalment?"

"The what?" said Stanley, his mind still on Caroline Snow.

"Don't give me that," said Pilbeam loudly. "You heard. The first instalment of this capital of yours we hear so much about."

"There's been a hold-up at my solicitor's."

"Well, you'd better get twisting your solicitor's arm, then, hadn't you?"

"It's coming. A week or two and we'll be able to get started."

"O.K. But just remember I'm an impatient man. I've got the lease and I had to touch the missus for the lolly. She'll want it back and quick, make no mistake about that."

"I won't," said Stanley feebly, and then more firmly, "your round, I reckon."

"We'll drink to a glorious future," said Pilbeam more amiably and he fetched two more whiskies.

"By the way," said Stanley, remembering Caroline Snow who might be a policewoman and might have a search warrant or something, "by the way, I've got a few bits to show you, pieces we might flog."

"That's my boy. What sort of bits?"

"A carriage clock and some china stuff."

"Where are they?"

"Back at my place."

"I tell you what," said Pilbeam. "Why don't you and me go back there now and give the stuff the once over? Your wife there, is she?"

"My wife's away."

"No kidding? You nip round the Off, Stan old boy, and get us a bottle of Haig and we'll make an evening of it."

Stanley had to tell him he hadn't got any money and Pilbeam, his bad temper returning, said in a very nasty tone that he'd buy it just this once but Stanley would have to stump up his share when they got to Lanchester Road.

Still in an ill humour, Pilbeam hardly spoke until they were inside the house and then he said he wasn't impressed by Stanley's domestic arrangements.

"Don't do yourself very well, do you?" Pilbeam looked scornfully at the worn carpet and Vera's framed photographs. "No wonder you've capital. You haven't spent much on this place."

"I'll get the stuff I told you about. It's upstairs."

"You do that, old man. And while you're about it, I'll relieve you of twenty-six and nine."

"That's upstairs too," Stanley muttered.

There was no help for it. He'd have to use a couple of Ethel's notes. Stanley opened the crossword annual for 1954 and took two from between the pages. Then he got the parcels out of his wardrobe and went back to Pilbeam who was already drinking whisky from one of Vera's sherry glasses.

"Funny pong they've got about them," he said, sniffing the notes. "Where've you kept them? In a tin of talcum powder? Right old miser you are, Stan." He pocketed the notes but he didn't produce any change.

"Are you going to have a dekko at these, then?"

Pilbeam examined the shepherdess, the bowl, the jug and the clock, sniffed and pronounced them saleable but of no great value. Then he put his feet up on the sofa and, without waiting for an invitation, told Stanley the story of his life.

It made an interesting narrative, full as it was of

accounts of Pilbeam's brushes with the law, his escapades with women and the fortunes he had nearly made. But Stanley found his attention wandering constantly back to Caroline Snow. Who was she? What was she going to ask him? Would she come alone? Stanley drank for comfort until his head was thick and fuddled and when Pilbeam reached a point in his story where he had nearly married an heiress old enough to be his mother, he nodded off into a jumpy stupor.

The last thing he remembered that night was Pilbeam getting up, pocketing the three-quarters empty bottle and saying, "I'll give you a ring in a day or two."

"No good," Stanley murmured thickly, "before next week."

"You leave that to me, Stan old boy. I'll twist your arm so as you know how to twist your stockbroker's."

It was noon the next day before Stanley came down after a night spent stretched on his bed, fully clothed. Pilbeam had left all Ethel's property behind, but he had taken the bottle and Stanley's change.

Unused to heavy drinking, Stanley had a blinding headache. He felt as if there was someone standing inside his head, pressing with all his force against the bony walls of his prison in a splitting effort to get out.

The sight of food made him give a slow, painful retch. Tentatively, he peeled the paper from the joint of beef Vera had left him and which he had forgotten to leave, soaking in salt water, on the tiled larder shelf the night before. It was on the turn, not exactly high but too far gone to eat when you felt as queasy as he did. He tipped it into the bin to join the beans. Well, he didn't feel up to eating anything, anyway. Instead he took two aspirins and wandered out into the garden.

Suddenly, for the first time since he got up, he was aware that it was a very hot day, blindingly, oppressively hot for late April, the kind of day that makes weather records and gives rise to newspaper articles about people fainting from the heat and the tar melting on the roads. The garden was virtually without shade. Never a

sun worshipper, Stanley gave a malevolent glare over
the fence to where the Macdonalds sat, eating their Sunday lunch under a striped awning. Some people didn't
know what to do with their money, he thought, eyeing
their new garden furniture with scorn and Mrs. Macdonald's bikini with disgust. She was forty-five if she
was a day and she ought to know better, she with a son
of fifteen. The boy, who was wearing nothing but a pair
of swimming trunks, glared back at Stanley and Stanley
went indoors.

The dining room, shut up since the night before, its
french windows beaten on by the sun since seven, was as
hot as a furnace and it stank of Pilbeam's cigars. Stanley
retched again and staggered into the cooler kitchen. He
might have taken a chair out on to the concrete into the
shade by the back door but he didn't want to be over-
looked by John Blackmore who, still painting his house,
was perched on his ladder.

Presently he made himself a cup of tea and took it
upstairs. He lay on the rumpled bed, sweating profusely,
but he couldn't relax. In seven hours' time he was going
to have to deal with Caroline Snow.

His feelings about the coming interview were considerably less sanguine than they had been on the previous evening. It was difficult to understand how a few
words on the telephone and the revelation of certain as-
pects of Pilbeam's character could have drawn so sudden and so dark a cloud across his happiness. Only
hours, not years, had passed since he had sat without a
care in the world on the steps of the war memorial.

At last he fell into an uneasy sleep and dreamed
that he could hear Maud snoring through the wall. It
was only the Blackmores' lawn mower, he discovered
when he awoke, but the notion that his subconscious
was translating commonplace sounds into aural halluci-
nations of his late mother-in-law upset him. That was
the first dream he had had of her since the night of her
death.

The sun had moved round to the front of the house
and penetrated the thick curtains, suffusing the bed-

room with hot glowing light. All Stanley's clothes seemed to be sticking to him. When it was nearly six he got up and put on a clean shirt. He went downstairs and re-wrapped Ethel's bowl and jug and clock and china and pushed them inside the sideboard.

He hadn't had a thing to eat all day but the very thought of food made him queasy again. Maybe he'd go out, go for a bus ride or see what was on at the pictures. Then Caroline Snow would find an empty house and serve her right. But Stanley knew he wouldn't go. To postpone for another day or even days finding out who Caroline Snow was and what she wanted would be unbearable.

At half-past seven he found he had started to pace up and down. It was cooler now but not very much and he kept the french windows shut. The Macdonalds were still outside, still laughing and playing with a beach ball and exchanging badinage with John Blackmore on his ladder as if, because they hadn't a care in the world, they thought no one else should have either. Stanley forced himself to sit down. A muscle in the corner of his mouth had started to twitch and jump.

Suppose she brought her husband with her? Or Mrs. Huntley or—God forbid—a policeman? She'd be at the station by now, he thought, looking at his watch, just about to catch the bus up. Ten minutes and she'd be here. Stanley went upstairs and looked out of all the windows which gave on to the street. It was deserted, but for one brave spirit washing his car down. That'll be me in a week or two, Stanley told himself for comfort, me with my Jaguar and my van parked side by side. By that time Caroline Snow would be in the past, a bad dream. . . .

What could they do to him, anyway? What could anyone do? Ethel Carpenter was a handful of ashes in an urn and he'd yet to learn any clever sod could analyse ashes and find out whose they were. In any case, he hadn't laid a finger on her. Was it his fault she'd fallen down dead in his lounge? He'd given her a damn' good funeral, far better than she'd have had if that Mrs.

Huntley had found her dead in her own room. Really, he'd done her a service. Very dignified that cremation had been and in the best of taste. The way he worried you'd think he was a murderer or something.

Five past eight. Stanley found that his heart had begun to grow very gradually lighter as the crucial hour passed by. He went downstairs and opened the french windows. The Macdonalds were packing up their furniture and their stupid toys. Stanley felt almost sufficiently well and relaxed to mow the lawn. He muttered something in reply to Blackmore's greeting and got the mower out of the shed. Up and down the lawn twice, the shorn grass spraying into the box. Perhaps it would be just as well to pop indoors and check she hadn't turned up, after all.

Stanley ran quite lightly up the stairs, leaving a trail of grass cuttings behind him. His bedroom windows showed him a deserted street. Even the car washer had finished and gone in. A beautiful, calm evening. Not normally a man to derive peace and tranquillity from communing with nature, Stanley now felt that nothing bad could happen on such a serene and tender night. The sky was a cloudless pastel violet, the shadows long and still. How beautiful his lawn would look when close-cut, its edges trimmed with the long shears.

Almost placid now, he returned to it.

The mower cut smoothly in long clean sweeps and Stanley worked evenly and methodically, for he liked his lawn to have a neat ribbed look like a piece of corded velvet or a very expert sample of knitting. The heather garden was in shadow now, sleeping under its quilt of peat and mowings. Up and down, up and down . . . Twenty-five past eight. What a fool he had been to get into a state!

He came down towards the house, pushing the machine. What the hell was Blackmore up to, making signs to him?

"There's someone at your door, mate."

Stanley's mouth dried.

"What?"

"A young lady ringing your door bell."

"O.K., O.K.," said Stanley. His palms were running with sweat. He wiped them on his trousers and went into the dining room. The whole house seemed to reverberate with the vibration of the bell. Momentarily, Stanley put his damp hands over his ears. Why shouldn't he just go upstairs and keep his ears covered until she had gone? But Blackmore had seen her, Blackmore would tell her where he was. . . .

"Oh, Christ!" Stanley moaned. "All right, all right," he said, "I'm coming."

The ringing stopped. He opened the door.

"Mr. Manning? Oh, good evening. I'm Caroline Snow. I'm so sorry I'm late. I had a job finding your house."

Stanley gaped at her. For a moment his terror had left him. It wasn't fear which made him speechless. He had seen such creatures as she before, of course, seen them on television in the Miss World contests or on the covers of the magazines Vera sometimes bought, even sometimes seen near copies of them driving up to the pumps at the Superjuce garage. But no one like this had ever until now rung the bell at 61, Lanchester Road.

"Isn't it hot? May I come in? Oh, thank you so much. I'm afraid I'm being a terrible nuisance."

"That's all right," Stanley mumbled.

He followed her into the dining room. Even from behind she looked nearly as good as from in front. Her long pale blonde hair covered her shoulders in a thick gold veil. Stanley didn't think he had ever seen such a straight back or such legs, legs which were so long and smooth and exquisite that it was almost painful to look at them.

When she was in the room and had turned to face him he wondered how he could ever have thought her back view was as nice. Her skin was tanned a smooth, even and satiny brown, much darker than her hair. Swedish or something, Stanley thought feebly. His eyes met sea-green eyes, as cool and calm as northern waters, and a wave of perfume floated over him so that he felt slightly faint.

"Can I get you a cup of tea?" he said.

"That would be great."

He went into the kitchen and put the kettle on. It wasn't just the beauty of that face that had made him stare at her. He stared because he felt it wasn't entirely unfamiliar to him. Somewhere he had seen it, or a face very like it though somehow changed and spoiled, in the recent past. In a film? In the paper? He couldn't remember.

"First I'd better explain," said Caroline Snow when he went back to her, "why I've come."

"Well, I did wonder," said Stanley.

"Naturally, you did. But I didn't feel I could talk about something so—well, personal and private on the phone. Did you know your kettle's boiling?"

Stanley got up and went out to turn it off. He meant to go on being tactful and polite but when he came back he found himself blurting out involuntarily, "Who are you?"

She smiled. "Yes, well, that's the embarrassing part. I may as well tell you and get it over. I'm Ethel Carpenter's granddaughter."

14

"You can't be," Stanley said. "She wasn't ever married."

"I know, but she had a baby at seventeen just the same."

Stanley, who had held his mouth open ever since

Caroline Snow's revelation, now closed it, swallowing
some air. At last he said, "Now you mention it, I did
know. My wife must have told me."

Caroline Snow said, "I think I'd better tell you the
whole story."

"O.K.," said Stanley, resigning himself. Having got
so far, he'd better know the worst. "I'll get the tea." Her
granddaughter, he thought miserably as he poured on
the boiling water. Almost as bad as a policewoman.

She smiled at him. Stanley thought she looked less
pretty when she smiled, for her teeth were uneven. She
also looked much more like Ethel Carpenter and now
Stanley knew whose face hers had reminded him of.

"Let's have it, then," he said.

"My people live in Gloucester," Caroline Snow began, "but I'm at training college in London. I'm training
to be a teacher and I'm in my second year. Well, we had
to do a special study this term, Greek myths or genealogy, and I chose genealogy." Stanley looked at her suspi-
ciously. He knew quite well what genealogy was, for his
passion for crossword puzzles had given him a large vo-
cabulary and, in any case, he was fond of words. But he
couldn't see what genealogy had to do with teaching kids
to read and write and he wondered if Caroline Snow
was lying. "Honestly, I'd have chosen the myths if I'd
known what I was letting myself in for. Our lecturer wanted us all to make family trees, one for the paternal side
and another for the maternal. You do follow what I
mean?"

"Of course I do," said Stanley, offended. "I'm not
ignorant."

"I didn't mean that. Only it's a bit complicated.
Well, doing Dad's tree was easy because all his people
came from a village outside Gloucester and I got hold of
the parish records and everything. I got that all finished
by half-term. Then I came to Mummy's. She was very
shy about it, didn't want to give me any help at all,
which isn't a bit like Mummy. She's a marvellous person, absolutely terrific. You'd adore her."

"I daresay," said Stanley. When was she going to come to the point? The last thing he wanted was to hear about marvellous adorable Mummy whom he was sure he'd loathe at sight.

Caroline Snow crossed her long legs and lit a cigarette. Gimlet-eyed, Stanley watched the packet returned to her handbag with mounting rage. "Anyway, to cut a long story short, I rather nagged Mummy about it all and then she told me. She said she was illegitimate. I'd always understood her parents were dead and that's why she'd been brought up in an orphanage, but she said she'd just told me that. The truth is her mother's still alive and she never knew who her father was. Well, at last I got it all out of her.

"Her mother was Ethel Carpenter, a housemaid who'd had her when she was only seventeen. My mother was brought up by Ethel's aunt until she was seven and then the aunt got married and the new uncle sent Mummy to this orphanage. Wasn't it awful? Mummy never saw her own mother and for years the only member of her family she did see was a cousin who came to visit her. He was Ethel's cousin actually and he was very kind to Mummy.

"Well, Mummy had brains, thank goodness, and went to training college—the same one as I'm at actually—and when she was teaching in a school in Gloucester she met Dad and married him and they lived happily ever after. It's rather a terrible story, though, isn't it?"

"Yeah." Stanley watched her stub out her cigarette. "I don't see where you come into it," he said.

"I've had my grandmother on my conscience," said Caroline Snow. "I felt so bad about her, you see. Mummy's never wanted to meet her. I suppose she thought it would be too heartbreaking for both of them. But now I've come so far I've just got to find her. Think what it would mean to her, Mr. Manning, a poor lonely old woman suddenly finding she'd got a whole family of her own."

Stanley could well understand Mummy's feelings, although most of his sympathy went to Mr. Snow.

That'd be a fine thing, he thought, having the good luck to marry an orphan and then getting an old mother-in-law thrust on you when you were middle-aged. Probably have to part out with money for her too. If I were in his shoes, Stanley said to himself, I'd smack that girl's bottom for her. Interfering little bitch of a do-gooder.

"I'd give the whole idea up if I were you," he said aloud. "It stands to reason, if she'd wanted a family she'd have hunted all you lot up long ago." It was, he thought, a good line to take, charitable to the unfortunate Mr. Snow as well as opening up a let-out for himself. He warmed to it. "She won't want to be reminded of her past, will she? The disgrace and all? Oh, no, you give it up. I reckon your dad'd say the same. It's always a mistake, stirring things up. Let sleeping dogs lie is what I say."

"I'm afraid I disagree with you," Caroline Snow said stiffly. "You must read the papers. You know what a terrible problem we have in this country with our old people, how lonely some of them are and how friendless. I'd never forgive myself if I gave up now." She smiled, giving him an indulgent look. "Anyway, you don't really mean it. Mrs. Huntley told me you'd had your own mother-in-law living with you for years and having to be looked after. You didn't abandon her now, did you? And now she's dead you've got nothing to reproach yourself with. Well, I don't want to reproach myself either."

This little speech temporarily took Stanley's breath away. He gaped at her, frowning. Her zeal and her innocence were beyond his understanding. He cleared his throat. "How did you get on to Mrs. Huntley?"

Serene again, Caroline Snow said, "The cousin who used to visit Mummy in the orphanage is still alive, although he's a very old man. I went to see him first and he said he'd lost touch with my grandmother but he knew her last place had been with some people called Kilbride. I found them and they told me she had a room with a Mrs. Huntley."

"And she put you on to us?"

"Well, she said you'd know where my grandmother was, on account of she and Mrs. Kinaway being such close friends. And she said my grandmother had been coming to stay here with you but she'd changed her mind and now she's got lodgings in Croughton with a Mrs. Paterson but she'd forgotten the address. I thought—I thought if you could just give me that address I'd go round now and introduce myself and . . . Oh, I feel so nervous and excited! I'm quite sick with nerves. Just imagine, Mr. Manning, what she'll think when she sees me. I'm going to tell her she'll never be alone again. We've got quite a big house in Gloucester and I want Daddy to turn the attics into a flat for her. I want to take her home myself and show her her new home and just see her face."

I'd like to see Daddy's, thought Stanley. Poor sod. It was one thing for this silly little piece, arranging people's lives for them. She wouldn't be there to listen to Ethel banging on the floor with her stick and demanding meals at all hours and monopolising the T.V., she'd be living it up in London at her college. That poor devil, he thought with indignation. It was his, Stanley's, duty to prevent anything like that happening, his bounden duty. . . . He was so outraged that for a moment he had forgotten the impossibility of Snow's house ever being invaded by a mother-in-law. Then, suddenly, he remembered. Ethel was dead, all that remained of her some fifteen feet away from them in an urn on the mantelpiece. It didn't matter where Caroline Snow went or where she looked, for Ethel had vanished from the face of the earth.

"Mrs. Paterson's address is 52, Green Lanes," he said, "but I don't think you'll find her there. My wife said she'd found somewhere new."

Caroline Snow wrote down the address. "Thank you so much," she said fervently. "I'm sure I'll be able to trace her now. But wasn't it odd her telling Mrs. Huntley she was coming here and then suddenly changing her mind?"

Stanley frowned. "When you've had as much experience of old people as I have," he said with feeling, "you won't be surprised by any of the funny things they do."

She got up, first looking at him in rather a woe-be-gone way, her ardour perhaps a little dampened, and then eyed herself critically in the mirror. "I wonder if I look at all like her? I'm the image of Mummy and Mummy's supposed to look like her."

"Yeah, you do a bit," said Stanley.

Caroline Snow swung round to face him. "Then, you do know her? You have seen her?"

Stanley could have bitten his tongue out.

"She was at my wedding," he muttered.

"Oh, I see." She picked up her bag and Stanley saw her to the door. "I'll let you know how I get on," she said.

From his bedroom window Stanley watched her hurrying along in the direction of Green Lanes. Somewhere he had once read that most of the things one has worried about have never happened. How true that was! When the girl had disappeared from view he finished mowing the lawn in the half-light, whistling an old tune which he later realised had been Tennyson's "Maud."

Vera was enjoying her holiday. She had met some nice people, a married couple about her own age and who were also staying at Mrs. Horton's. They insisted on taking her about with them in their car, along the coast to Beachey Head and inland to Arundel Castle, and they laughed and asked Vera if she thought they were on their honeymoon when she demurred and suggested she was intruding. They wanted her to share their table but Vera wouldn't do that. She ate alone, sitting in the window and watching holidaymakers coming up from the beach, and she enjoyed her food, relishing every scrap because she hadn't had to cook it herself.

There was only one thing that troubled her and that was that neither her new friends, the Goodwins, nor Mrs. Horton had once asked about Stanley, where he

was and why he hadn't come with her. Vera felt
rather piqued. She couldn't help thinking that in the early days of her marriage when Maud had still come to
Bray for holidays, she had poisoned Mrs. Horton's mind
against Stanley. I shan't mention him, if that's the way
they want it, Vera said to herself. She felt no pressing
need to talk about him. Now he was far away, she found
she hardly thought about him and this made her so
guilty that she sent him a postcard every day.

At a loss to know how to amuse herself one wet
afternoon, Mrs. Goodwin took Vera up to her bedroom
where she washed and set her hair, made up her face,
and, while Vera was waiting for the set to dry, turned
the hem of Vera's blue and white spotted dress up two
inches.

"You've got very nice legs. Why not show them
off?"

"At my age?" said Vera.

"Life begins at forty, my dear. You'll look ten
years younger, anyway, when I've finished with you."

Vera did. She stared in wonderment and unease at
her new self, at the bouffant golden-brown hair, the
pale blue eyelids and the pink mouth Mrs. Goodwin had
created with a lip-brush. The dress barely reached her
knees. Feeling half-naked, she went down to dinner and
hid herself in her alcove away from the other diners.

She was waiting for Mrs. Horton's maid to bring
her second course, when a man came into the dining
room and wandered about, evidently looking for someone. Vera watched his reflection in the window. She was
so busy staring at this that she nearly jumped out of her
skin when a hand touched her shoulder. She turned and
looked upwards, flushing slightly.

He was a stranger, quite unfamiliar to her, a man
of fifty perhaps with a rather haggard face, fair hair
gone pepper and salt, a long lean man with an anxious,
even forbidding, look. Vera half-rose. She must have
done something wrong. Forgotten to pay for her deck
chair perhaps. . . .

"I'm sorry . . ." she hesitated, stammering. "What —er . . . ?"

He smiled at her and it made him look much younger.

"Hallo, Vee."

"I don't think . . . I don't know you, do I?"

"You used to know me. I know I've changed. You haven't, not very much. I'd have recognised you anywhere. May I sit down?"

"Oh, yes, of course."

He pulled up a chair, offered her a cigarette. Vera shook her head.

"My aunt told me you were here. I meant to come yesterday but, I don't know . . . I suppose I was shy. It's been so long. How are you?"

Confidence suddenly came to Vera and a poise she didn't know she possessed.

"I'm very well, thank you, James. It's good to see you."

"Oh, Vee, you don't know how glad I am to see you," said James Horton.

15

Gradually, as the week went on, Stanley's small panic receded. For the first few evenings he sat close to the phone, the crossword puzzle on his knees, expecting a call from Caroline Snow. But no call came. In fact nothing came from the world outside at all but daily postcards from Vera. She wrote that she was having a wonderful time, meeting new people, going out and about with them every day. Stanley felt very bitter towards her and resentful.

As soon as she got back she could go down to that Finbow and get Maud's money out of him. It was downright diabolical, solicitors hanging on to other people's rightful inheritances for weeks on end.

"How's your head, Stan?" said Pilbeam when he phoned on Thursday.

"There's nothing wrong with my head," said Stanley.

"Bet there was Sunday morning. One sniff of a barmaid's apron and you're out like a light."

"I told you," said Stanley, "it was no good ringing me this week. I'll have the money on Tuesday like I said."

"You never did, in point of fact, me old love. But let it pass. Tuesday, you said?"

"That's a promise."

"I sure am glad to hear that, Stan. I've been out knocking today—got a lend of a van—and some of the things I've picked up'll make your hair curl." It was a funny thing about Pilbeam, Stanley thought. The mere sound of the man's voice brought him vividly before one, snub nose, sausage-like finger and all. "How about a sniftah in the Lockkeeper's tomorrow night, so as I can get a clearer picture of the state of your finances?"

Stanley was obliged to agree. Pilbeam would get a clear picture of his finances all right when he turned up in the Lockkeeper's with all he had left of last Friday's pay, ten bob.

The whole Macdonald family and the two Blackmores were outside the Macdonalds' gate, admiring Fred Macdonald's new car, when Stanley left the house to keep his appointment. He would have marched past them without a word but the Macdonald boy, Michael, barred his way, holding both arms outstretched.

"Look what my dad's just brought home, Mr. Manning."

"Very nice," said Stanley, but still they wouldn't let him get away. Macdonald got out of the car and invited

Stanley to take his place and examine the arrangements for the automatic gear change. Unable to think of an excuse, Stanley got sulkily into the car and contemplated the control panel.

"No more wearing my left foot out on the clutch in a traffic jam," said Macdonald jubilantly. "Comfortable, isn't she? I've only got one complaint. When I sink into that I'll fall asleep behind the wheel."

The women were nattering nineteen to the dozen, scuttling around the car and pointing out the mirror-like gloss on its bodywork, the vast capacity of its boot and the workmanship of its chrome. Mrs. Macdonald was swollen with pride. Wait till they see my Jag, Stanley thought, after this tin can. Then they'll laugh on the other side of their faces.

"The mirror adjust at the touch of a finger," said Macdonald, thrusting his head through the window.

Stanley put it to the test. He moved the mirror an inch down and glanced into it. Then he stared harder, going hot all over. From the High Street end of Lanchester Road Caroline Snow was walking along the pavement in the direction of his house. She wore large round sunglasses with mauve lenses and a skirt several inches shorter than the one she had worn on Sunday. Stanley looked down, twiddling knobs and pulling small levers. One of these operated the windscreen washers and a fountain of water gushed across the glass.

"Here, here," said Mrs. Macdonald. "Mind what you're doing. I shall have to get a leather to that." She frowned spitefully at Stanley and pulled the card door open. "Anyway, you're wanted. There's someone come to call on you."

Stanley got out very slowly, not looking behind him. Macdonald slapped him on the shoulder. "When the cat's away the mice will play, eh, old man? Very good taste you've got, if I may say so."

"I don't know what you're talking about," Stanley muttered. Six faces confronted him, the children's inquisitive, the women's indignant, the men's frankly prurient. John Blackmore gave a crooked grin and then he slowly winked. "Excuse me," Stanley said. "Got to go in."

He scuttled up the path to where Caroline Snow stood waiting for him on the doorstep. Behind him he heard Mrs. Blackmore say, "Well, really! How disgusting."

"I just had to come and see you again, Mr. Manning. I do hope it's not inconvenient?"

The air in the house smelt stale. Stanley flung open the french windows. The girl followed him.

"Perhaps we could sit in the garden? It's so hot, isn't it? And your garden's lovely."

"I haven't got time for any sitting about," said Stanley hurriedly. He looked at his watch. "I've got an appointment at half-past six."

"I've really come to you," the girl said, taking no notice of all this, "because—well, you were very kind to me on Sunday and you're really the only responsible man I can talk to. You see, I've relied on Daddy all my life but Daddy's such a long way away."

Let me be your father, Stanley thought eagerly, forgetting for the moment all about his date with Pilbeam. "What exactly d'you want me to do, Miss Snow?"

"I went to see Mrs. Paterson," Caroline Snow said earnestly, "and she said Miss—er, my grandmother had got a room with a Mr. Smith but she doesn't know his address. Now college comes down on Tuesday and I have to go home so I wondered . . . My grandmother's bound to come and see you and your wife sometime, isn't she? I thought if you'd be kind enough to tell her about me if she does and—well, write to me, I could look her up when I get back to London."

"Yeah, I could do that," Stanley said slowly. Of course he could. He could tell her he'd seen Ethel and Ethel had moved again or even that Ethel didn't want to make contact with her relatives. Suddenly he was inspired. Making his voice sound as confident as he could and infusing into a hint of the paternal, he said, "Why don't you ask your father's advice? Have you told him anything of all this?"

"Well, no . . . As far as Mummy and he know, I just wanted my grandmother's name for this family tree."

Wonderful. Just what he'd hoped for. He could just imagine Snow's horror when he heard of this search for his mother-in-law and his relief when he learned she wasn't to be found. "Your dad's a man of experience. He'll know what's the best thing to do." He will, Stanley thought, if he's in his right mind. "He might feel rather hurt if you went over his head like this. She is his mother-in-law after all. He might not . . ."

"Oh, but Daddy's a marvellous person. He's got a terrific social conscience. He couldn't bear to think . . ."

"Can you be quite sure of that, Miss Snow?" Stanley leaned earnestly towards her. "Certainly your father'll want to know all the details you've told me, but isn't it likely he'll want to do any further investigating himself? Besides, he and your mother may feel your grandmother's got a right to privacy, if that's what she wants and it seems she does want it. No, he wouldn't like it at all if you put people's backs up and got the police on a wild goose chase."

"I wonder if you're right?" Caroline Snow looked nearly convinced. "You've put things in a different perspective for me, Mr. Manning. Actually, I've just remembered something. Once, years ago when I was quite young a gipsy came to our door when Mummy was out and I gave her some clothes and made her a cup of tea and when Daddy heard about it he was *furious*. He said the state should look after people like that. He'd got quite enough supporting his own family."

The man with the terrific social conscience! Stanley almost laughed aloud.

"Of course, it's not really a parallel case, but it does make me think I ought to ask Daddy before I go any further." She got up and held out her hand. "You've really been very kind, Mr. Manning. I'm sure you've given me the right advice. I won't do another thing be-

fore I've asked Daddy." She held out her hand. "I'm
afraid I've made you late for your appointment."

"Better late than never," Stanley said cheerfully.
"I'll walk with you. It's on my way."

They left the house together. John Blackmore, who
was trimming his hedge, favoured Stanley with another
wink. Stanley talked about the weather and the car he
was going to buy and the business he was going into to
take the girl's mind off Ethel Carpenter.

"I wonder now why I got this idea something terrible might have happened to her? I suppose it was because Mrs. Huntley said she was carrying fifty pounds
on her."

"She'll be living it up on that without a care in the
world," Stanley said reassuringly.

Caroline Snow smiled at him and in that smile he
saw Ethel grinning up at him and waving her umbrella.
She gave him the address of her father's house and they
parted cordially.

That, Stanley thought, was the last he would ever
see or hear of her. He walked to the Lockkeeper's because he couldn't afford the bus fare. The little shop
was still boarded up but the agent's placard had been
taken away.

Pilbeam wasn't alone but surrounded by a circle of
friends, all of whom seemed extravagantly big men. He
didn't introduce any of them to Stanley but moved away
from them without a word. For some indefinable reason
this made Stanley uneasy.

Without asking Pilbeam's preferences—he knew
them—Stanley bought two halves of bitter and, flounder-
ing in a mass of prevarication, set about giving his new
partner a picture of his finances.

Pilbeam said only, "Next week, me old love. First
thing next week."

Some of Vera's ideas about James Horton had
been right and some wrong. He was manager of Barclay's Brayminster branch; he was well-off, for he had

inherited money both from his father and his uncle; he
did live in a nice house. But he wasn't married to a
woman in her handsome early forties and he hadn't a
family of teenage children. His wife had died of cancer
five years before, leaving him with one son, now at uni-
versity.

"A lonely life, James," Vera said on her last evening as she and James sat in the cocktail lounge of the
Metropole hotel.

"It gets lonely sometimes."

"You never thought of marrying again?"

"Not until lately," said James. "You know, Vee,
you haven't told me a thing about yourself. We've been
out together every night—oh, mostly with the Goodwins, I know—but all the time I've seemed to do nothing but talk of my life and I haven't given you a chance
to tell me about yours. I'm afraid I've been very self-
centred."

"Oh, no. I've been so interested."

"I suppose it's living alone that makes one want to
talk. But your life must have been as lonely as mine."

"What makes you say that?" Vera looked at him,
puzzled.

"Aren't we almost in the same boat, Vee? I a wid-
ower and you a widow, you childless and I . . ."

"James," Vera said loudly, "whatever made you
think I was a widow?"

He turned rather pale and stammered, "But my
aunt said . . . You came down here alone and you never . . ."

"I'm afraid Mrs. Horton's got it wrong. I'm not a
widow. My husband just couldn't get time off from
work. Oh dear, now I begin to see a lot of things I didn't
understand."

"You mean you live with your husband? You and
your husband . . ."

"Of course. I'm going home to him tomorrow."

"I see," said James Horton. "I've been rather foolish and obtuse."

16

All Vera's cards were on the mantelpiece but not displayed. They were tucked in a stack behind a vase. Stanley hadn't asked her if she had enjoyed herself and she was very hurt.

"How's the job?" she asked quietly.

"I've resigned, if you must know. I'm going into the antique business. There's pots of money to be made out of antiques and we're taking a shop in the old village. Me and my partner, that is."

"Your partner?" said Vera. "What partner? Who is he, Stan? Where did you meet him?"

Vera looked so aghast that it would hardly have made matters worse to tell her he had met Pilbeam in the street and founded the partnership in a pub. But Stanley was one of those men who never tell their wives the truth if a lie will serve instead. "He was put in touch by a mutual friend," he said vaguely. "A client of mine at the Superjuce gave him my name." He knew Vera wouldn't believe him but at the moment he hardly cared. He shifted his eyes sullenly. Two hours before she came home he had telephoned Finbow and Craig only to be told by a secretary that Mr. Finbow had a matter he wanted to discuss urgently with Mrs. Manning and a letter on the subject would reach her on Monday morning. Another hold-up. God knew what Pilbeam would say if the money wasn't forthcoming in the Lockkeeper's on Tuesday night.

Vera said astutely, "Has this man got any capital?"

"Be your age," said Stanley. "He's rolling. Would I get involved with him if he hadn't?"

"I don't know what you'd do, Stan. But I reckon you're a child when it comes to business. I know more about business than you do. Promise me you won't do anything silly."

Stanley didn't answer her. He couldn't get that letter out of his mind and the more he thought about it the more he felt the tiny muscles around his eyes twitching. On Sunday night he slept badly, being visited by troubling dreams of Maud. In one of them he and she were discussing the contents of her will and Maud told him she hadn't finished with him yet, that Mr. Finbow's letter would be concerned with a clause in that will designed to upset any business schemes he might have.

He was therefore less indignant than he might otherwise have been when Vera brought him a cup of tea and read aloud to him.

Dear Mrs. Manning,

With regard to your inheritance from the late Mrs. Maud Kinaway, I have been in touch with the firm of stockbrokers acting for the late Mrs. Kinaway. Owing to the recent fall in the stock market, I feel it my duty to inform you that I consider it inadvisable to sell the stock in which your late mother's monies are invested, at the present time. I am, however, reliably advised that the market is once more rising and that it would be expedient to retain these stocks for a further few weeks.

No doubt, you will wish to discuss this whole question with me as soon as possible. I should like to stress that should you desire this stock to be sold forthwith, I will naturally proceed to instruct your late mother's stockbroker accordingly. Perhaps you could arrange to call at my office early this week.

I remain,
Yours sincerely,

CHARLES H. FINBOW.

"I just hope he's on the level," Stanley said gloomily, "and not playing ducks and drakes with our money. You can tell him to sell that stock right away."

"Don't be silly, dear," Vera said mildly. "Mr. Finbow's only acting in our interests. He means that if he sold those shares now he'd get hundreds less than if we waited a few weeks."

Stanley sat up, choking over his tea. "You what? We've got to have that money. God knows, we've waited long enough." He felt quite sick with horror. Imagine Pilbeam's face if he was asked to wait weeks. The whole enterprise would go up the spout. "You'll go there today," he spluttered, "in your lunch hour and I'm coming with you."

"I can't, Stan. Doris is off and I can't get away for lunch."

"If you won't, Vee, I will." Stanley threw back the covers. "I'll go down there alone and get that money if I have to knock his teeth in."

"I'll see what I can do," Vera sighed.

Alone in the house, Stanley paced up and down, sweating. In the pub on Friday he had confidently promised Pilbeam money to buy a van, money for decorating and furnishing the shop and enough ready cash to stock it. Finbow would have to cough up. His eye fluttered painfully and to calm himself he sat down and did the crossword puzzle.

He was just filling in 26 across "Last Post" eight letters, four and four, "Ultimate mail before leaving the field" when the doorbell rang on a sharp peremptory note.

Stanley never answered a doorbell naturally and innocently as other people do. He always debated whether it was wise to answer it at all. Now he crept into the front room and peeped through the curtains. Pilbeam stood on the doorstep with a large heavily built man who looked no more than twenty-eight and who was recognisable as one of those henchmen who had moved silently away from Pilbeam in the pub on Friday.

Stanley let the curtain fall, but not before Pilbeam's

eyes had met his. There was no help for it. The door would have to be answered. He opened it and Pilbeam put his foot inside and on to the mat like a pushing salesman.

He didn't introduce his companion. Stanley didn't expect him to. They all knew why the friend had come. There was no need for hypocritical formalities.

"I told you Tuesday," Stanley said.

"I know, old man, but what's a day one way or the other? We all realise the big lolly's coming tomorrow. What I want is fifty on account now."

They came in. Stanley couldn't stop them.

"I haven't got fifty," he said, very conscious of the friend's size and youth.

"Thirty, then," said Pilbeam. "It's in your own interest, Stan. Me and my mate have got our eye on a couple of *famille rose* vases. It'd be a sin to let them go."

"I'll see," said Stanley feebly. The friend's mammoth shoulder was nudging his. "Sit down. Make yourselves at home. The money's upstairs."

He scuttled up the stairs and made for the bookcase. Leafing thirty notes from the pages of the crossword annual, he became aware of a step behind him and then that Pilbeam was standing in the doorway, watching the operation with interest and a certain bewilderment.

"So that's your little safe deposit, is it? By gum, it stinks of violets."

Speechless, Stanley handed over the thirty pounds. There were now only thirteen notes left in the annual.

"This is my husband," Vera said when they were admitted to Mr. Finbow's office. It wasn't an introduction she had often had to make. She and Stanley hadn't lived in a world where many introductions were called for. But whenever she had to say those words she was conscious of a little creeping feeling of shame, a feeling which was even more intense today as she glanced at Stanley and noticed the belligerent set of his chin and the calculating suspicious gleam in his eye. "He wanted to come with me."

"How do you do, Mr. Manning?" said Mr. Finbow. "Won't you both sit down? Now then, I think my letter explained the situation, but if you'd like any further details I'd be glad to give them."

Stanley said, "We would. That's why we're here."

Mr. Finbow raised his eyebrows slightly and turned his attention pointedly in Vera's direction. "The position is this, Mrs. Manning. The money your late mother bequeathed to you is principally invested in two stocks, Euro-American Tobacco and Universal Incorporated Tin. Both very sound investments, as safe, if I may say so, as houses. You are, however, no doubt aware of the effect on the stock market of the recent Arab-Israel crisis."

He paused, perhaps for some comprehending response from Vera. But Vera, although vaguely aware that there had been a lot on television about the Middle East during recent weeks, had been too involved with personal crises to pay much attention, and she could only give a rather helpless nod.

"I am told," said Mr. Finbow, "that to sell at this juncture would result in a loss of several hundred pounds, owing to the considerable fall in prices."

Vera nodded again. "But these—er, investments, they'll get back to what they were before?"

"I am assured they will. You see, Mrs. Manning, the two companies I've mentioned are vast world-wide concerns which generally maintain their shares at a steady level. There's absolutely no question of any long-term deterioration in their value. The point is that the current price is temporarily unsatisfactory. In other words, any knowledgeable person would tell you it would be unwise to sell at present. But wait, say, six weeks and we should see a considerable improvement in . . ."

"Six weeks?" Stanley interrupted. "What about the interest? What's happening to all that?"

"As I have just explained," the solicitor said less

patiently, "the price is currently reduced. The price of each individual share is lowered but your wife's income is unaltered as there has been no change in the dividend policies of the companies."

"O.K., O.K.," said Stanley. "So you say. But how do we know there won't be more of these crises? You can keep us hanging on like this month after month. It's our money you're playing with."

"I *beg* your pardon?"

"Well, isn't it? My wife told you to sell. Weeks ago that was. And now, because you've been hanging about, there's not so much money there as what you said at first. Seems plain enough to me."

Mr. Finbow got up out of his chair and turning his back on Stanley, addressed Vera in a cold courteous voice, "If you're dissatisfied, Mrs. Manning, perhaps you would prefer to find another firm of solictors to act for you?"

Red with shame, afraid to look at Stanley, Vera stammered, "Oh, no. No, you mustn't think that. I don't think my husband quite . . ."

"I understand all right," said Stanley, not at all put out. "Not that any of that matters a damn. We said we wanted you to sell and we do. You can sell the lot right now, this afternoon. It's our money and that's what we want. Right?"

For a moment Mr. Finbow looked as if he would have a seizure. Then he said very icily, "I am not a stall-holder in a street market. I am a solicitor and senior partner in a firm of unblemished reputation. Never— never have I been spoken to in those terms before in my own office." Momentarily he closed his eyes as if in pain. Stiffly, he addressed Vera, "May I have your instructions, Mrs. Manning?"

Vera looked down. Her hands were trembling in her lap. "I'm sorry, Mr. Finbow. Really, I'm very sorry." She raised her eyes miserably. "Of course, you must do whatever's best. We're not in actual need of the money. It's just—just that there were one or two things . . ."

Mr. Finbow said quickly and slightly more sympathetically, "There are several insurance policies also which matured at your mother's death. If it was a question of, say, five hundred pounds, I will be happy to give you a cheque for that immediately."

"Five hundred pounds would do very nicely," said Vera more happily. She waited, her head turned away from Stanley, while Mr. Finbow drew the cheque. "And please don't do anything about selling those shares until you and the stockbroker think it's right."

"Very well," said Mr. Finbow, shaking hands with her and behaving as if Stanley wasn't there. "May I say I think you've been very wise, Mrs. Manning? Good afternoon."

"Oh, Stan, how could you?" Vera said as they went downstairs. "I don't know what Mr. Finbow must have thought of you."

"Blow that for a lark. He can think what he likes, pompous old bastard. Now, if you'll just write your name on the back of that cheque I'll take it along to Barclay's and open an account. Here'll do, on that table. You'd better get back to the shop or you'll be late."

Vera stopped, but she didn't open her handbag. "I don't have to be back till two. I thought I'd miss lunch today and go and look at some fridges in the Electricity Board."

"Good idea. Get cracking, then." Stanley held out his hand expectantly.

"When I said 'look at,' I meant buy. You know I've been longing to get a fridge. I can't buy one without any money and I shan't have any money till I get a cheque book. We'll both go to the bank first. Don't you think it would be nicer to have a joint account?"

"Nicer," in Stanley's mind, was hardly the word. He saw, however, that under the circumstances it was inevitable and they entered the Croughton branch of Barclay's together.

The manager wasn't in the least like James Horton to look at, being short and stout, but he reminded Vera of James perhaps because, like James, he was a manager of another branch of James's bank. She hadn't thought

much about James since her return but now he returned
vividly to her mind, a gentle, courteous and thoughtful
man, and she couldn't help contrasting his civilised behaviour with Stanley's conduct at Finbow and Craig.

"There you are, Mrs. Manning," said the chief
clerk, bending over the manager's desk. "Your cheque
book, and Mr. Manning's too. And a paying-in book for
each of you. Naturally, we'll send you cheque books
with your names printed on them as soon as they come
through."

The manager showed them to the door.

"That," said Stanley, "is what I call a gentleman."

He had deciphered the last clue in the crossword
puzzle ("Golden Spaniel"—"The marksman's 9-carat
companion") when Vera came in, pink with excitement.

"I've bought it, dear, a lovely refrigerator with a
place to keep salads. And, oh, I know it's very extrava-
gant but I've bought an automatic washer, too. They're
sending both of them up tomorrow."

"What did all that lot cost?" said Stanley, replacing
the cap on his pen.

"Just on a hundred. Having all that money went to
my head, I suppose. But I've made up my mind, I shan't
touch another penny until the rest comes through from
Mr. Finbow."

"It's your money," said Stanley graciously. "It's
you your mum left it to, after all."

"You mustn't say that, darling. It's ours. I want
you to buy yourself a new suit and any little thing you
fancy. You've got your own cheque book now."

Stanley put his hand in his pocket and fingered it,
the crisp green book, hard and as yet untouched in its
plastic folder. Very generous of Vee really, to look at it
in that light, giving him *carte blanche* as it were. He
would have dipped lavishly into the account, anyway,
but it was nice getting permission first.

The washing machine and the refrigerator arrived
at nine-thirty the following day. Stanley was still in bed
and getting up to let the men in put him in a bad tem-

per. Then he reflected that it was Tuesday, a good day
for him in two ways. He was going to keep Pilbeam happy and Caroline Snow was off to Gloucester. At one
o'clock he put the wireless on for the news, thinking
wistfully how one problem would be off his mind forever if the Paddington-Gloucester train crashed. It was
amazing what a lot of trains did crash these days. Rail
travel was getting as dangerous as going in aircraft. But
the news was all about the negotiations taking place to
quieten down the Middle Eastern ferment and trains
weren't mentioned.

Vera was too occupied playing with her new kitch-
en toys to enquire closely into his reasons for going out
at a quarter to eight. He told her casually that he had a
business appointment without adding that it was to take
place in a pub, a venue which rather detracted from the
respectable air with which Stanley wanted his new ven-
ture imbued.

Pilbeam was already there. He always was already
there.

"Sorry about yesterday's little *contretemps,* Stan,
but needs must when the devil drives. I got the vases
and some *very* pleasing Georgian silver. Time you came
down to the shop and looked over the loot. Now, about
this van. A mate of mine's offered me a smart little job.
It's ours tomorrow if we fancy it and only two hundred
and fifty quid."

"I reckon I can find that," Stanley said.

"Well, I should hope so, old man. After your
promises, I really should hope so. I've the wife to pay
back, you know, and if we're off to Barnet in our van
tomorrow . . ."

"Leave it to me," said Stanley.

They bought the van in the morning. Stanley gave
Pilbeam's friend a cheque for it and drew another to
cash. The van wasn't his idea of a smart little job, being
battered about the bumpers and chipped on the bodywork, but it started first go and carried them as far as
Croughton old village.

Pilbeam didn't say much on the journey and Stanley supposed he was sulking. But when he pulled up outside the shop he realised he'd been wrong. Far from sulking, Pilbeam had been silent from suppressed excitement and now, as he got out, he said proudly, "Well, old man, what d'you think? Surprise, surprise, eh? You can see I haven't been idle."

Stanley could hardly believe his eyes. When he'd last seen the shop the bow window had been cracked and dirty and the doorway boarded up. Now the window was repaired and every pane highly polished, affording a delectable view of treasures within. Above it, expertly lettered in gilt, was the name *The Old Village Shop,* and there was more gilt lettering on the door, a glass and wrought iron affair with a curly brass handle.

Pilbeam unlocked it and let him in.

Inside, the walls were papered in a Regency stripe and the floor was carpeted in dark red. On an oval table stood a pair of candelabra and a big glass rose bowl. Wide-eyed, Stanley tiptoed about, looking at hunting prints and Crown Derby plates and unidentifiable pieces of bric-a-brac. What he saw cheered him enormously, for he had begun to lose faith in Pilbeam. The man's arrival on the previous day to extort money from him by violence if necessary had shaken him, and the knocked-about old van had been almost the last straw. Now, gazing around him at polished wood and gleaming china, he felt his faith revewed.

"Who did all this decorating, then?" he asked.

"Couple of mates of mine." Pilbeam seemed to have dozens of friends. "I got them to do a rush job as a special favour. Like it?"

"It's grand," said Stanley.

"I told them to send the bill to you. That all right?"

"Oh, sure," Stanley said less comfortably. "About what sort of—er, figure will it be?"

"Say fifty, old man. About fifty. That won't break you, eh? Then there's the carpet. Lovely drop of Wilton that is, as you can see. But I don't reckon you'll get the bill for that before the autumn. Open up tomorrow, shall we?"

"Why not?"

They celebrated with a drink at the Lockkeeper's Arms and then they took the van up north into the villages of Hertfordshire. At the houses they called on Pilbeam did the talking. He seemed to like best the shabbier among the ancient houses and those occupied by a lone middle-aged or elderly woman whose husband was away at work.

His method was to ask this housewife if she had any old china or silver and mostly she had. While she was up in the loft turning it out, Pilbeam had a quick glance round at her furnishings, and when she came down again he bought everything she showed him, paying good prices until she was bemused by the sudden influx of cash given in exchange for what she thought of as rubbish. Just as they were leaving Pilbeam would offer her ten or twenty pounds for the piece he had had his eye on all the time, a wing chair or a writing desk, and in her greed and delight she usually agreed to his offer. Pilbeam took the attitude that he didn't really want this particular piece, he was doing her a favour in taking it off her hands.

"I'll give you twenty, lady," he would say, "but it'll cost me the same again to do it up, then I can sell it for forty-five. You see, I'm being completely honest with you. I'm in this for a profit."

"But I could have it done up and make the profit myself."

"I said it'd cost *me* twenty to do it up. That's not the price a cabinet-maker'd charge you. More like thirty or forty."

"Well, *you* know," the woman would say. "I'm sick of it, anyway. I'm glad of the chance to get rid of it. The last lot of stuff I cleared out I had to pay them to take it away."

The cash for these transactions came out of Stanley's pocket.

"It's not falling on stony ground, old boy," said Pilbeam. "Now, if you could just let me have twenty-five for the wife, we'll call it a day, shall we?"

Stanley had to write a cheque for Mrs. Pilbeam.
He had no cash left. "Just make it to H. Pilbeam," said
her husband. "Hilda's her name, the old battleaxe."

Well, he'd got through the four hundred remaining
in the bank all right, Stanley thought. The decorators
would have to wait. Still, he wouldn't have to part out
with any more for a bit and Vera had said she wouldn't
touch another penny. In any case, by the end of the
week, he'd take his first money out of the business.

The next day he took Ethel Carpenter's ornaments
with him down to the Old Village Shop and arranged
them tastefully on the oval table.

17

It was no good Stanley going out with the van. He
wouldn't know, as Pilbeam put it, a Meissen vase from a
baby's chamberpot, so while his partner plundered
drawing rooms, Stanley stayed behind to mind the shop.
The price of everything was marked on its base or one
of its legs and Pilbeam said not to drop at all, not to
haggle. They could take it or leave it.

They left it. Stanley made only one sale on his first
day and that was a silver teaspoon, sold to a putative
godmother for fifteen bob. He went home rather crest-
fallen to find a tight-lipped red-eyed Vera who answered
him in monosyllables when he told her about his day.

"What got into you?"

"You know very well what's got into me."

"No, I don't. You were all right this morning."

Surely she couldn't have found out about the money he'd had? His cheque book was safe in his own pocket. "I'm not a thought reader."

Vera sat down, picked at her food and burst into tears.

"For God's sake!" said Stanley. "What's wrong with you?"

"You are. You're what's wrong with me, you having your girls in this house while I was away." She lifted to him red eyes full of bitter reproach. "How could you, Stan?"

"Girls?" said Stanley. "What the hell are you on about? I never had any girls here. You must be round the twist."

"Well, girl, then. One girl, if that makes it any better. The whole neighbourhood's talking about it. They're all laughing at me, the lot of them. They always say the wife's the last to know, don't they?"

Caroline Snow. Damn, she was a jinx, an evil genius if ever there was one. Trouble after trouble she was making for him.

"I suppose Mrs. Macdonald told," he said.

"As a matter of fact, it was Mrs. Blackmore, but they all know. They're all talking about it. How this tall blonde girl came here on Sunday, the day after you'd got me out of the way, and then how she was back again on the Friday. Stayed for hours, Mrs. Blackmore said, and she saw you go off down the road together."

"I can explain," said Stanley classically. "She's—she's a girl me and my partner are thinking of taking on to do the books. I had to interview her, didn't I?"

"I don't know. But if that's true, why did you say no one came here when I was away. Those were your words, not mine, I didn't ask you. Nobody came here, you said."

"I forgot."

"Nobody ever comes here," Vera said wearily. "We haven't got any friends, or hadn't you noticed? Nobody but the neighbours come in here for years on end, but that girl came and you forgot to tell me. You *forgot*. How d'you think I feel? What am I supposed to think?"

"You ought to believe me," said Stanley. "Me, not the neighbours, bloody gossiping mob. I'm telling you the truth, Vee."

"Are you? You wouldn't know the truth if you saw it, Stan. Lies or truth, it's all the same to you. Suppose I ring up this Pilbeam, this partner of yours, and ask him if you're engaging a girl to do your books?"

"He's not on the phone," Stanley muttered. Christ, he'd have to prime Pilbeam in the morning just in case she made good her threat. "I reckon you ought to trust me, Vee."

"Why? Have you ever given me any reason to trust you the whole of our married life?"

That night Vera slept in the bed she had got ready for Ethel Carpenter.

As the weeks went on the shop did better. Because their funds were exhausted Pilbeam served in the shop on Thursday and Friday and his presence made a difference to their sales. Stanley could see he was a good and relentless salesman with a fine line in persuasive talk. He sold the oval table and the four chairs which each had a fragment of Hepplewhite concealed about them as genuine unblemished Hepplewhite to a woman who claimed her house was furnished throughout with Swedish white wood, and the candelabra as a present for a teenage tear-away. Pilbeam said he could sell central heating to tribesmen in equatorial Africa and Stanley believed him. But when he asked for his cut out of their week's takings, Pilbeam said they mustn't touch a penny for a long time yet. All their cash was needed for buying in.

Stanley went home empty-handed.

His relations with Vera had improved but they weren't restored to normal. Feeling relaxed and happier one evening, he'd rested his arm lightly round her shoulders while she was standing by the cooker, but she'd flinched away from him as if his arm were red hot.

"Isn't it time we let bygones be bygones?" he said.

"Do you swear that girl was nothing to you, just a girl after a job? Will you swear you never touched her?"

"I can't stand the sight of her," Stanley said truthfully, and after that Vera was nicer to him, asking about the business and planning what they'd do with the money when it came, but sometimes when they were watching television or he was at work on a crossword, he'd look up and catch her staring at him in a strange way. Then she would drop her eyes in silence.

She was beginning to look forward to the arrival of the money now and while Stanley did the *Telegraph* puzzle she begged the city page from him and studied the markets, well-satisfied that from day to day Euro-American Tobacco and International Tin showed a steady improvement. Maud would have wanted her to have the money, she thought, wanted her above all to have the things that money would buy. She had had one of those snapshots of Maud enlarged and hung on the dining room wall and now when she looked at it she often reflected how sensible and perceptive Maud had been, seeing Stanley from the first for what he was. Money wouldn't improve her daughter's marriage, Maud had always known that, but it would make her life as an individual rather than as a wife easier. It was something to be miserable in comfort.

It was nice now to sit at the table while Stanley was engrossed in his puzzle and write out cheques for the gas bill and the electricity instead of having to empty one of the tins she kept in the kitchen dresser and take the money all in coins down to the showrooms. Marvellous just to write eight pounds, nine and three and sign it without having to wonder whether you couldn't make it less next time by turning the light out every time you left a room. . . .

That week Stanley took ten pounds home with him.

"It could be five times that, me old love," said Pilbeam, "only we need all the capital we've got for fresh stock. The fact is we're hamstrung till you cough up."

And Stanley, who had been doubtful about his

partner right up until the time the shop opened, now saw that every forecast Pilbeam had made was true. He *did* know what he was talking about; he *was* an expert in the antique business. The whole thing was the gold-mine he had promised, a quarry of rich ores which could only be dug out and converted into coin when a sizeable capital sum was invested in it. The terrible thing was that his capital, his own legitimate capital was invested elsewhere in footling tin and tobacco, untouchable until Finbow gave the word.

His nerves were in a bad way. His hands didn't shake and he no longer had those attacks of sick fainting but something even more upsetting had happened to him. The twitch in his eye had become permanent.

The twitching had come on again when Vera had questioned him about the girl's visits. Then it had been in the muscles of his right eye. His eyelid jumped up and down especially when he was tired. Stanley went into the public library and looked up his symptoms in the medical dictionary he had first consulted when he had had designs on Maud. The dictionary said the twitching was commonly known as "live flesh" and was brought about by tiredness and worry but usually stopped after a short time. If it didn't it might be more serious, an early sign, in fact, of some disease of the central nervous system.

What, anyway, was a short time? Hours, days, weeks? There was no sign of this twitch abating and he'd had it for a fortnight now. The only time it stopped was when he was doing a crossword. The trouble with that as therapy was that he could now do the puzzle in ten minutes. Perhaps a better idea would be to begin at the other end, as it were, and make up crosswords himself.

Two or three years before he had tried doing this but there was no peace with Maud always there in the evenings and he had given it up. Now it was different. Sitting in the shop, whiling away time between customers, he sketched out crossword frames on the pad Pilbeam and he used for their bills. Sometimes Pilbeam was out on the knock, sometimes tapping away in the little workshop at the back. His eye was obedient and still while he invented clues and slotted in the words, for the task was a challenge to his mental powers. It preoccupied him, often to the exclusion of all else, and he found himself devoting whole hours together to the problem of finding a word to fit blank, R, O, G, blank, blank, S, blank, blank, before finally coming up with prognosis.

It was becoming something of an obsession, but Stanley knew it would go, just as the twitching would go, when the money came. Then he'd attend to the shop with real vigour, knowing that Pilbeam wouldn't appear from the back every few minutes to make nasty cracks about people who couldn't honour their obligations. Meanwhile, his crosswords were harmless enough and they kept his mind off the money and his eye from twitching.

Nearly a month had passed after opening the joint account when a letter came for Vera from the bank. Stanley had already gone to work, muttering under his breath E, blank, G, H, blank, and quite unable as he had been for three days now to find a word to fit this five letter puzzle. He passed the postman but he was too involved with this apparently insoluble cypher even to suppose he might at last be bringing news from Finbow and Craig.

The envelope was addressed to Mr. and Mrs. Manning and Vera hesitated before opening it on her own but at last she did and a shiver of disbelief ran through her.

Dear Mr. and Mrs. Manning,
    I am sorry to have to inform you that your joint current account is overdrawn to the sum of £35. I feel sure that you will wish to rectify this matter as soon as possible and am confident of receiving a remittance to cover the outstanding amount within the next few days.

                        Yours sincerely,
                        ARTHUR FRAZER (Manager).

But it couldn't be! She had only drawn cheques for the refrigerator and the washer and to pay the fuel bills. The account stood at five hundred pounds when opened and there ought to be at least three hundred and seventy there now. She had told Stanley to buy himself a suit, but he hadn't. Could it be a mistake? Oh, it must be. Did banks make mistakes? Everyone did sometimes, so banks must too.

Again Vera was aware of her ignorance of so many of those matters the average person takes in his stride. Perhaps she had written one of those cheques wrongly, put in an extra nought. But wouldn't the gas or the electricity people be honest about it? Or would they just hang on to what they'd got like Stanley had once when a greengrocer had handed him change for a fiver and not the single pound note he'd given him?

Worse than that, could the bank prosecute her? Somewhere she remembered hearing that it was an offence, actually against the law, to write cheques that couldn't be honoured. If only there was someone she could turn to, someone she could ask.

Maud would have known. Vera looked desperately at the photograph of her mother on the wall. Maud had been a good businesswoman, a marvellous manager, as sharp as any accountant, but Maud was dead. There was only Doris at the shop or Mrs. Blackmore or Mrs. Macdonald. Vera didn't want any of those women knowing her business. It was bad enough their discussing her married life among themselves and Stanley's deceit.

She didn't know anyone else, unless . . . Well, why not? James had said he was her friend. "Don't let's lose touch now, Vera," he'd said. Of course, that was before she'd told him her husband was alive and living with her, and they *had* lost touch. Not a word had passed between them since she came back from Bray.

But if she didn't ask James, what was she going to do? Lose three hundred and seventy pounds? More than that, because she was overdrawn by another thirty-five.

Almost distraught, Vera telephoned the dry-cleaner's and told Doris she wouldn't be in. She didn't feel well, she said truthfully. There was no point in hesitating any longer, pacing up and down and re-reading that letter. Vera got out her address book and then she dialled the long string of numbers that would put her directly through to Brayminster.

The bank wasn't open yet and James was free. He seemed very pleased to hear Vera's voice, not sad or disillusioned as he had been at their last encounter.

"You're not putting me out at all, Vee. Of course, I'll give you any advice I can."

Rather haltingly and with many apologies for troubling him, Vera explained.

"I see. What does your husband say?"

It had never occurred to Vera to get in touch with Stanley.

"I haven't told him yet."

There was a short silence at the other end of the line. Then James said, "It's a joint account, you say?"

"Yes, but Stanley doesn't need money. He's in business, he's doing well."

Why did James suddenly sound so sympathetic, so gentle?

"I really think you should speak to your husband, Vee. But I'll tell you what I'll do. I've met Mr. Frazer once or twice and I'll give him a ring now and say you're a friend of mine and that you'll be in to see him at eleven. Will that be all right? You'll have time to get in touch with your husband first."

"You're awfully kind, James."

"I'd do anything for you, Vee. You know that. Would you like me to lend you thirty-five pounds just to tide you over?"

"I couldn't think of it," Vera said vehemently. "No, please, I didn't want to speak to you for that."

"You're welcome if you need it. Now, Vee, don't *worry*. The bank has honoured these cheques so there's no question of their being returned to drawer or anything of that sort. Mr. Frazer will be quite understanding. Just ask him to give you a statement and show you

the cheques that have passed through your account.
D'you understand?"

"Yes, of course."

"Good. Nobody is going to lecture you or threaten
you in any way. I suppose as a bank manager I
shouldn't say this, but thousands upon thousands of people are overdrawn every month and they don't even turn
a hair. I only wish they would. Get in touch with me tomorrow, will you?"

"I wouldn't think of it," said Vera.

James said calmly, "Then I'll phone you. Yes, I
will. It's been lovely talking to you, Vee. Give me that
pleasure again tomorrow."

Vera felt a good deal better and very pleased that
she had plucked up the courage to talk to James. But
she wouldn't be able to see Stanley before she went into
the bank. He had told her he'd be out in the van till
noon.

She made up her face carefully in the way Mrs.
Goodwin had taught her and put on the blue and white
spotted dress. By five to eleven she was in a waiting
room at the bank and after a few minutes Mr. Frazer
himself put his head round the door and invited her into
his office. His manner was quite pleasant and cordial.

"I had a call from your friend, Mr. Horton," he
said. "But you mustn't ever be afraid to come and see
me, Mrs. Manning."

Vera blushed hotly. What a fool they must both
think her!

"Perhaps you'd like to see your statement," said
Mr. Frazer.

While it was being fetched he chatted easily about
the weather and about Brayminster where he had once
spent a holiday. Vera could only answer him in monosyllables. She felt anything but at ease. The bank had a
serious air about it and she suddenly wondered if she
was on the threshold of something immensely serious in
a personal sense to herself.

The statement was brought in by a girl clerk. Mr.
Frazer sent her away and then he passed the statement

with its batch of cheques enclosed over to Vera. He lit a cigarette but Vera shook her head when he offered one to her.

It was the first time she had ever seen a bank statement and she didn't understand it. Bewildered, she picked up the top cheque, expecting to find it as incomprehensible as the statement, and then she saw her own handwriting. It was the one she had sent to the Gas Board. I suppose they pay it into their bank, she thought, and the money's marked to their credit there and then it somehow gets to my bank and they subtract the money from what I've got. Straightforward, really.

Back to the statement. The Gas Board had their money all right but only because the bank had paid, not because she had the money. She hadn't had any money before she'd written that cheque. She blushed again.

Here was her cheque for the refrigerator and the washer and another one to the electricity people. Vera turned up the last but one. She drew in her breath sharply. Verity Vehicles, she read, two hundred and fifty pounds, £250.0.0, Stanley G. Manning. There was one more. To cash, £150. Stanley G. Manning.

"My husband," she stammered. "I'd forgotten . . . He did say . . . Oh, dear, I'm so sorry. . . ."

"Well, we like to think we don't make many mistakes, Mrs. Manning."

"I'm the one who made the mistake," Vera said and the words suddenly meant far more than just an apology for extravagance. "I'll try to pay it back—well, next week. I don't know how but I'll try."

"My dear Mrs. Manning, we're not bloodsuckers. You mustn't be so upset. As long as you've managed to straighten matters out by the end of the month . . ."

"You're very kind," said Vera. Everyone was very kind, very understanding, bending over backwards to help her because—because they pitied her so. And, of course, they knew what had happened. James had guessed from the start. Mr. Frazer had seen through her clumsy little covering up tactics. They all knew she was married to a man she couldn't trust an inch.

As soon as he saw Vera's face, Stanley realised he was in trouble again. This time he wasn't going to put up with being ignored, more or less sent to Coventry. He flung his coat over the back of a chair, scowled at Maud's picture on the wall—she might as well be still alive for all the good her death had done him—and said:

"I suppose those bloody interfering women have been giving you a few more details about my so-called girl friend."

"I haven't seen Mrs. Blackmore or Mrs. Macdonald today."

"What is it, then?"

Vera poured herself a cup of tea and sipped it in silence. Silence, thought Stanley. "Permission is possibly quiet." Anagram on "licence" . . . God, he'd have to control himself, not keep seeing every word as part of a crossword puzzle. For the first time in their married life Vera had helped herself to a cup of tea without pouring one for him.

"What's up with you?" he said, his nerves on edge.

Vera turned round. She looked old and ugly, deep shadows ringing her eyes, deep lines scored from nose to mouth. "I may as well have it out," she said. "I've been to the bank his morning. I had a letter from the manager."

"Oh, that."

"Yes, that. Is that all you can say?"

"Look Vee, you said I could have some of the money. You said, buy yourself anything you want."

"I said a suit or any little thing you wanted. I didn't say draw out four hundred pounds. Stan, I don't mind you having the money. But couldn't you have told me? You wanted it for the business, didn't you? Couldn't you have just said? Did you have to make me look a fool in front of the bank manager and nearly worry myself to death?"

"You said you wouldn't write any more cheques. How was I to know you'd start paying bills?" Why was she staring at him like that? Her eyes were fixed on him so that he had to look away.

"What's wrong with your eye?" she said coldly.

"Nothing. The muscles keep jumping, that's all. It's my nerves."

Silence again. Then Vera said, "We can't go on like this, can we? God knows, I didn't want Mother to die, but when she was dead, I thought—I thought things would be better. I thought we'd have a proper marriage like other people. It hasn't worked that way, has it?"

"I don't know what you're on about," said Stanley, edging his way into the dining room. He sat down on the sofa and began doodling on a sheet of paper. Vera followed him. "Look, I'm sorry about the money, but there's no need to make a song and dance about it. I can easily get it back out of the business."

"Can you, Stan? We haven't seen much out of the business yet, have we? Come to that, I don't even know there is a business. You haven't taken me to the shop or introduced me to Mr. Pilbeam or . . ."

"Do me a favour," said Stanley huffily. His eye was opening and shutting like an umbrella. "Can't you take my word for it?"

Vera laughed. "Take your word? Stan, you can't be serious. I can't take your word for anything. You just say the first thing that comes into your head. Truth or lies, it's all the same to you. I don't think you know the difference any more. And Stan, I can't bear it. I can't bear to be left in the dark and humiliated and deceived just because doing that to me is easier for you than telling the truth. I'd—I'd rather be dead or not with you."

Stanley hadn't paid much attention to all this. Vera's remark about his eye had affected him more than all her analysis of his shortcomings. Drawing a crossword puzzle frame and inserting a couple of words, he had heard nothing since then but her last sentence. It leapt at him like a red warning light.

Alarmed, he said, "What d'you mean, not with me?"

"When people reach the stage we've reached, they separate, don't they?"

"Now, look, Vee, don't you talk like that. You're my wife. And all this—well, it's six of one and half a dozen of the other. If I keep you in the dark it's on account of the way you nag me. A man can't stand nagging." Can't stand, either, having no control over his own face. Stanley covered up his eye and felt the lid jerk against his hand. "You're my wife, like I said, and have been for twenty years. There's a good time coming, Vee, I promise you. We'll both be in clover by the end of the year and . . ."

She stared at him even harder.

"Do you love me?"

What a question! What a thing to ask a man when he was tired and worried and maybe on the verge of Parkinson's Disease. "Of course I do," Stanley muttered.

Her face softened and she took his hand. Stanley dropped his pencil reluctantly and laid his other hand on her shoulder. His eye was aching. For a long time Vera said nothing. She held his hand tightly and then, without letting it go, sat down beside him. Stanley fidgeted nervously.

"We'll have to make a fresh start," Vera said suddenly. He sighed with relief. A fresh start. "Beginning with a new jump"? Surreptitiously he felt among the cushions for his pencil. That S could be the S in business, the word going down. "After public transport I'm on a Scottish loch. . . ."

"Yes, we'll have to start again," Vera said. "We'll both have to make an effort, Stan, but that won't be so hard now we've got all this money coming to us."

Stanley smiled at her, his eye quite normal.

"We'll sell this house and buy a new one and we'll scrap all this old furniture. Mother would have liked to see us in a modern house." That "us," Stanley thought, was a mere courtesy. Maud would have liked to see *him* in a modern concentration camp. "And we'll have prop-

er holidays together and a car. I'll promise never to nag
you again if you'll promise to be open with me. But I
have to trust you, Stan. You do see that?"

"I'll never tell another lie to you, Vee, as long as I
live."

She stared at him, wishing she could believe what
he said, that at last he was being sincere. Stanley returned her gaze glassily. He had thought of his word. E,
blank G H blank. Eight, of course, the only English
word surely to fit that particular combination. And all
day long he'd been wondering if he could alter the H to
O—change the word across from phone to Poona—and
make 18 down ergot. Triumphantly Stanley wrote in
"eight" and beside it, "One over it is too many drinks."

18

The bill came in from the decorators and someone had
written across the top of it: "Prompt settlement will be
appreciated." They would have to take their apprecia-
tion elsewhere. Stanley didn't at all appreciate the de-
mand for £175, instead of the fifty Pilbeam had spoken
of so confidently. Vera and he, making their fresh start,
sat side by side on the sofa, studying the market.
Euro-American Tobacco had dropped a couple of
points overnight. Stanley's eye fluttered lightly, then began a rhythmic blinking.

"You want to put some more money into the business, don't you, Stan? I only hope it'll be safe."

"You said you wouldn't nag me," said Stanley. He

reached for the sheet of paper on which he was composing a larger and more ambitious crossword. Nag would fit into that three-letter space, he thought. Nag, nag, nag. How about, "The horse may pester?" Yes, that would do. Nag meant "horse" and "pester" . . .

"I don't mean to nag. But have you formed a sort of company or a partnership? Have you had it done legally, Stan?"

"I trust my partner and he trusts me," said Stanley. "Pity I can't say the same for my wife." He printed in "nag" and then tacked "wife" on to the W in "window." Wife: "If in two compass points find a spouse." Vera was looking at his eye now, although the twitching had stopped.

"Don't you think you ought to see the doctor about that tic you've got?" she said.

James was as good as his word. He phoned Vera at home and, getting no reply, phoned the cleaner's.

"Well, Vee, I said he wouldn't eat you, didn't I? What was it all about, a simple mistake on someone's part?"

"My husband forgot to tell me he'd written rather a large cheque." Loyally, Vera lied, "He's put it all back out of his business."

"That's fine." James didn't sound as if he thought it was fine at all. He sounded as if he didn't believe her, a notion which was confirmed when he said, "Vee, if you're ever worried about anything, you'll get in touch with me, won't you?"

"I've got Stanley," Vera said.

"Yes, of course. I hadn't forgotten. But there might be a time when . . . Good-bye, Vera. Take care of yourself."

It was time she did, Vera thought, time she took care of herself. Really, it was ridiculous for a woman in her financial position, or prospective financial position, to keep on working in a cleaner's. She handed a customer two newly cleaned pairs of trousers and then she sat down to write her resignation as manageress of the Croughton Laundry.

Thursday. Her afternoon off. Vera left the shop at one and called in at the nearest estate agent. He would be pleased to handle the selling of her house, he said. What kind of figure had she thought of asking? Vera hadn't thought about it at all, but the estate agent knew the type of house and suggested four thousand, five hundred pounds. He promised to come to Lanchester Road during the afternoon and look the place over.

Vera made herself some scrambled eggs for lunch and finished up the chocolate mousse they could now keep overnight because they had the refrigerator. It was unlikely the estate agent would get there before three and that would give her an hour to make things look a bit shipshape upstairs.

Before the house was sold she'd have to make an effort and clear out Maud's room properly, all those clothes that Aunt Louisa didn't want, all those papers and the bottles and jars whose contents had kept Maud alive for four years.

After the funeral Vera had shut them up in one of the dressing table drawers. She opened it now and contemplated Maud's various medicines, anti-coagulants, diuretics, mineral salts, vitamins, sleeping tablets and tranquillizers. I wonder if the chemist would take them back? Vera thought. It seemed a wicked waste just to throw them away.

Now for the clothes. She was packing them into an old bolster case when the doorbell rang. Vera was expecting the estate agent and she was surprised to see a young woman on the doorstep.

"Good afternoon. I'm collecting for the Chappell Fund."

Vera thought she said "chapel fund" and was about to say she was Church of England when she remembered the young policeman who had been shot during the Croughton Post Office raid. She opened her purse.

"Thank you so much. Actually, we're trying to get a

thousand pounds collected privately for Mrs. Chappell and some of us are getting up a few stalls at the Police Sports next week. If you do happen to have . . ."

"Would you like some cast-off clothing?" Vera asked. "My mother died recently and all her clothes were good. Nobody wants them now and I'd be glad if you'd take them off me."

The young woman looked delighted, so Vera went upstairs, fetched the bolster and handed it to her.

"These were your mother's, you say?"

"That's right. I've no use for them, really."

"Thank you very much. You've been a great help."

The only thing that worried him now was the money. Once get his hands on that and life would be serene. It was obvious he was never going to hear another word from Caroline Snow.

Relishing the picture, Stanley imagined her bursting into her home in Gloucester and pouring out the whole story to Snow, tired, poor devil, after a hard day's work toiling to keep women in luxury. Probably Snow was watching the box or even doing a crossword. In his mind's eye, Stanley saw the man's face fall when he heard how he was expected first to find a mother-in-law he had never before considered as a serious menace and then welcome her to his hearth and home.

"We must find her, mustn't we, Daddy? You're so marvellous in a crisis. I knew you'd know what to do."

Stanley chuckled at this piece of silent mimicry. And what would Snow say?

"You leave it to me, darling." Soothing tone, brain sorting it all out like a computer. "I'd like to talk it over, with your mother when we're alone."

Shift to scene with marvellous Mummy, tête-à-tête, lights dimmed, Caroline off somewhere with dog or boy friend. ·

"She's such an impetuous child, dear."

"Yes, I know. But I can't destroy her faith in me, can I?"

"She adores you so, darling. I must say for my

part, I don't exactly relish a reunion with a mother I haven't seen for forty years."

"There's no question of that. Nothing would induce me to pal up with the old lady and have her here. Good heavens, I'm not a glutton for punishment. . . ."

"Why not just say you've got in touch with the police, dear? Say they're making enquiries. Caroline will have forgotten the whole thing when she's been home a week."

"Of course she will. You're so marvellous, darling."

Stanley laughed uproariously at this invented cameo of the set-up and dialogue *chez* Snow. He could almost see them sitting there among their refined middle-class G-plan furniture. It was a pity he had to keep it to himself and couldn't tell anyone about it. He wiped his eyes and when he had stopped laughing his eye began to twitch ferociously.

He was trying to hold the eyelid steady, seeing if he could control it by an effort of will, when Pilbeam walked into the shop, holding a plastic bag full of horse brasses.

"You want to get that eye of yours seen to, old man. I had an aunt with the same trouble, St. Vitus's Dance."

"What happened to her?"

Pilbeam tipped the horse brasses on to the floor and sat down. "She got to jerking all over. It was embarrassing being with her." He scratched his nose with the nailless finger. "Why don't you go and see the quack? I can cope here."

The group practice whose list he was on held an afternoon surgery three times a week. His worry over getting his hands on his inheritance had long since driven any apprehension over the part he had played in Maud's death from Stanley's mind so, after waiting forty minutes, he walked more or less serenely into the surgery where Dr. Moxley sat behind his desk.

"What seems to be the trouble?"

The swine might take the trouble to look at me,

Stanley thought sourly. He explained about his eye and as he spoke it fluttered obligingly.

"They call it 'live flesh.' "

"They do, do they? And who might 'they' be?"

"A medical book."

"Oh, dear, I wish you lay people wouldn't be always poking about in medical books. You only frighten yourselves. I suppose you thought you'd got muscular dystrophy."

"Well, have I?"

"I shouldn't think so," said Dr. Moxley, laughing breezily. "Been worrying about something, have you?"

"I've got a lot on my mind, yes."

"Stop worrying, then, and your twitch'll stop." Just like that, Stanley thought indignantly. As if telling someone not to worry would stop them. Bloody doctors, they were all the same. He took the prescription for a sedative and was halfway to the door when Dr. Moxley said, "How's your wife? Getting over Mrs. Kinaway's death all right?"

What business was it of his? Stanley muttered something about Vera being all right. The doctor, a past master, Stanley thought, at switching moods, smiled and said genially, "I ran into old Dr. Blake the other day. He was quite upset to hear Mrs. Kinaway had died. Surprised, too. He said he'd seen her in the street only a couple of days before and she looked very fit."

Stanley was speechless. The scare over Caroline Snow, now past, had been bad enough. The last thing he had anticipated was that questions might be asked at this late date about Maud. Why, it was weeks and weeks . . .

"He couldn't understand Mrs. Kinaway having another stroke when she was on Mollanoid." Moxley gave an innocent yet somehow sinister smile. "Still, these things happen. Dr. Blake's very conscientious. I advised him not to give it another thought."

Stanley walked out in a daze. Who would have thought Maud's old doctor would still be hanging about the neighbourhood? Probably it meant nothing. He had enough troubles without bothering about that.

To get his prescription made up Stanley went in to the same chemist he had been to when buying Shu-go-Sub and suddenly he remembered that two and a half tubes of saccharine tablets still remained in Maud's Mollanoid cartons. The first thing he'd do when he got home was get hold of those tablets and burn them just in case Moxley and the conscientious Blake were planning to make a swoop on the house and investigate.

"What's happened to all your mother's stuff," he asked Vera.

"All gone. I've been having a turn-out. The estate agent said we could get a better price if the place was smartened up so I thought I'd do some decorating."

Decorating was a dirty word to Stanley. Sourly he watched Vera come down the steps, wipe her brush and put the lid on the distemper tin. Distemper was a good word for a puzzle and he couldn't remember ever doing one in which it had been used Distemper: "Paint prescribed for the dog's disease." Very good.

"You've thrown everything out?" he asked casually.

"Everything but her clothes. Someone came round collecting for the police."

Stanley felt the sweat break out on his upper lip. "The *what?*"

"Whatever's the matter? You're jerking all over."

Stanley clenched his hands. Even they were jumping. He couldn't speak.

"Well, not the police really, dear." Vera was sorry she had put it that way. Stanley had always been afraid of the police. "They were collecting for that policeman's widow, Mrs. Chappell, and they were so pleased when I gave them Mother's clothes. Stan, dear, let me make you a cup of tea. You're overwrought, you're worrying about your eye. Come along. You can do your crossword while I'm making the tea."

"I've done it."

"Then make one up. You know you like doing that."

Still jumping and shivering, Stanley tried to sketch a crossword frame. He wrote in "distemper" and then "policewoman" going down from the P. Perhaps the woman had come on an innocent errand; perhaps Moxley had meant nothing sinister. But suppose instead that Moxley had dropped a hint or two to the police and they had sent this woman round because . . . What could they find out from Maud's clothes? Perhaps there was some substance present in a person's sweat when they had high blood pressure or when they were taking saccharine or weren't taking Mollanoid. For all Stanley knew, Moxley might be an expert in forensics. He wrote "forensics" in, going down from the R in distemper.

They might go round all the chemists and find that a man answering his description had bought a lot of saccharine. . . . Then they'd dig Maud up. The gash on her head might be gone by now. They'd analyse the contents of her stomach and find Shu-go-Sub, masses of it. But no Mollanoid. Maud hadn't taken any since early March.

His eye winked, half-blinding him, so that he couldn't see the words he had printed across the white squares.

3. Down

19

It was high summer now, a fine, beautiful summer. Hot day succeeded hot day and this sameness was reflected in the Mannings' life. Nothing changed for the better or —Stanley comforted himself—for the worse either. The police showed no further interest in him and he hadn't been back to Dr. Moxley, although his eye still twitched. He couldn't stop worrying about the money.

Letters went back and forth between Vera and Mr. Finbow but there was no hint in anything the solicitor wrote that it would now be prudent to sell those tin and tobacco shares. Vera refused firmly though kindly to sell them against Mr. Finbow's advice or to ask for another advance, even though Stanley had shown her the reminder which had come from Pilbeam's decorators with "please settle outstanding payment at once" scrawled across it. Pilbeam made Stanley's life a misery with his nagging about the shop's need for more capital.

A "For Sale" board had been put up outside the house. No one came to view it. It lacked, the agent told Vera, certain amenities which these days were indispensable.

"We might have a garage built," said Vera. "Only it would mean sacrificing your heather garden."

"Doesn't matter," said Stanley. A garage would keep Maud hidden forever. On the other hand, how much unearthing would the builders have to do to lay foundations?

"I'll see about it, then, and I'll carry on with my decorating. We ought to get an offer soon. The agent says sales are booming."

"Dare say it to the goose in front of the vase for a big bang. . . ."

"What did you say, dear?"

"A clue in my crossword. Booming. Dare say it to . . . Oh, never mind."

"You don't seem to think about anything but crosswords these days," said Vera.

It was true. Puzzles, inventing them and solving them, had become an obsession with him. He even did them secretly in the shop while Pilbeam was out, so that when his partner came back his head was full of floating words and puns and anagrams, and when Pilbeam started afresh on his demands, as he did every day, he could turn a vague, half-deaf ear.

"Remember that old bag we flogged the Georgian table to?" Pilbeam would say. "She wants to do her whole flat over in period. With me working day and night and you coming up with the cash to buy in, we could make five hundred on this deal alone." Or, "We're hamstrung, Stan. It makes me weep the opportunities we're missing." And always he ended up with, "We've got to have that money. Now, Stan, not in the sweet by-and-by."

Stanley was too much in awe of Pilbeam to do more than placate him with soothing promises. He saved his rage for Vera.

"I tell you, I've got to have that money for the business. It's ours but we can't touch it. We're as poor now as when your bloody old mother was still alive. The business'll go bust if I don't have the money. Can't you get that into your head?"

Vera flinched away from him, afraid of his greed and the wild light in his eyes. His face twitched dreadfully when he was angry. But she was most frightened when instead of answering her properly he replied with some meaningless conundrum.

One day towards the end of July Vera started work

on the small spare bedroom and as she was turning out she came upon Maud's collection of pills which she had put in here while she was painting her mother's room. It seemed wasteful to discard them all, especially as one of the little plastic cartons hadn't been opened and the other was only half empty. There would be no harm in asking the chemist about them while she was out shopping.

As she left the house she encountered the builders bringing in bags of cement and a concrete mixer.

"No need to wait in for us, lady," said the foreman. "We shan't make a start on your garage till next week what with this strike at the brickworks. You won't mind us leaving our gear in readiness, will you?"

Vera said she wouldn't. She went straight into the chemist and asked if it would be all right to return the carton of tablets as none of them had been used.

The pharmacist smiled. "Sorry, madam, we don't do that. We advise our sutomers to throw away all un-used drugs. To be on the safe side, you see." He re-moved the cap and looked at the contents of the carton.

"They're called Mollanoid, I believe."

Pharmacists, like doctors, prefer lay people to be in utter ignorance of such esoteric matters. This one was no exception. He frowned at Vera. Then he took out a single tablet, looked closely at it and said:

"What makes you think these tablets are Mollan-oid?"

Vera said rather tartly, "You made up the doctor's prescription and you wrote Mollanoid on the label. My mother always took Mollanoid for her blood pressure."

"Certainly I made up the prescription and *wrote* the label, but these are not the tablets I put in the car-ton. Mollanoid is what we call an anti-coagulant; in oth-er words it helps prevent the formation of clots in the bloodstream. As I say, these tablets aren't Mollanoid."

"What are they, then?"

The pharmacist sniffed the tablet he was holding and put it to his tongue. "Some compound of saccha-rine, I imagine."

"*Saccharine?*"

"The stuff slimmers use to sweeten tea and coffee," the pharmacist said in the tone of one addressing a
retarded child.

Vera shrugged. Rather confused and puzzled, she
finished her shopping. Was it possible that the pharmacist himself had made a mistake in his dispensing and
the carton had always contained saccharine? It seemed
unlikely but more probable than that Maud had been
secretly taking saccharine. If that had been the case,
what had she done with the Mollanoid? Certainly she
wouldn't have stopped taking them. She depended on
them utterly as a lifeline and often said that but for them
she would have had a second stroke.

Choosing a cheap but pretty wallpaper and deciding on a colour scheme distracted Vera's mind but, for
all that, she decided to mention the matter to Stanley
when he came in. He was rather late and as soon as
Vera saw him she knew he was in no state to be interested in other people's medical problems.

"My eye's killing me," he said.

For the first time in their married life he left his
dinner, lamb chops, chips and peas, untouched, and
Vera, who formerly would have been anxious and solici-
tous, hardened her heart. If she told him to go to the
doctor again he would only snap at her. She couldn't
talk to him, they had no real communication any more.
Often these days she thought of James Horton who was
sympathetic and gentle and with whom it was possible to
have conversation.

"What's the matter with you now?" she asked at
last, trying to keep her tone patient.

"Nothing," said Stanley. "Nothing. Leave me
alone."

His eye blinked and squeezed shut as if fingers inside his head were squeezing it. The something that was
doing the squeezing seemed to laugh at him and at the
success of its tricks which he couldn't combat. But that
something must be himself, mustn't it? God, he thought,
he'd go off his rocker at this rate.

Vera was watching him like a hawk. He couldn't

tell her that he was trembling and twitching and off his food because he was terribly frightened, because something had happened that day to reduce him to a far worse state than he had been in when the Chappell Fund woman had called or even when he had first seen Maud fall to her death. His teeth were chattering with fear and he ground them tightly together as if he had lockjaw.

That afternoon, while he was out in the van, a policeman had called at the Old Village Shop.

He had been to Hatfield to relieve an old woman of an eighteenth-century commode for approximately a fifth of its true value, and driving back had tried to calm his pulsating eye by finishing off an imaginary crossword. Stanley could now invent and complete crosswords in his head just as some people can play chess without a board. He drove the van into the yard at the back of the shop, murmuring under his breath, Purchase: "An almost pure hunt for this buy," when he saw a uniformed policeman leave the shop and cross to a waiting car. His eye moved like a pump, jerked and closed.

"What was that copper doing in here?" he asked Pilbeam in a strangled thin voice.

"Just checking on the stock, old man." Pilbeam stroked the side of his nose with the nailless sausage-like finger. He often did this but now Stanley couldn't bear to see it. It made him feel sick. "They often do that," Pilbeam said. "In case we're harbouring stolen goods in all innocence."

"They've never done it before. Did they ask for me?"

"You, old boy? Why would he ask for you?" Pilbeam smiled blandly. Stanley was sure he was lying. He was always up to something when he stared you candidly in the eye like that. "Been a good day, me old love. I reckon we can each take ten quid home with us tonight."

"I see that china and silver of mine went."

"A lady from Texas, she had them. Crazy about anything English, she was. I reckon she'd have paid anything I'd asked." Pilbeam laid his hand on Stanley's sleeve, the finger stump just touching the bare skin at the wrist. His eyes weren't frank and friendly any more. "I promised my old woman I'd pay her back next week. Money, Stan, loot, lolly. My patience, as the old exfuhrer put it, is getting exhausted."

Stanley wanted to ask him more about the policeman's visit but he didn't dare. He desperately wanted to believe Pilbeam. Surely if the policeman had wanted to talk to him he would have called at Lanchester Road. Perhaps he had called and found no one in.

If he'd been right and somehow or other they'd analysed Maud's clothes, if Moxley had been shooting his mouth off, if Vera had boasted to all the neighbours about the garage they were going to have built . . . Suppose, all these weeks, the police and the doctors had been building up a case against him from hints and hearsay. . . . He was afraid to go home, but he had nowhere else to go. All the evening he could sense Vera had something she wanted to tell him but was too sulky or too subtle to come out with it. Maybe the police had been getting at her too.

He couldn't sleep that night. Every muscle was twitching now and the remedy seemed almost worse than the disease. He began to wish he'd never done a crossword in his life, so compulsive was this need to keep inventing clues, to slot words across, fit others down. All that night and Saturday night he had a chequer board pattern in front of his eyes.

He felt he was on the edge of a nervous collapse.

Vera couldn't stay in the same bed with him when he twitched like that. He slept on Sunday night, from sheer exhaustion, she guessed, and his whole body rippled galvanically in sleep. In the small hours she made tea but she didn't wake him. Instead she took her tea into the spare room.

She switched on the light, stepped over paint pots

and got into the spare bed. As soon as she saw Maud's pills all her bewilderment of the morning came back to her. She reached for the half-empty carton of Mollanoid, the ones Maud had been taking right up to her death, and removed the lid.

I wonder, she thought, if Mother planned to stop taking sugar because Dr. Blake told her she should lose weight? Perhaps she had bought saccharine and had used a Mollanoid carton to keep it in.

It was beginning to get light. Vera could hear a thrush singing in the Blackmores' laburnum. The meaningless and not really musical trill depressed her. She felt very cold and she pulled the bed covers up to her chin.

But as she prepared to settle down and snatch a couple of hours' sleep, her eye fell once more on the carton she had opened. Mollanoid. Of course they were Mollanoid. They looked exactly like the tablets Maud had been taking three times a day, every day, for four years. But they also looked exactly like the ones she had taken to the chemist on the previous morning. Again Vera sat up.

Maud hadn't touched those, hadn't taken a single one of them. These, on the other hand, were three-quarters used, and the carton which contained them had stood by Maud's plate at her last breakfast. Vera knew that. In the increasing light she noticed the smear on the label the chemist had made, handing her the carton before the ink had quite dried. And casting her mind back to that breakfast—would she ever forget it or forget Maud's elation?—she recalled her mother's taking two of the tablets just after spooning sugar plentifully into her tea.

Her heart began to pound. Slowly, as if she were a forensic expert about to test poison at some risk to himself, she picked out one of the tablets and rested in on her tongue.

For a moment there was no taste. Vera's heart quietened. Then, because she had to know, she pressed the tip of her tongue with the tablet on it against the roof of her mouth. Immediately a rich sickly sweetness spread across the surface of her tongue and seeped between her teeth.

She spat the tablet into her saucer and then lay face downwards, numb and very cold.

It was ten when Stanley woke up. He stared at the clock and was out of bed and half across the room before he remembered. This was the day he was going to the doctor's. He'd told Pilbeam he wouldn't be in before lunch.

Just thinking the word doctor started his eye twitching again. He cursed, put on his dressing gown and went into Maud's room to see if the builders had started work yet. It was imperative to keep an eye on them in case they got too enthusiastic and began digging the earth they were to cover. But the garden was empty and the concrete mixer idle.

It wasn't like Vera not to bring him a cup of tea. Perhaps she hadn't wanted to disturb him. Poor old Vee. She wasn't much to look at any more and, God knew, she'd always been as dull as ditch-water, but a man could do worse.

No breakfast tray either. Come to that, no Vera. The house stank of paint. Stanley felt the beginnings of a headache. He'd missed Moxley's morning surgery but there was another one at two and he'd go to that. Everywhere was tidy and clean. Obviously, Vera had cleaned the place and gone out shopping.

He mooched back to the kitchen, his eye opening and shutting in a series of painful winks. She hadn't even left the cornflakes out for him. He got the packet out of the larder, poured out a dishful and looked around for the *Telegraph*. Might as well do the puzzle. There was no question any more whether he could do it or not or even whether he could do it at a single sitting. The only amusement it still afforded Stanley was seeing if he could beat his record of seven minutes.

The newspaper was folded up, lying on top of the refrigerator. Stanley picked it up and saw that under-

neath it was a letter poking half out of its envelope. The
envelope was addressed to Vera but that had never de-
terred him before and it didn't deter him now. He
pulled it out with shaking fingers and read it.

The money had come through.

Mr. Finbow would expect Vera at her earliest convenience and would hand her a cheque.

Stanley rubbed his eyes. Not because they were
twitching but because tears were running down his face.

20

Years and years he had waited for this moment. Ever
since he'd first set eyes on Maud and heard how well-
heeled she was, he'd dreamed of today, now or long ago,
now or in time to come, the shining hour when it would
all be his. Twenty-two thousand pounds.

His eye hadn't twitched once since he had read that
letter. He also now saw clearly that in imputing sinister
motives to a harmless housewife collecting for a sale and
a policeman on routine duty he had been letting his
imagination run away with him. Money cured all ills,
mental and physical. No doctors for him. Instead he
would take a bus down to the old village.

Pilbeam was in the shop, polishing a brass warming
pan. "You're early," he said morosely. "What did the
quack say?"

Stanley sat down on the piecrust table. He felt like
a tycoon. Laconically he said, "I've got a thousand quid
for you. I may as well write a cheque for the decorators

at the same time and you can give it to them. There'll be loads more next week if we need it. We're laughing now, boy. No more worries. No more struggling on a shoe-string."

"You won't regret it, Stan. I'll promise you you won't regret it. My God, we knew what we were doing when we started this little lark!" Pilbeam slapped him on the back and pocketed the cheques. "Now, I'll tell you what. We'll go down the Lockkeeper's and we'll split a bottle of scotch and then I'll treat you to a slap-up lunch."

Not quite half a bottle, but four double whiskies on an empty stomach, followed by a heavy meal of steak, fried potatoes, french beans, carrots, mushrooms, rasp-berry pie and cream, sent Stanley reeling towards Lanchester Road at half-past two. He badly wanted to burst into song as he made his way unsteadily along the respectable streets of dull little villas, but to be arrested on this glorious golden day, one of the happiest days of his life, would be a disastrous anti-climax.

The sky which, when he first got up, had been overcast had cleared while they were in the Globe and now it was very hot. One of the hottest days of the year, Stanley thought, immensely gratified that the weather matched his mood. He passed the Jaguar showrooms and wondered whether it would be possible to buy a car that very afternoon. That scarlet Mark Ten, for instance. He didn't see why not. It wasn't as if he was af-ter some little mass-produced job like Macdonald's tin can which lesser mortals, miserable wage-earners, had to wait months for. He must sober up. Have a cup of tea perhaps and then he'd buy the car and take Vera for a ride in it. Maybe they'd go out Epping Forest way and have a meal in a country pub.

These pleasant fancies sliding across the surface of his fuddled brain, he marched into the kitchen and called, "Vera, where are you?" There was no answer. Sulking, he thought, because I didn't hang about to tell her what the doctor said. Doctor! The last thing he needed.

He could hear her moving about upstairs. Probably she was toiling away painting that bedroom. Well, she'd have to buck her ideas up, expand her horizons. People with his sort of money didn't do their own decorating. He moved carefully into the hall. Better on the whole not to let her see he'd been drinking.

He called her name again and this time he heard a door close and her face appear over the banisters. For a woman who had just come into twenty-two thousand pounds, she didn't look very happy.

"I thought you'd gone in to work," she said.

"The doctor said I was to take the day off. Come down here. I want to talk to you."

He heard her say something that sounded like, "I want to talk to you, too," and then she came slowly down the stairs. She was wearing the blue and white spotted dress and she hadn't any paint on her hands. A sudden slight chill took the edge off his joy. What a moody, difficult woman she was! Just like her to find something to nag about on this day of days. He knew she was going to nag. He could see it in the droop of her mouth and her cold eyes.

"Did you get the money?" he said heartily. "I couldn't help seeing old Finbow's letter. At last, eh?"

She was going to say she hadn't got it. She'd asked Finbow to hang on to it, re-invest it, something diabolical. Christ, she couldn't have!

"You *did* get the money?"

He'd never heard quite that tone in her voice before, that chilling despair. "Oh yes, I got it."

"And paid it into the bank? What's up, then, love? Isn't this what we've been waiting for, planning for?"

"Don't call me love," said Vera. "I'm not your love. You mean you've been planning for, don't you? But you haven't planned quite well enough. You should have disposed of your saccharine tablets after you'd killed my mother."

Momentarily Stanley thought that this couldn't be real. He'd drunk too much and passed out and that bloody awful puzzle dream was starting again. But we always know when we are awake that we cannot be dreaming even though when actually dreaming we feel all this may be real and Stanley, after the first sensation of nightmare unreality, had no need to pinch himself. Vera *had* said what she'd said. They were in the kitchen at 61, Lanchester Road and both were wide awake. She *had* said it, but he asked her to repeat it just the same.

"What did you say?"

"You said for two pins you'd kill her and she said you would and, God forgive me, I didn't believe either of you. Not until I found what was in those medicine cartons."

There is a great difference between anticipating the worst, dreading, dreaming and living in imagination through the worst, and the worst itself. Stanley had visualised this happening, or something like this, over and over again, although usually his accuser had been a doctor or a policeman, but he found that all these preparations and rehearsals did nothing to mitigate the shock of the reality. He felt as if he had been hit on the head by something heavy enough to half-stun but not heavy enough to bring blissful unconsciousness.

In a feeble trembling voice he said what he had planned to say when "they" started asking, "I didn't kill her, Vee. Just taking saccharine didn't kill her."

"She died of a stroke, didn't she? *Didn't she?* Isn't that what she had while I was out? You know it is. Dr. Moxley came and said she'd died of a stroke."

"She'd have had that stroke, anyway," Stanley muttered.

"How do you know? Have you got medical degrees? You know very well you wanted her to die, so you took away her tablets and put saccharine in the carton and she died. You murdered her. You murdered her just as much as if you'd shot her."

Vera went out of the kitchen and slammed the door behind her. Alone, Stanley felt his heart pounding against his ribs. Why hadn't he had the sense to burn those bloody saccharines after Maud had died? And how had Vera found out? That hardly mattered now.

He put his head into the sink and drank straight from the cold water tap. Then he went upstairs.

She was in their bedroom, throwing clothes into a couple of suitcases. He fumbled in his mind, trying to find the words. At last he said, "You wouldn't go to the police about this, would you, Vee?"

She didn't answer. Her hands went on folding mechanically, slipping sheets of paper between the clothes, tucking in a pair of rolled-up stockings. He stared at her stupidly and suddenly the meaning of what she was doing came home to him.

"Are you off somewhere, then?"

She nodded. There were little beads of sweat on her upper lip. It was a very hot day.

Stanley managed a hint of sarcastic bravado. "May I ask where?"

"I'll tell you whether you ask or not." Vera marched into the bathroom and came back with her sponge-bag. "I'm leaving you," she said. "It's all over for us, Stanley. It was over years ago really. I could take you treating me like a servant and having that girl here and living off my money, but I can't stay with a man who murdered my mother."

"I did not murder your mother," he shouted. "I never murdered anyone. Anyone'd think you liked having her here. Christ, you wanted her out of the way as much as I did."

"She was my mother," Vera said. "I loved her in spite of her faults. I couldn't live with you, Stanley, even if I managed to forget what you've done. You see, I can't stand you near me. Not now. Not any more. After what I found out last night, you make me feel sick just being in the same room with me. You're really wicked, you're evil. No, please don't come near me." She moved away as he came towards her and he could see that she was trembling. "Mother always wanted me to leave you and now I'm going to. Funny, isn't it? It was what she wanted and now she's getting what she wanted but not until after she's dead. I suppose you could say she's won at last."

Stanley's head was splitting. "Don't be so stupid," he said.

"You've always thought me stupid, haven't you? I know I'm not brainy, but I can read, and once I read somewhere that people mustn't be allowed to profit from their crimes. I can't think of anything worse than letting you have any of Mother's money when it was you that killed her. So I'm sorry, I didn't mean to lead you on and then let you down. Up till this morning I meant the money to be yours as much as mine, more yours than mine if you wanted it. But I've hardened myself now." Vera closed the lid of one of the suitcases and looked at him. "Mother left it to me and I'm keeping it."

"You can't!" Stanley shouted, one triumph left to him. "You can't keep it. That bank account's a joint account. I can draw the lot out tomorrow if I like and, by God, I will!"

Vera said quietly, "I didn't pay it into the joint account. That account was more or less closed, anyway, thanks to you overdrawing on it. I opened a new one this morning, a private account for me only."

21

Vera picked up the cases and carried them downstairs. Stanley remained sitting on the bed, the hot sun striking the back of his neck through the closed windows. Again he was aware of a sense of unreality, of nightmare. Nightmare. He said the word over and over to himself.

Nightmare, nightmare, nightmare . . . "Nasty dream of
a nocturnal charger"? Christ, not that again!

His left eye had begun opening and shutting involuntarily, tic, tic, tic. Stanley swore and clenched his
hands. He listened. She was moving about downstairs.
She hadn't gone yet. He'd have to talk to her, make her
see reason.

She was standing in front of the dining room mirror, applying lipstick.

It is hard to say nice things to someone you hate.
Stanley hated Vera at that moment far more then he had
ever hated Maud. But the things had to be said. Most
men will say anything for twenty-two thousand pounds.

"You've been the only woman in my life, Vee.
Twenty years I've been devoted to you. I've taken everything for your sake, your parents insulting me and then
your mother moving in here. I'm a middle-aged man
now. I'll go to pieces without you."

"No, you won't. You've always been in pieces.
Having me here never made you pull yourself together
yet. God knows, I tried and now I'm sick of trying."

He began to plead. He would have gone down on
his knees but he was afraid she'd walk away and leave
him there on all-fours like an animal. "Vee," he said
pulling at her sleeve, "Vee, you know I'm making a go
of this business, but I have to have a bit of capital." It
was the wrong thing to say. He could tell that from the
look on her face, the contempt. Like a really distraught
husband, he moaned at her, "Vee, you're all I've got in
the world."

"Let's call a spade a spade," said Vera. "My money's all you've got in the world." She pulled on a pair of
navy-blue gloves and sat down on an upright chair as if
she were waiting for something or someone. "I've
thought about that," she said. "I've thought and thought
about it all. And I've decided it wouldn't be right to
leave you without anything." She gave a heavy sigh.
"You're so hopeless, Stan. Everything you touch turns
out a mess except crossword puzzles. You've never held

a job down yet and you won't hold this one. But I wouldn't like to think of you penniless and without a roof over your head, so I'm going to let you have this house. You can keep it or sell it, do what you like. If you're silly to sell it and hand the money over to that Pilbeam—well, that's your business."

"Christ," said Stanley, "thanks for bloody nothing." She was going to give him this house! She was taking everything that was his and leaving him this end-of-a-terrace slum. And suddenly what she was doing and that she meant it came fully home to him. Vee, his wife, the one person he was sure he could keep under his thumb and manipulate and get round and persuade that black was white, Vee was selling him down the river. He said wildly, "You don't think I'm going to let you get away with it, do you? Let you go just like that?"

"You haven't got much choice," Vera said quietly, and suddenly there was a sharp knock on the door. "That'll be the driver of the car I've hired."

She bent down to pick up her cases. Stupefied, Stanley would have liked to kill her. As she lifted her face, he struck her hard with the flat of his hand, first on one cheek, then the other. She made a whimpering sound and tears began to flow over the marks his hand had made but she didn't speak to him again.

After the car had gone he wept too. He walked about the room, crying, and then he sat down and pounded the sofa arm with his fists. He wanted to scream and break things but he was afraid the neighbours would hear him.

Crying had exacerbated the twitch in his left eye. It continued to water and pulsate after he had stopped crying. He tried holding the lid still in two fingers but it went on moving in spite of this as if it wasn't part of his body at all but a trapped fluttering insect with a life of its own.

He had lost the money. *He had lost it, all of it.* And now, his face working terrifyingly and uncontrollably, he realised amid the turmoil of his thoughts that for

almost the whole of his adult life the acquiring of that
money had been his goal, its possession the dawning of a
golden age. At first he had thought of it in terms of only
a thousand or two, then eight or nine, finally twenty with
a bonus of two added. But always it had been there, a
half-concealed, yet shimmering crock at the end of a
rainbow. To possess it he had stayed with Vera, put up
with Maud and, he told himself, never bothered to carve
out a career. He had wasted his life.

He thought of it all but not calmly and panic kept
returning by fits and starts, making him catch his breath
in loud rasping gasps. At last he knew the true meaning
of living in the present. Everything behind him was
waste and bitterness while ahead there was nothing.
Worse than nothing, for now that Vera knew of his at-
tempt on Maud's life and the police had somehow been
alerted, now that Pilbeam would have to know that all
his vaunted capital amounted to just the roof over his
head, how could he even contemplate the passing of another hour, another minute?

He stared at the clock, watching, though not of
course, actually seeing, the hands move. That was what
his life had been, a slow, indiscernible disintegration towards the present utter collapse. And each moment, apparently leaving the situation unchanged, was in reality
leading him inexorably towards the end, something
which, though inconceivable, must be even worse than
present horror.

A little death would make the unbearable present
pass. With jumping twitching hand, he felt in his pocket.
Eight pounds remained out of the ten he brought home
on Friday. The pubs wouldn't yet be open but the wine
shop in the High Street would. He staggered into the
kitchen and rinsed his face at the sink.

Outside it was even hotter than indoors but the feel
of fresh air made him flinch. Walking was difficult. He
moved like an old man or like one who had been con-
fined to bed after a bad illness. There were only a few
people about and none of them took any notice of him
and yet he felt that the streets were full of eyes, unseen

spies watching his every movement. In the wine shop it was all he could do to find his voice. Speaking to another human being, an ordinary reasonably contented person, was grotesque. His voice came out high and weak and he couldn't keep his hands from his face as if, by continually wiping it, smoothing the muscles, he could still those convulsive movements.

The assistant, however, was accustomed to alcoholics. His own face was perfectly smooth and controlled as he took the five pounds from Stanley for two bottles of Teacher's and another pound for cigarettes.

Back at the house he drank a tumblerful of the whisky, but without enjoying it. Instead of making him feel euphoric, it merely deadened feeling. He took one of the bottles and a packet of cigarettes upstairs with him and lay on the bed, wishing in a blurred, fuddled way that it was winter and not nearly mid-summer so that the dark might come early. Stanley found he didn't like the light. It was too revealing.

Words came unbidden into his mind and he lay on his back splitting them and anagramming them and evolving clues. He found he was saying the words and the clues out loud, slurring them in a thick voice. But the twitch, temporarily, was gone. He went on talking to himself for some time, occasionally reaching for the bottle and then growing irritable because the drink was making him forget how to spell and lose the thread of words in black spirals which had begun to twist before his eyes.

A whole night of deep sleep, total oblivion, was what he needed, but instead he awoke at nine with a headache that was like an iron hand clamped above his eyebrows. It was still light.

The dream he had just had was still vividly with him. It hadn't been what one would call a nasty dream, not in the sense of being actually frightening or painful, and yet it belonged nevertheless in the category of the worst kind of dreams a human being can have. When we are unhappy we are not made more so by nightmares of

that unhappiness; our misery is rather intensified when
we dream of that happy time which preceded it and of
people, now hateful or antagonistic, behaving towards us
with their former affability.

Such had been Stanley's recent experience. He had
dreamed he was back in the Old Village Shop distribut-
ing largesse to Pilbeam and had seen again Pilbeam's
joy. Now, wide awake, he realised that four hours before, thinking he had reached the depths, he had under-
estimated his situation. Not only had he been robbed of
his expectations and left penniless; he had also given his
partner a cheque for a thousand pounds and another, to
be handed to the decorator, for one hundred and seven-
ty-five. Both those cheques would bounce, for the money was all Vera's, stashed away in a private account.

There seemed no reason to get up. He might as
well lie there till lunchtime. Somewhere he could hear
water running, or thought he could. The night had been
so full of dreams, dream visions and dream sounds that
it was hard to sort out imagination from reality.

He had forgotten to wind the clock and its hands
pointed to ten past six. It must be hours later than that.
Pilbeam would wonder why he hadn't come in but Stanley was afraid to telephone Pilbeam.

His head was tender and throbbing all over. At the
moment he wasn't twitching and he didn't dare think
about it in case thinking started it up again. He lay staring at the ceiling and wondering whether there was any
point in going down to fetch the *Telegraph,* when a
sharp bang at the front door jolted him into sitting up
and cursing. Immediately he thought of the police, then
of Pilbeam. Could it be his partner, come already to say
the cheques were no good?

He rolled out of bed and looked through the crack
in the curtains, but from there he couldn't see under the
porch canopy. Although there was no lorry in the street,
it occurred to him that his visitor might be one of the
builders. Whoever it was knocked again.

His mouth tasted foul. He slid his feet into his

shoes and went downstairs without lacing them. Then he opened the door cautiously. His caller was Mrs. Blackmore.

"I didn't get you out of bed, then?" Presumably she inferred this from the fact that he was still wearing his day clothes, although these were rumpled and creased. "I just popped in to tell you the pipe from your tank's overflowing."

"O.K. Thanks." He didn't want to talk to her and he began to close the door.

She was back on the path by now but she turned and said, "I saw Mrs. Manning go off yesterday."

Stanley glowered at her.

"She looked proper upset, I thought. The tears was streaming down her face. Have you had another death in your family?"

"No, we haven't."

"I thought you must have. I said to John, whatever's happened to upset Mrs. Manning like that?"

He opened the door wider. "If you must know she's left me, walked out on me. I slapped her face for her and that's why she'd turned on the waterworks."

That wives sometimes leave their husbands and husbands strike their wives was no news to Mrs. Blackmore. Speculating about such occurrences had for years formed the main subject of her garden fence chats, but no protagonist in one of these domestic dramas had ever before spoken to her of his role so baldly and with such barefaced effrontery. Rendered speechless, she stared at him.

"That," said Stanley, "will give you something to sharpen your fangs on when you get nattering with old mother Macdonald."

"How dare you speak to me like that!"

"Dare? Oh, I dare all right." Savouring every luscious word, Stanley let fly at her a string of choice epithets, finishing with, "Lazy, fat-arsed bitch!"

"We'll see," said Mrs. Blackmore, "what my husband has to say about this. He's years younger than you,

you creep, and he hasn't ruined his health boozing. Ugh,
I can smell it on your breath from here."

"You would, the length of your nose," said Stanley
and he banged the door so hard that a piece of plaster
fell off the ceiling. The battle had done him good. He
hadn't had a real dingdong like that with anyone since
Maud died.

Maud . . . Better not think about her or he'd be
back on the bottle. He wouldn't, he'd never think of her
again unless—unless the police made him. His eye was
still twitching but he was getting used to it, "adapting"
himself, as some quack of Moxley's ilk would put it.
One thing, the police hadn't come yet. Would they
search the house before they started on the garden?
Stanley decided that probably they would. Not that
there was anything for them to find, as Vera was sure to
have taken that carton of Shu-go-Sub away with her.
Might as well check, though . . .

He went into the room where Vera had spent her
last night in Lanchester Road. The carton with the little
smear on its label was still beside the bed. Stanley could
hardly believe his eyes. What a fool Vera was! Without
that no one could prove a thing. The police wouldn't
even get a warrant to dig up the garden.

Stanley took the cap off the carton and flushed the
tablets down the lavatory. Then he ran the basin and the
bath taps. Often this simple manoeuvre had the effect of
freeing the jammed ballcock and making it rise as it
should do as the water came in from the main. He listened. The outfall pipe had stopped overflowing.

The phone bell made him jump, but he didn't consider not answering it. Letting it ring and then wondering for hours afterwards who it had been would be far
worse. He picked up the receiver. It was Pilbeam and
Stanley swallowed hard, feeling cold again.

But Pilbeam didn't sound angry. "Still under the
weather, old boy?" he asked.

"I feel rotten," Stanley mumbled.

"Bit of a hypochondriac you are, me old love. You
don't want to dwell on these things. Still, I'm easy. Take

the rest of the week off, if you like. I'll pop round to see you sometime, shall I?"

"O.K.," Stanley said. He didn't want Pilbeam popping round but there was nothing he could do about it.

Just the same, the call had put new heart into him, that and his discovery and destruction of the tablets. Maybe those cheques wouldn't bounce. That man, Frazer, the bank manager, was a good guy, a real gentleman. He mightn't like it but surely he'd pay up. What was a mere £1,175. to him? Probably that private account business was just a polite sop to silly women like Vera. He and she were still man and wife, after all. Frazer had seen them together and given them a cheque book each. Those two cheques would come in and Frazer wouldn't think twice about them. He'd pay up and then perhaps he'd write to Stanley and caution him not to be too free with writing cheques. Absurd, really, how low he'd let himself get yesterday. Panic and shock, he supposed. Very likely Vera would come back, asking for his forgiveness.

There was someone knocking at the door again. John Blackmore, come to do battle on his wife's behalf. The fool ought to know better, ought to thank his stars someone with more guts than he had had put his wife in her place at last.

Stanley had no intention of answering the door. He listened calmly to the repeated hammering on the knocker and then he watched Blackmore return to his own house. When he went downstairs again he found a scribbled note on the mat:

"You have got it coming to you using language like that to my wife. You came from a slum and are turning this street into one. Don't think you can get away with insulting women.

                                        J. BLACKMORE."

This note made Stanley laugh quite a lot. Slum indeed! His father's cottage was no slum. He thought once more of the green East Anglian countryside, but no longer of going back there as a conquering hero. Go back, yes, but as the prodigal son, to home and peace and forgiving love. . . .

Through the kitchen window he could see that water was again beginning to stream from the outfall pipe. It looked as if he would have to go up into the loft. Vera had always seen to things of this kind but Stanley had acquired, mostly from her accounts, a smattering of the basic principles of plumbing. He fetched the steps from where she had left them, mounted them and pushed up the trap-door. It was dusty up there and pitch dark. He went back for a torch.

This was the first time he had ever been in the loft and he was surprised to find it so big, so quiet and so dark. Vera had said you must stand on the cross-beams and not between them in case you put your foot through the plaster, and Stanley did this, encountering on his way to the tank, the skeleton of a dead bird lying in its own feathers. It must have come in under the eaves and been unable to find its way out. Stanley wondered how long it had been there and how long it took for newly dead flesh to rot away and leave only bones behind.

He lifted off the tarpaulin which covered the tank and plunged his arm into the water. The ball on the end of its hinged arm was some nine inches down. He raised it and heard the cocks close with a soft thump.

Having washed his hands in a dribble of water—he didn't want the ballcock to stick again—he fetched the paper and took it back to bed with him to do the crossword. As if he were a real invalid, he slept most of the day away and during the afternoon, dozing lightly, he several times thought he heard someone at the door. But he didn't go down to answer it and when he finally left the bedroom at half-past six there was no one about and the builders' equipment hadn't been moved. By now he was light-headed with hunger so he ate some bread and jam. This place, he thought, is more like Victoria station in the rush hour than a private house. There was some-one at the door again. Blackmore. He'd heard a car draw up. Adrenaline poured into Stanley's blood. If he wanted a fight he could have it. But first better make sure it was Blackmore.

Once more he stationed himself at the window, one eye to the division between the curtains. There was a car there all right but it wasn't Blackmore's old jalopy. Stanley waited, gazing down. The man retreated from the porch. He was tall and dark and in his middle thirties. Stanley didn't know him but he had seen him about, mostly going in and out of Croughton police station.

Christ, he thought, Vera hasn't wasted much time.

Stanley prayed the policeman would go back to his car but instead he made for the side entrance, going out of his watcher's line of vision. Quaking, Stanley crept into Maud's room. From there he watched the policeman walk slowly round the lawn. He by-passed the heather garden but stopped in front of the cement mixer. Then he walked round it, rather as a man may walk round an isolated statue in an exhibition, looking it up and down with a thoughtful and puzzled expression. Then he gave his attention to the cement sacks, one of which he kicked so that the paper ripped and a thin stream of grey dust trickled out.

Back in his own bedroom, Stanley stood as still as he could, which wasn't very still as his whole body was twitching and quivering with fear. It was a job to bring the front garden into focus, particularly as his eyelids weren't under control. At last he got a blurred image of the policeman going back to his car. But instead of getting into it, he unlatched the Blackmores' gate and walked up their path.

Stanley had reached a stage of fear when no stimulant could help him. If he drank whisky he knew he would throw it up. His thoughts raced incoherently, The Blackmores would pass on everything they knew of his relations with Maud. Mrs. Macdonald would tell of finding him prone on the earth after filling in the trench he'd prepared in advance. Flushing away those tablets wouldn't help him, for there had been at least one other carton, now no doubt handed over to the police by Vera. That would be enough for them to get a warrant and dig and find Maud, bones maybe among her outer coverings like the bird in the loft.

The loft! He could hide in the loft. It wouldn't matter then if they broke down the doors to get in. He'd be safe up there. The steps were still where he had left them under the trap-door. Cigarettes in one pocket, bottle in the other, he went up the steps and hoisted himself on to a beam. Then, looking down, he knew it wouldn't work. Even if he closed the trap, they'd see the steps.

Unless he could pull the steps up after him.

Stanley lay down flat, bracing his feet against the galvanised wall of the tank. At first, when he grasped the steps, he thought he'd never do it, but he thought of the policeman and renewed fear brought strength. Dragging them straight up was no use. He'd have to use a sort of lever principle. Who was it said, Give me something to stand on and a long enough pole and I will move the earth? Well, he was only trying to move a pair of steps. Use the edge of the trap as a fulcrum, ease them slowly towards him, then pull them down to rest on the joists. Careful . . . Mustn't make a mark on the plaster. He felt as if his lungs would burst and he grunted thickly. But it was done.

When he was shut in he kept his torch on for a while but he didn't need light and he found he could listen better in the dark. With the extinction of light he felt something that was almost peace. There was no sound but a tiny lapping in the tank.

Sitting there in the dark, he felt the twitches beginning again like spirit fingers plucking at his eyelids, his knee, and delicately with the gentleness of a caress, across the skin of his belly. Stanley found that he was crying. He only knew it because the fingers holding his cigarette encountered tears.

He wiped them away on his sleeve and then, although he couldn't see them, he spoke silently the name of every object in the loft: joists, beams, bottle, matches, stepladder, storage tank. Clues formed themselves expertly. "Storage tank," eleven letters, seven and four. "It holds water but rots up with age on the armoured vehicle." "Stepladder": "Snake spelt wrong at first for a means of climbing."

Oh God, he thought, he must be going mad, sitting in the dark in a loft, setting clues for puzzles that would never be solved, and he rested his cheek against the cold metal in despair.

4. Last Word

22

When Stanley came down from the loft the whole neighbourhood was asleep, not a light showing anywhere. He rolled into his unmade bed, certain he wouldn't sleep, but he did and very heavily until past nine in the morning. Fumbling his way downstairs, still in his soiled and sweaty clothes, he found a letter on the front door mat.

It was from Vera and headed with the address of that boarding-house at Brayminster.

> Stanley,
>
> After what you did you will probably think I have changed my mind about the house. Don't worry, you can still have it. I promise you can and I am putting it in writing as I don't suppose you would take my word. I am staying here until I find somewhere else to live. Please don't try to find me. I have been told I could ask for police protection if you did and then get a court order. I never want to see you again.
>
> VERA.

Cursing, Stanley screwed it up. It more or less proved she'd been to the police, the bitch. Who else would have told her about getting court orders? Better keep the letter, though. Carefully he smoothed out the creases. Once he got out of this mess, he'd sell the house all right. Get four thousand for it and put the lot in the business. Maybe in the long run he'd make as much money that way as if he'd had Maud's money and when he did he'd take care Vera got to know about it.

After another meal of bread and jam, he had a bath and put on clean clothes, and as he had foreseen, the pipe started overflowing again. By this time he had become an expert in getting quickly in and out of the loft and he could manage it without getting too dirty. Stanley passed a reasonably serene day, lying on the sofa, gently sipping whisky and drawing, on the plain side of a sheet of wallpaper, an enormous crossword, eighteen inches square.

Pilbeam came round about eight. Having first checked that this wasn't another representative of the law, set on his trail by Vera, Stanley let his friend in. Together they finished the whisky.

"You look a bit rough, old man." Pilbeam studied him with the disinterested and unsympathetic curiosity of a biologist looking at a liver fluke through a microscope. "You've lost weight. That must be trying, that eye."

"The doctor," Stanley said, "says it'll just past off."

"Or you'll pass on, eh?" Pilbeam laughed uproariously at his joke. "Not before we've made our packet, I trust."

Stanley thought quickly. "Would you have any objection if I took a bit of time off? I'm thinking of going away, maybe down to the South Coast to join my wife."

"Why not?" said Pilbeam. "I may go away myself. We can close the shop for a week or two. One way of whetting our customers' appetites. Well, I must be on my way. All right if I have twenty of your classy fags off you? I haven't got a bean on me but we're more or less one flesh, aren't we, like it says in the marriage service?"

Pilbeam laughed loudly all the way up the path.

The cheque was all right, then. He'd given it to Pilbeam on Monday and today was Thursday, so it must be all right. And in the morning he would go away. Not to Vera but to his mother and father. I'm going home, Stanley thought. Even if I have to hitch all the way, even if I arrive penniless on the doorstep, I'm going home. But he cried himself to sleep, weeping weakly into the dirty pillow.

Early on Friday morning, when Vera was told that she was urgently needed at Croughton police station, she went to catch the first train but Mrs. Horton had alerted James and he was waiting for her with his car. They reached Croughton by ten-thirty.

Pilbeam had already been with the police for two hours by then.

She passed him coming out as she was taken into the superintendent's office but neither knew the other. There were a great many people coming and going whom Vera didn't know but whom she suspected were connected with the case against her husband. She avoided Mrs. Blackmore's sharp eye and the curious fascinated gaze of young Michael Macdonald. The superintendent questioned her closely for an hour before he let her go back to James and weep in his arms.

Stanley awoke with a splitting headache. Another hot day. Still, better to stand by the roadside in sweltering heat than pouring rain. His reflection in the mirror showed him a seedy, nearly elderly man with a pronounced and very apparent tic. Maybe his appearance would arouse pity in the heart of those arrogant bastards of motorists from whom he hoped to cadge lifts.

He bundled up a spare pair of trousers and the two clean shirts he had left and stuffed them into a suitcase. It was nearly noon. God, how deeply he slept these days! He was sitting on the bed, combing his hair, when he heard a car draw up. Blackmore home for lunch. Without getting up, he shifted along the bed and put his eye to the crack between the curtains.

All the blood receded from the muscles of his face. He crushed the comb in his hands and a bunch of teeth came off into his palm. A police car was parked outside. As well as the man who had been there before, there were three others. One of them opened the boot and took out a couple of spades. The others marched up the path towards his front door.

Stanley climbed up the steps, clutching his suitcase. At the moment his hand touched the trap-door he heard his callers hammer on the front door. He gave a violent shiver. Almost as soon as the hammering stopped the door bell rang. Someone was keeping his finger on the button. Stanley clambered through the square aperture, lay across the joists and hauled on the steps. Afterwards he didn't know how he'd managed to lever the steps up without dropping them to ricochet over the banisters, or how he lifted them at all, his whole body was jumping so violently. But he did lift them and, almost by a miracle, succeeded in laying them soundlessly down beside him. He wiped his hands on his trousers to avoid making marks on the outer surface of the door, and then he dropped it into its frame.

When it was done he rolled on to his back and lay in the dark, murmuring over and over, "Oh, Christ, Christ, Christ . . ."

Stanley pressed his ear to a very thin crack, more a join than a crack, between the boards of the door and listened. Yes, he could hear something now, the sound of someone forcing open the back door. He heard the lock give and footsteps in the kitchen. How much of his movements could they hear? Would even the most mi-nute shifting on the old joists send a great reverberation to those on the ground floor?

They were coming up the stairs.

The wood creaked under his ear and then someone spoke.

"I reckon he's gone, Ted. Pilbeam said he'd do a bunk and Pilbeam wouldn't lie to us. We've got too much on him."

Judas, thought Stanley, bloody double-crossing Ju-das with his "me old love" and his Stan this and Stan that. Footsteps moved across the landing. Into the bath-room, Stanley thought. Ted's voice said: "They've started digging, sir. There's quite a crowd in the Macdonalds' garden. Shall I put up screens?"

"They'd have to be sky-hooks, wouldn't they?"

They stopped talking and Stanley heard "Sir"—an inspector? A chief inspector? A superintendent?—moving about in the bedrooms. Ted went downstairs.

So they knew now. Stanley held his body as still as he could, clenching his hands. They knew. Vera had told them and Blake had put his spoke in and somehow or other Moxley had supported them. In a minute they would scrape away the peat and find Maud's body.

No one would hear him now if he struck a match. They weren't looking for him, anyway, they had said so, but searching the house for evidence of how he had killed Maud. Without getting up, he felt for the box, took out a match and struck it in front of his face. The flame sent strange long shadows like clasping and unclasping fingers rippling across the beams and up into the roof. He looked at his watch. He thought that hours and hours had passed but it was only twelve-thirty. Would they go away when they had found what they had come to find, or would they leave a man in the house? He could do nothing about it but continue to lie between the joists, walled in by wood as if he were already in his own coffin.

Stanley had no idea how much time passed before "Sir" and his assistants returned to the landing. Again it seemed like many hours. His limbs ached and every few seconds sharp burning pains stabbed his knees, his shoulders and the joints of his arms. He wanted to scream and scream to let the fear out of him, for he was like a man possessed of a devil which could only be released in a scream. He clasped his hand over his mouth to stop the screaming devil leaving him and tearing down through the floor to those below.

Someone slammed the back door.

Feet, many feet, tramping up the stairs, sent vibrations through his body. There was about eight feet, he thought, between the landing floor and ceiling and he was perhaps a foot above the ceiling. That meant "Sir's" head might be only three feet away from his. He pressed his mouth against raw splintery wood to muffle his ragged gasping breath.

"Thirteen quid in pound notes, sir," someone said. "They were between the pages of this annual."

For a second the words were meaningless. They were nothing like those he had expected. Why didn't they speak of Maud? Maud, Maud, he mouthed into the wood. She must be lying down there now amid the ruins of his garden, bones in her own feathers.

"Sir's" voice broke up the fantasy and Stanley felt his body stiffen. "They smell of violets like the inside of that handbag."

"And the thirty Harry Pilbeam handed over to us, sir."

"Yes. I never thought I'd say, thank God for Harry Pilbeam. But he knows which side his bread is buttered, that lad. Shop his own wife for a quid if she hadn't divorced him ten years back. When I told him we were on to his little game, faking antiques and selling them for the genuine article, he couldn't wait to get back in good with us by passing over the carriage clock and that piece of china."

Someone laughed.

"I must say it's given me some satisfaction to know that he conned Manning properly. The moron's actually handed Pilbeam—Pilbeam, I ask you!—nearly two thousand quid all told. God knows where he got it from."

"What had Pilbeam in mind, d'you know?"

"Bleed him for as much as he could get and then do a bunk's my guess."

Silence fell. Stanley lay as still as a corpse, letting the words flow and pass over him. He didn't understand. What were they doing there? What were they hoping for? They had dug but they hadn't found Maud. Why not? A tiny thrill of hope touched him. Was it possible that they hadn't been looking for Maud at all but for stolen goods, something that Pilbeam had put them on to?

From a long way away a voice came. Unidentifiable, the words a jumble of sound. They were in Maud's room now, now moving back to the landing. The muzzy sound cleared into distinguishable words like a picture coming into focus.

"That'll have been the mother-in-law's room, Ted."

"What's happened to her, then? Gone off with the wife?"

"No, no. The old woman's dead. Died of a stroke round about the time Manning . . ."

Again the voices swam away into a jumble and the footfalls receded. Stanley had been holding his breath. Now he let it out carefully. His heart was hammering. It was true, they hadn't found Maud. They hadn't found anything but a handful of pound notes. He was hiding in vain. They only wanted to question him about Pilbeam. And he'd tell them, everything they wanted to hear and more besides. An eye for an eye . . . Revenge on Pilbeam would be sweet indeed. They had nothing on him, nothing. By a miracle they had guessed nothing, found nothing, and they thought Maud had died a natural death.

He moved his right hand and brought it in silence across to the handle on the inside of the trap-door. The cramped fingers closed over the handle and then Stanley hesitated. If he came down now they'd think he had something to hide. Better let them go, let them leave the house, then come down and tell them what they wanted of his own volition. "Sir" and his assistants were directly underneath him again now and someone was descending the stairs. They were leaving. Once more Stanley held his breath.

More than anything in the world now he wanted one of them to speak the words that would tell him he was free, cleared of any suspicion, just a fool who had allowed himself to be taken for a ride by a con man. The briefest sentence would do it. "We only need Manning for a witness" or "I reckon Manning's paid enough already for trusting Pilbeam." They must say it. He could almost hear them saying it.

The footsteps went down the stairs.

Ted said, "I suppose we'll have to get Mrs. Huntley for the identification, sir," and "Sir" said softly and slowly, "There's not much doubt, though, that this is the body of Miss Ethel Carpenter."

23

"You poor dear," said Mrs. Huntley. In the police station waiting room she moved her chair closer to Vera's and touched her hand. "It's far worse for you than any of us."

"At least I didn't have to identify her. That must have been awful."

Mrs. Huntley shuddered. "But for the little ring, I wouldn't have known her. She'd been in the ground for —oh, I can't bear to speak of it."

"He—my own husband—he killed her for fifty pounds. They found the wound on her head where he struck her. If there's any comfort for me at all, it's that Mother never knew. I'll tell you something I won't ever tell anyone else. . . ." Vera paused, thinking that there was one other person she might tell, one person to whom in time she might tell everything. "I thought," she said softly, "I thought he'd killed Mother for her money, but now I know that was wrong. There's a mystery there that'll never be cleared up. You see, if he'd killed Mother, he wouldn't have needed that fifty pounds. Thank God, Mother never knew anything about it."

"There were a good many things poor Mrs. Kinaway never knew," said Mrs. Huntley thoughtfully. "Like who was the father of Miss Carpenter's child. She told me one day when she was feeling low. You know now, don't you?"

"I guessed. I guessed as soon as I saw that girl this morning. She must be my niece. If Mother had ever met that girl, and she would have if . . ." Vera half-rose as Caroline Snow came into the room. In spite of the shock of it all and the horror, she smiled, gazing at the face which might have been her own twenty years ago.

"This is my father," said Caroline Snow. "He helped me. He went to the police when we couldn't find her. Daddy is absolutely marvellous. He promised that when we found her she could come and live with us, but we didn't find her. Well, not until . . ."

The man's eyes met Vera's. He looked kind, patient, capable of great endurance. He was her brother-in-law. She had a whole family now.

"I'm sorry, I'm sorry," was all she could say.

"It wasn't your fault." George Snow's blue eyes flashed. "Mrs. Manning, you're all alone. Come and stay with us. Please say you will."

"One day I'd like to," said Vera. "One day when this is all past and gone." And meet my sister, she thought. "But I have somewhere to go to, somewhere and someone."

The police wouldn't let her go yet. They questioned her and questioned her as to where Stanley might be but Vera couldn't help them. She could only shake her head helplessly. There were so many people in the police station, so many faces, Mrs. Paterson, Mrs. Macdonald and her son, an important key witness, Mrs. Blackmore, the man who delivered peat, and they all reminded her of that old unhappy life in Lanchester Road. She wanted only one person and at last they let her go out to the car where he was waiting for her.

"One day," he said, echoing her own words, "when this is all past and gone, you'll get a divorce and . . ."

"Oh, James, you know I will. It's what I want more than anything in the world."

Stanley stayed in the loft until his watch told him it was ten o'clock. He used his last match to see the time, but it was pain rather than the loss of light that drove him down. His body ached intolerably in every joint and he would have come down in any circumstances, even if, he told himself, the house had still been full of policemen.

Very clearly now he saw the trap he had made for himself. He had murdered no one but the body he had hidden had died by violence; by burying Ethel's cases and Ethel's ring with it, by using Ethel's money, he had irrevocably branded himself as a killer and a thief. There was his record too, the record which showed he was capable of such an act. No use now to ask for an examination of the real body of Ethel. By his own desire that body was reduced to ashes, a fine soft powder, delicate and evanescent, far more elusive of analysis than the cobwebby dust which now clung to his clothes and his skin.

Standing on the landing in the shadowy gloom of the summer night, Stanley tried to brush this dust off his clothes until the air was filled with soot-smelling clouds. He wanted to cleanse himself of it entirely, for he felt that it was Ethel who clung to him, enveloping him in ashy vapour. For months Maud had haunted him, appearing in dreams, but Maud was gone now for ever. He seemed to feel Ethel standing beside him as she had stood on the day of her death, listening to Maud's snores, about to admonish him as she was admonishing him now. He shivered and whimpered in the dusk, brushing Ethel off him, wiping her off his face with shaking hands.

His own body had a smell of death about it. Afraid to use water and set the pipe overflowing again, he made his way down the stairs. His limbs were gradually losing their stiffness and their pain. Life was returning to them and with it fear. He had to get away.

The house was full of creaks and whispers. In the dark Stanley bumped into furniture, knocking the telephone off its hook so that it buzzed at him and made him whimper abuse at it. Ethel was in here too, the very essence of Ethel, waiting quietly for him on the mantelpiece. The room was full of greenish sickly light from the single street lamp outside. He took hold of the urn in fingers which shook and twitched and threw it on to the floor so that grey powdery Ethel streamed across the carpet. And then he had to go, run, escape, leave the house and Ethel in possession of it.

Nobody followed him. No one had been waiting for him. He ran, his heart pounding, until he was far from Lanchester Road, across the High Street and into the hinterland of winding, criss-crossing roads where everyone went to bed early and nearly all the lights were out. Then he had to stop running, stand and hold his aching chest until he could breathe normally again.

Just to be out of that house, to be free of it and not pursued, brought him a tiny shred of something like hope. If he could get hold of some money and some means of transport . . . Then he could go home to Bures and his river. They wouldn't look for him there because Vera would tell them how he didn't get on with his parents and had run away and never wrote. He leant against a wall, bracing himself, trying to get his thoughts into some sort of coherent order, trying to make his brain work realistically, calmly. I'm going home, he said, going home, and then, shuffling at first, then moving faster, he turned his steps in the direction of the old village.

The shop was in utter darkness. Steadier and saner now that he was doing something purposeful, Stanley made his way round the back, checked that the van was there and unlocked the back door. Thank God, he said to himself, he always carried the shop key and the van key in his jacket pocket. In his absence, Pilbeam had got rid of nearly all their stock, and apart from a few hideous and probably unsaleable pieces, the place was empty. Pale light from a metal-bracketed antique street lamp filtered waterily across a huge mahogany table and lay in pools on the floor.

A couple of cars passed in the street and one stopped outside, but it wasn't a police car. Stanley looked at it vaguely across the shadows and the flowing citron-coloured light and then he opened the till. It contained twenty pounds in notes and just short of another five in silver. He was transferring them to his pocket when he heard footsteps coming round the back. There was nothing to hide behind but a pair of maroon velvet curtains Pilbeam called portieres and which he had rigged up on one of the walls. For a moment Stanley's body refused to obey him, he was so frightened and so dreadfully weary of being frightened and hunted, but at last somehow he got behind the curtains and flattened himself against the wall.

The back door opened and he heard Pilbeam's voice.

"That's funny, me old love, I could have sworn I locked that door."

"Did you leave anything in the till?"

"You must be half-cut, Dave. That's what we've come for, isn't it? Should be near enough thirty quid."

Stanley trembled. He couldn't see anything but he felt their presence in the room where he was. Who was Dave? The huge man Pilbeam had brought round with him to Lanchester Road? He heard the till open with a squeak like an untuned violin string. Pilbeam said, "Christ, it's empty!"

"Manning," said Dave.

"How could it be? They'll have him behind bars."

Dave said, "You think?" and ripped aside the left-hand portiere. Leadenly, Stanley lifted his head and looked at them. "Turn out your pockets," Dave said sharply.

A little courage returned to Stanley. There is always a little left in reserve right up to the end.

"Why the hell should I?" he said in a thin high voice. "I've a right to it after what he's had out of me."

Dave's shadow was black and elongated, the shadow of a gorilla with pendulous hands. He didn't move.

Pilbeam said, "Oh, no, Stan, old man. You haven't got a right to nothing. You never had nothing, did you? It's easy giving away what's not your own."

Stanley edged behind the table. Nobody stopped him. "What's that supposed to mean?" he said.

"Cheques that bounce, Stan, that's what it means. I don't think you've ever been properly introduced to my friend, Dave. Let me do the honours. This is Stan, my partner, Dave old boy. Dave, Stan, is the—er, managing director of the firm that did our decorating."

Stanley's mouth went dry. He cleared his throat but still he had no voice.

"What d'you expect me to do?" Dave said. "Shake hands with him? Shake hands with that dirty little murderer?"

"You can shake hands with him in a minute," said Pilbeam. "I promise you you shall and I will too. First I'd like to tell my friend Stanley that both his cheques, mine and Dave's, came back yesterday marked Returned to Drawer. Now I might overlook a thing like that, old man, being as we're old mates, but Dave . . . Well, Dave's different. He doesn't like sweating his guts out and then being made a monkey of."

Stanley's voice came out as a squeak, then grew more powerful. "You shopped me," he said. "You bleeding copper's nark. You did dirt on me behind my back. Nothing but lies you've told me. You haven't got a wife, haven't had a wife for ten years. You . . ."

His voice faltered. Pilbeam was looking at him almost gently, his eyes mild, his mouth twitching at the corners. Even his voice was indulgent, kindly, when he said, "Let's shake hands with him now, Dave, shall we?"

Stanley ducked, then overturned the table with a crash so that it made a barricade between him and the other two men. Dave kicked it, planting his foot in the centre of its glossy top. It skidded back until its legs struck the wall and Stanley was penned in a wooden cage.

They came for him, one on each side. Stanley thought of how he had fought with Maud, centuries, aeons ago. He felt behind him for a vase or something metal to throw but all the shelves had been emptied. He cringed, arms over his head. Dave pulled him out, holding him by a handful of his jacket.

When he was in the middle of the shop, Dave held him, locking his arms, and as he kicked and wriggled, Pilbeam caught him under the jaw with his fist. Stanley sobbed and kicked out. For that he got a kick on the shin from Dave, a kick which made him scream and stagger.

In wordless dance, the three men edged round the overturned table, Stanley hoping for a chance to grab its legs and send the heavy mass of wood toppling to crush Dave's feet. But he was limping and shafts of pain travelled from his shin up through his body. When he was back against the wall again he cringed back cunningly to make them think he was done for, and as Pilbeam advanced slowly upon him, Stanley twisted suddenly and grabbed the velvet portieres. There was a scrunch of wood as the rail which held them came apart from the wall. Stanley hurled the heavy mass at his assailants and for a moment they were enveloped in velvet.

Right at the back of the shop now, within feet of the door, Stanley found a weapon, a nine-inch-long monkey wrench Pilbeam had left under the till counter. As Dave emerged, struggling and cursing, Stanley threw the wrench as hard as he could. It missed Dave's head and struck him in the chest, just beneath the collar bone. Dave howled with pain. He flung himself on Stanley as Stanley reached the door and was struggling with the handle.

For perhaps fifteen seconds the two men grappled together. Dave was much taller than Stanley but he was impeded by the pain in his chest and even then Stanley might have got away but for the intervention of Pilbeam who, creeping along the floor, suddenly grabbed Stanley's legs from behind and threw him face downwards.

Dave picked him up, held him while Pilbeam pummelled his face and then, holding him by the shoulders, banged his head repetitively against the wall. Stanley's knees sagged and he dropped, groaning, into the pile of velvet.

When he came to he thought he had gone blind. One of his eyes refused to open at all, and with the other he could see only implacable blackness. He put his hand to his face and it came away wet. With blood or with tears? He didn't know because he couldn't see. His fingers tasted salty.

Then gradually something took vague dark shape before him. It was the table, set up on its legs again. Stanley sobbed with relief because he wasn't blind. The place was so dark only because the street lamp had gone out.

The velvet he was lying on was soft and warm, a tender gentle nest like a woman's lap. He wanted to bury himself in it, wrap it round his tired body and all the hundred places that ached and throbbed. But he couldn't do that because he was going home. The green Stour was waiting for him, the fields that were silver with horse beans and emerald with sugar beet.

He sat up in the darkness. The place he was in seemed to be a sort of shop without any goods for sale. What was he doing there? Why had he come and where from? He couldn't remember. He knew only that he had passed through a time of great terror and pain and violence.

Had he always trembled and jumped like this, as if he had an incurable disease? It didn't matter much now. The beckoning of the river was more urgent than anything. He must get to the river and lie on its banks and wash away the tears and the blood.

Vaguely he thought that someone was after him but he didn't know who his pursuers were. Attendants in a hospital perhaps? He had run away from a hospital and fallen among thieves. When he stood up he rocked badly and walking was difficult. But he persevered, shuffling, his arms outstretched to fumble his way along by feel. Outside somewhere he thought there was a car and it was his car because he had an ignition key in his pocket. He found the car—in fact, he bumped into it—and opened the door with his key.

When he was sitting in the car he switched on the light and looked at his face in the mirror. It was black and bruised and there was dried blood on it. Over his left eye was a cut and under the cut the eye jerked open and shut.

"My name is George Carpenter," he said to the stranger in the mirror, "and I live at . . ." He couldn't remember where he lived. Then he tried to recall something—anything—out of the past, but all he could see were women's faces, angry and threatening, swimming up out of darkness. Everything else had gone. No, not quite . . . His own identity, he hadn't lost that. His name was George Carpenter and he had been a setter of crossword puzzles, but he had become very ill and had had to give it up. The illness was in his brain or his nerves and that was why he twitched so much.

An unhappy life, a life of terrible frustration. The details of it had gone beyond recall. He didn't want to remember them. When he was a boy he had been happy, fishing in the river for miller's thumbs and loaches. The miller's thumbs had faces like coelacanths. They were fish left over from another age when there were no men in the world. Stanley found he liked to think of that time; it eased the pressure in his head.

Loach was a funny name. Useful if you were setting a puzzle and had to fit a word into "l" blank "a" blank "h." "Loach: For this fish the Chinese pronounces another." He turned the ignition key and started the van.

Stanley had been driving for so long that by now he drove quite mechanically, as if the van were not some-

thing he had to operate but an extension of his own
body. He had no more need to think about driving than
he had to think about walking when he moved across a
room. The streets he drove through seemed familiar but
still he couldn't place them. On the bridge by the lockkeeper's house he stopped and looked down into the canal. He wasn't far from home then, for here was the
Stour, lying limpid between its green willows, his green
river, cold and deep and rich with fish. It wasn't green
now but black and ripple-free, a metallic gleam on its
flat surface.

Soon the dawn would come and then the river
would go bright as if its green came, not from the awak-
ening sky, but from some hidden inner source of colour.
And people would appear from those black unlighted
houses, whose outlines he could just see cutting into the
horizon, and walk in the fields as the morning mist rose
and spread and pearled the grass.

There was a white police car on the other side of
the bridge, a stationary car with its headlights full on but
trained away from him. A speed trap, he thought, although there were no cars but his to trap. They must be
waiting for someone, some runaway villain they were
hunting.

They would have no chance to trap him, for he
wasn't going their way. He was going to take the towpath
and drive slowly along it until the dawn came and then,
when the river became a dazzling green, lie on the bank
and bathe his hurt face in the water.

The surface of the path was hard and bumpy like
ridged rock. Each time the van shuddered a spasm of
fresh pain made him wince. Soon he would stop and
rest. The dawn was coming up ahead of him, the black
sky shredding apart to disclose the thin pale colour behind it. Bures and the Constable villages lay before him.
He could see the shape of them now in a crenellated horizon.

Stanley switched off his lights, and in the distance
he saw another car following him. They must be com-

ing, he thought, to warn him off the river. Someone had fishing rights here and he'd be poaching. When had he ever cared for anyone else's rights?

They wouldn't be able to see him now his lights were off. He knew his river better than they did. Every bend in it, every willow on its banks was as familiar to him as a solved crossword.

Once he was home and safe he'd start doing crosswords again, bigger and better ones, he'd be the world's champion crossword puzzler. Even now, weak and trembling as he was, he could still make up puzzles. He found he had forgotten the words that made up his own name, but that didn't matter, not while he had his skill, his art. "Undertake the fishing gear": "Tackle." "Sport a leg in fruity surroundings": "Fishing." "Undertake . . ." Stanley shivered. There was some reason why he couldn't find a clue for that word, that ugly word which had dealings with death. He drove faster, the van's suspension groaning, but his mind was calmer, he was almost happy. Words were the meaning of existence, the panacea for all agony.

"Panacea": "Cure is a utensil with a twisted card." "Agony": "The non-Jew mixes with an atrocious pain." He could do it as well as ever.

There was a bend ahead at this point. Very soon the bank veered to the left, following the river's meander, and when you could see his village, just a black blot it would be on the grey fields, you had to brake and turn to the nearside. "Meander"—a beautiful word. "I and a small hesitation combine to make the river twist." Or better perhaps, "Dear men," (anag. seven letters) or, how about "Tough mean and red, the river has a curve in it?"

Stanley's body ached and his eyes glazed with weariness. He was afraid he might fall asleep at the wheel, so he shook himself and forced his eyes to stare hard ahead. Then, suddenly, he saw his village. It was floating in grey mist, peaceful, beckoning. Now, at this point, the river meandered.

"The winding river," he heard himself whisper, anagramming, "is a dream need." He groaned aloud with pain and longing and then he pulled the wheel feebly to follow the way the path should go.

The van slid and sagged, running out of control, but gradually and slowly. Stanley's hands slipped weakly from the wheel. It was all right now, he was home. No more running, no more driving. He was home, cruising gently downhill to where his village loomed in front of him.

And the dawn was coming, rising bright and green and many-coloured like a rainbow, pouring in through the van's open windows with a vast crunching roar. Stanley wondered why he was screaming, fighting against the wet dawn, when he was home at last.

The police car screeched to a halt on the canal bank. Two men got out, running, slamming doors behind them, but by the time they reached the shored-up edge the water was almost calm again with nothing to show where the van had gone down but dull yellow ripples spreading outwards in wide concentric rings. The dawn showed muddy red over the warehouses and the first few drops of rain began to fall.

ABOUT THE AUTHOR

RUTH RENDELL has won three major awards: The Mystery Writers of America "Edgar Allen Poe" Award for *The Fallen Curtain*, the Crime Writers Association "Golden Dagger" for *A Demon in my View* and *Current Crime* magazine's reader poll named *Shake Hands Forever* as the best book of the year, over contenders such as Agatha Christie and Len Deighton.

A FATAL INVERSION

Barbara Vine

1.

The body lay on a small square of carpet in the middle of the gun room floor. Alec Chipstead looked around for something to put over it. He unhooked a raincoat from one of the pegs and, covering the body, reflected too late that he would never wear that again.

He went outside to see the vet off.

"I'm glad that's all over."

"Extraordinary how painful these things can be," said the vet. "You'll get another dog, I suppose?"

"I expect so. That's really up to Meg."

The vet nodded. He got into his car, put his head out of the window, and asked Alec if he was sure he didn't want the body taken away. Alec said no, thanks, really, he'd see to all that. He watched the car move off up the long, sloping lanes that in those parts was called a drift, under the overhanging branches of the trees, and disappear around the bend where the pinewood began. The sky was a pale silvery blue, the trees still green but touched here and there with yellow. September had been a wet month, and the lawns that ran gently to meet the wood were green too. On the edge of the grass, where a strip of flower border separated it from the paved drive, lay a rubber ball dented with toothmarks. How long had that been there? Months, probably. It was a long time since Fred had been up to playing with a ball. Alec put it into his pocket. He walked around the house, up the stone steps on to the terrace, and in by the french windows.

Meg was sitting in the drawing room, pretending to read *Country Life*.

"He didn't know a thing," Alec said. "He just went to sleep."

"What fools we are."

"I held him on my lap and he went to sleep and the vet gave him the injection and he—died."

"We couldn't have kept him any longer. Not with that chorea. It was too painful to watch and it must have been hell for him."

"I know. I suppose if we'd had a family, love—I mean, Fred was just a dog and people go through this with kids. Can you imagine?"

Meg, who was made sharp-tongued by distress, said, "I've yet to hear of parents calling in the doctor to put their sick children down."

Alec didn't say any more. He went back through the house, across the large, finely proportioned hall, with its pretty, curved staircase, under the wide arch to the kitchen area, and then to the gun room. The front kitchen and the back kitchen had been converted into one, lined with the latest in cupboards and gadgets. You couldn't have imagined, while in there, that the house was two hundred years old. It was the real estate agent who had called the place where the freezer lived and where they hung their coats the gun room. No guns were kept there now. No doubt there had been in the Berelands' time, and some old Bereland squire had sat in here in a windsor chair at a deal table, cleaning them. . . .

He twitched the corner of the raincoat and had a last look at the dead beagle. Meg had come up behind him and was standing there. Sentimentally he thought, though did not say aloud, that the white and tan forehead was still at last, would suffer no more brutal spasms.

"His was a good life."

"Yes. Where are we going to bury him?"

"On the other side of the lake, I thought, in the Little Wood."

Alec wrapped the body up in his raincoat, wrapped it like a parcel. The raincoat had seen better days, but it had come originally from Aquascutum, an expensive shroud. Alec had an obscure feeling that he owed this last sacrifice to Fred, this final tribute.

"I've got a better idea," Meg said, putting on her parka. "The Bereland graveyard. Why the little wood when we've already got an animal cemetery? Oh, do let's, Alec. It seems so *right*. It's been a traditional burying place for pets for so long. I'd like Fred to be there, I really would."

"Why not?"

"I know I'm a fool. I'm a sentimental idiot, but I'd sort of like to think of him with those others. With Alexander and Pinto and Blaze. I am a fool, aren't I?"

"That makes two of us," said Alec.

He went across to the old stable block, where they kept the tractor and the wood stacked for winter, and came back with a wheelbarrow and a couple of spades.

"We'll mark the grave with a wooden plaque, I think. I could make one out of sycamore log, that's a nice white wood, and you could do the lettering on it."

"All right. But we'll do that later." Meg bent to lift up the parcel but recoiled at the last moment, straightening up again and shaking her head. It was Alec who put the dog into the barrow. They set off up the drift.

There were two woods, three if you counted the one below the lake. The lawn in front of the house in which a great black cedar grew ended at the old wood, five or six acres of deciduous trees, and beyond that, the ground rose, a green ride of turf separated it from the pinewood. This was a plantation, rows of cluster and knobcone pines, set rather too close together and now forming a dense forestation. It was larger than the deciduous wood, nearly twice the size of it, and forming a windbreak between it and Nunes Road, across which, since the uprooting of hedges, gales swept across unchecked from the prairielike fields.

Impenetrable the pinewood seemed to be from the drift and Nunes Road. But on the southern side an offshoot from the green ride led in between the ranked trees, led into the center, where it broadened out into a rough circular shape. Here both the Chipsteads had penetrated on one previous occasion, on a Sunday of exploration not long after they bought the house and land. If you have twenty acres of land it takes you a little time to learn exactly what your possession consists of. They had been a little moved by what they saw, gently derisive, too, to conceal their sentimentality even from the other.

"This could only be in England," Meg had said.

This time they knew exactly where they were going and what they would find. They left the drift by the green ride that was rather like a tunnel between the two kinds of wood and which at its distant end showed a little vista of green meadows piled in lozenge shapes, scraps of darker copse, a church tower. Underfoot, where the grass ended, was a slippery floor of pine needles. The air smelled of resin.

Turf covered the circular place, but here it was raised into a dozen or so small hummocks, shallow hills, grassy knolls. The monuments were mostly of wood, oak, of course, or it would not have lasted so long, but even some of these had fallen and rotted. The rest were greened with lichen. Among them was the rare stone: a block of slate, a slab of pink granite, a curb of bright white Iceland spar. On this last was engraved the name Alexander and the dates: 1901–1909.

What writing there might have been on the wooden crosses had been obscured by time and weather. But the inscription on the pink granite remained sharp and clear. *Blaze* was printed there in capital letters, and under it:

> They do not sweat and whine about their condition;
> They do not lie awake in the dark and weep for their sins . . .
> Not one is respectable or unhappy over the whole earth.

Meg stooped down to look at brushstrokes almost obliterated by yellow mold. " 'By what eternal streams, Pinto . . .' " she read. " 'Gone from us after three years.' Do you think Pinto was a water spaniel?"

"Or a pet otter." Alec lifted out Fred's shrouded body and laid it on the grass. "I can remember doing this sort of thing when I was a kid. Only it was a rabbit we were burying. My brother and I had a rabbit funeral."

"I bet you didn't have a ready-made cemetery."

"No. It had to be the back of a flower bed."

"Where shall we put him?"

Alec picked up the spade. "Over here, I should think. Next to Blaze. It seems the obvious place. I should think Blaze was the last to be buried here, the date's 1957. Presumably succeeding occupants didn't have pets."

Meg walked around, eyeing the graves, trying to calculate the order in which the plots had been used. It was hard to tell because of the collapse of so many of the wooden monuments, but certainly it seemed as if Blaze had been the last animal laid here, there being two rows of seven hummocks each behind his grave and three hummocks to the left of it.

"Put him on the right side of Blaze," she said.

Now Alec had begun to dig, Meg would have liked to get it over with as soon as possible. It was all folly; it was beneath their dignity as middle-aged, presumably intelligent people; it was what children did. Alec's recounting his pet rabbit's funeral brought this home to her. Why, at one moment she had almost been going to suggest uttering a few farewell words as Fred was laid to rest. They must bury him, they must replace the turf over him, forget all the nonsense about a memorial. White sycamore indeed! Meg seized the other spade and began digging rapidly, turning up the soft, needle-filled leafmold. Once the turf was penetrated, the ground yielded to the spade as easily as the sand on a beach above the water line.

"Easy does it," Alec said. "It's Fred we're burying, not a coffin six feet under."

These were unfortunate words that he was to remember in the days to come with a squeeze of the stomach, a wrinkling of the nose. His spade struck what he thought was a stone, a long flint. He dug around it and cleared a blade-shaped bone. There was an animal buried here already then. . . . Something that had a very big rib cage, he thought. He wasn't going to say anything to Meg but just cover up that rib cage and that collarbone quickly and start afresh up where she was digging.

Alec was aware of a crow cawing somewhere. Down in the tall limes of the deciduous wood, probably. The thought came unpleasantly to him that crows were carrion birds. He plunged the spade in once more, slicing into the firm dry turf. As he did so he saw that Meg was holding out her spade to him. On it lay what looked like the bones, the fan splay of metatarsals, of a very small foot.

"A monkey?" Meg said in a faint, faltering voice.

"It must be."

"Why hasn't it got a headstone?"

He didn't answer. He dug down, lifting out spadeloads of resin-scented earth. Meg was digging up bones; she had a pile of them.

"We'll put them in a box or something. We'll rebury them."

"No," he said. "No, we can't do that. Meg. . .?"

"What is it? What's the matter?"

"Look," he said, and he lifted it up to show her. "That's not a dog's skull, is it? That's not a monkey's?"

*   *   *

There was a big picture of the Princess of Wales visiting a home for handicapped children. The main story was about trouble in the Middle East and a subsidiary one about racial trouble in West London, street fighting mainly and breaking shop windows. Shiva's eyes traveled down the page. At the foot of one of the left-hand columns he read a headline. For the amount of text underneath it, a mere paragraph, it was a disproportionately large headline. It even rather spoiled the symmetry of the page.

The headline said: *Skeleton Found in Woodland Grave* and the story beneath it ran: *While digging a grave for his pet dog, a Suffolk landowner with a home near Hadleigh unearthed a human skeleton. The remains appear to be those of a young woman. Police declined to comment further at this stage and Mr. Alec Chipstead, a chartered surveyor, was not available for questioning.*

Shiva read it twice. It was rather strangely put, he thought. He felt this about most articles in newspapers. They didn't know much but they told you what they did know in the most cryptic way possible to whet your appetite and make you speculate. For instance, they didn't tell you if the landowner and Mr. Alec Chipstead were one and the same person, though you could tell that was what they meant.

He could feel sweat standing on his face, on his upper lip and forehead. Wiping it away with his handkerchief, he closed his eyes, opened them, and looked around the room, then back at the newsprint in front of him, as if he might have been dreaming or have imagined it. The paragraph, of course, was still there.

*   *   *

Zosie would steal something and Rufus wanted to see her do it. He found himself observing her as one might watch the behaviour of a laboratory animal in a drug trial. All desire he had ever had for her was dead. He would not even have cared to touch her.

In and out of shops they had wandered—or simply through the departments of stores? A food department he could remember and all those clothes and the crowds and the heat. So perhaps there had been no air conditioning or only part air conditioning. If Zosie took anything from a shelf or out of one of those bins filled with stockings, with panty hose, with underclothes, he didn't see her. He lit a cigarette and a man in a suit with a lapel badge came and asked him to put it out. Then the message came over the public address system. The exact words he had forgotten but the gist of it he remembered.

"Will the parent or person in charge of a small boy aged about three dressed in a white shirt, blue shorts and blue sandals, please come to . . ."

And there had followed directions to some manager's office where the child could be claimed. Rufus could remember perfectly where he had been when he heard the message, by some trick of memory—so arbitrarily selective, so lacking in respect for the recall one most needed—photographed forever and printed on some wall of the mind. On one side of a bank of shelves packed with cosmetics he had been and the black and silver Mary Quant packaging he could see now. Zosie was on the other side of it, hidden from him but no more than six feet away. He heard the message about the lost boy and immediately turned to find Zosie, but she was gone; she, too, was lost.

He looked for her. The place was very crowded. The curious thing was that though Zosie was beautiful she was not very memorable, she was not unusual to look at. Thousands of young girls looked like her—or superficially like her, they looked like her from a distance. They all wore jeans and T-shirts and sandals and no makeup and had hair that was very long or very short.

She knew where the van was as well as he did. She knew the time—or did she? Of course she didn't possess a watch. But he didn't care, he wasn't going to wait for her past ten past four. They were due to pick Vivien up at four-thirty. If Zosie got left behind in London, she would find her way back. Home is where you go when you have nowhere else to go. Home is the only port in a storm.

Rufus sat in the van, smoking. He saw Zosie coming toward him along the aisle between parked cars, the metal glittering, the tarmac surface quivering with heat distortion, her shadow and that of the little boy black, short, dancing. He was fair-haired, blue-eyed, bewildered. He had a white shirt on and blue shorts and blue sandals, and he was holding Zosie's hand.

"Open the door, Rufus, quick. He can come in back with me. Let's get away quickly."

Rufus wasn't often frightened. He prided himself on being easy, laid-back, cucumber-cool. But he was frightened then, fear hit him in the pit of the stomach, it was as physical as that. He jumped out, he slammed the van door.

"Are you mad?"

He knew she was. It wasn't a real question.

"Take him back. How did you get hold of him? No, never mind. I don't care. Just take him back. Put him inside the doors and leave him, anything."

"I want him, Rufus. He's called Andrew. He said he was called Andrew. He was saying Andrew wants Mummy so I walked in and I said here's

Mummy, Andrew, whatever happened to you? I said, and come on, let's go. They didn't stop me, they didn't ask anything, and he just came. Look, he likes me. We can take him back to Ecalpemos and he can live with us."

From the first Rufus had been always aware of his future career, that he must keep his hands clean. That, at any rate, he must appear to have clean hands. It ruled him, that principle, it kept him from the worst excesses. Shiva had it, too, but Shiva was a loser; Shiva, through not being ruthless enough, would go down. Rufus had nightmares about doing something or something happening to wreck his qualifying and prevent forever what might come after qualifying. They were nightmares, but he had them in the daytime when fully conscious.

"Take him back!"

The child, up till then stunned perhaps by events, began to cry. Rufus picked him up and held him up on his shoulders. His heart was in his mouth, he literally had that feeling of choking, of imminent nausea and throwing up. But he ran across the tarmac with the child in his arms, the child who by then was screaming, ran under some sort of covered way and in through glass double doors and into the first shop he came to, a shoe shop, where he thrust the little boy into the arms of an assistant and shouted: "He's the lost boy, he's called Andrew. There was a message . . ."

Between them they nearly dropped the boy. His screams shattered the air. Rufus turned and fled. He jumped into the van, aware that he was swearing aloud, muttering every obscenity he could think of, spitting out at Zosie that he would kill her, that she was criminally insane. She was crying, lying back on the seat with her head hanging back and weeping. He brought the van out as fast as he could, his heart knocking, his hands shaking. To think of it now even started his heart going.

*   *   *

The rain had eased up a little. In procession they went up into the pinewood, not yielding to the idea of using the heavy old wooden wheelbarrow that stood in the stables, but carrying the wrapped bodies. Adam and Shiva each carried tools, the heavy spade and a fork, the lighter spade they had used to bury the coypu in the Little Wood being unaccountably missing. Or it had been unaccountable then. Now Rufus knew it had been taken by the gardener who came to Wyvis Hall at dawn and whose footsteps sent Adam to the gun room and the gun, who was in a way responsible for Adam's using the gun.

Adam woke very early on Thursday morning, at about five. Waking had been preceded by a dream in which Hilbert and Lilian, with himself and Bridget and their parents in attendance, were burying the body of their only child in the cemetery in the pinewood. The body could not be seen, for it was sealed up in a tiny coffin of walnut veneered in a flame pattern. Lilian and Hilbert looked less like themselves, or after a time began to look less like themselves than like the parents in the picture. Adam knew he had dreamed this because of what his father had said to him the evening before about Blaze's funeral. He lay in the dark, wondering if this was the day on which his world would end. He had taken to wondering this every morning.

In the dream Hilbert and Lilian had been doing

the digging themselves, having selected the plot next to where Blaze was buried, and they were digging deep. They dug deeper than their own height, so that not even the tops of their heads showed above the brink of the grave. When they had dug, Shiva and Rufus, and then he had taken over from Shiva, they had not been so thorough, and had gone down no more than three feet. If we had dug deeper, thought Adam, if we had dug the statutory six feet down, none of this would have happened. . . .

But it had been three feet, not six. Even so it took them a long time and the worst part was putting the earth back, seeing the earth trickle into the folds of cloth, the strands of hair. If the grave had only been deep, deep enough for a man as tall as Rufus to stand in and his head not show above ground level. They had been oppressed with fear, and cold and wet, shivering in the rain, wanting to get on with it and get it over. A Monday morning at the end of summer and the end of the world. . . .

Up there you could just hear the traffic, what there was of it, a car or two passing, and once, horse's hooves. Shiva had cut the turf back carefully before they began digging, cut it out in squares with the spade. He had laid the squares on one side ready for replacement when the grave was filled. Rain, which had been falling intermittently all the time they worked, now came down in a glassy sheet. Yet it was as if the rain were on their side, falling swiftly on the grave to make the grass grow over it.

In the pinewood, among the dense growth of black tree trunks, they took refuge. It was bone-dry in there, dark, scented and close. You could hear the rain but not feel it. Hours seemed to have passed since anyone had spoken, it was as if they had all been stricken dumb, but inside the pinewood Adam spoke to Zosie.

"Are you all right?"

She moved out of the circle of his arm. "Oh, yes."

They put the turf back and trod on it, pressing it down. The sky was all clouds, the treetops swinging. The cedar was doing its witchlike dance, clapping its branches in their black sleeves, when they came out of the wood and approached the house.

Shiva hung up the fork in the stable where the tools were kept but Adam held on to the spade. He went into the house, into the gun room where the turtle was and the fox came bursting out of the wall, and fetched the four-ten, the lady's gun, and then he and Zosie went down to the Little Wood and buried it near the spot where they had buried the coypu. He had meant to bury both guns, the lightweight shotgun and the heavier pump action, the one he had used, but when it came to the point he was afraid.

Up in the cemetery he had spoken only to remark on the rain falling, the rain being on their side. But Rufus had said: "We should all go our separate ways as soon as we can. We should pack up now and go."

"I haven't got a separate way," Zosie said.

from Sue Grafton
author of "A" IS FOR ALIBI

"B" IS FOR BURGLAR
A Kinsey Millhone Mystery

KINSEY MILLHONE IS ...

"The best new private eye."   —*The Detroit News*

"A woman we feel we know, a tough cookie with a soft center, a gregarious loner."   —*Newsweek*

"Smart, sexual, likable, and a very modern operator."
—*Dorothy Salisbury Davis*

"A stand-out specimen of the new female operatives."
—*Philadelphia Inquirer*

"Thirty-two, twice divorced, and lives in a fifteen-foot-square room in a converted garage ... On the road she stays in crummy motels because she's cheap. She likes people for good reasons. She's smart but she makes mistakes ... I like Millhone."   —*The Detroit Free Press*

Finding wealthy Elaine Boldt seems like a quickie case to Kinsey Millhone. The flashy widow was last seen wearing a $12,000 lynx coat, leaving her condo in Santa Teresa for her condo in Boca Raton. But somewhere in between, she vanished. Kinsey's case goes from puzzling to sinister when a house is torched, an apartment is burgled of worthless papers, the lynx coat comes back without Elaine, and her bridge partner is found dead. Soon Kinsey's clues begin to form a capital M—not for missing, but for murder. And plenty of it.

Look for "B" IS FOR BURGLAR in your bookstore or use this coupon:

50 YEARS OF GREAT AMERICAN MYSTERIES FROM BANTAM BOOKS

Stuart Palmer

"Those who have not already made the acquaintance of Hildegarde Withers should make haste to do so, for she is one of the world's shrewdest and most amusing detectives."   —*New York Times*
                                                        May 6, 1934

☐ 25934-2 THE PUZZLE OF THE SILVER PERSIAN (1934) $2.95
☐ 26024-3 THE PUZZLE OF THE HAPPY HOOLIGAN
          (1941) $2.95
      Featuring spinster detective Hildegarde Withers

Craig Rice

"Why can't all murders be as funny as those concocted by Craig Rice?   —*New York Times*
☐ 26345-5 HAVING WONDERFUL CRIME $2.95
   "Miss Rice at her best, writing about her 3 favorite characters against a delirious New York background."
                                                      —*New Yorker*

☐ 26222-X MY KINGDOM FOR A HEARSE $2.95
   "Pretty damn wonderful!"   —*New York Times*

Barbara Paul

☐ 26234-3 RENEWABLE VIRGIN (1985) $2.95
   "The talk crackles, the characters are bouncy, and New York's media world is caught with all its vitality and vulgarity."   —*Washington Post Book World*
☐ 26225-4 KILL FEE (1985) $2.95
   "A desperately treacherous game of cat-and-mouse (whose well-wrought tension is heightened by a freakish twist that culminates in a particularly chilling conclusion." —*Booklist*

For your ordering convenience, use the handy coupon below: